## LOSING HIS MIND

I took out the second nurse with a chopstick jab and began clawing at Jin's straps. Releasing his buckles seemed to take long agonizing minutes, but when I started yanking at the wires connected to Jin's body, he woke up and shrieked in pain.

"That's arterial bleeding. He'll die in seconds." Merida stood in the doorway. I glanced around and saw all three cyberguards at her back.

For an instant, we hung silent. Bright red blood continued to pulse from Jin's neck, saturating the sheets.

Merida was losing her composure. "Fool! Your stupidity will kill him. Let me close that wound."

I said, "Move into the hall, and you can send a cybernurse to fix him. But don't try anything, or I'll stab his brain and destroy your whole project."

What could I do, leave him there for Merida to play with and wait in my cell till the guards came to kill me? For all I knew, Jin's mind might be locked in an endless nightmare of suffering. This was no time for logic. I felt a ferocious compulsion to get Jin away from Merida at any cost. And I wasn't about to give up.

# hyperthought

## M. M. BUCKNER

ACE BOOKS, NEW YORK

HYPERTHOUGHT

An Ace Book / published by arrangement with
the author

PRINTING HISTORY
Ace mass-market edition / February 2003

Copyright © 2003 by M. M. Buckner.
Cover art by Craig White.
Cover design by Rita Frangie.
Text design by Julie Rogers.

Visit our website at
www.penguinputnam.com
Check out the ACE Science Fiction & Fantasy newsletter!

ISBN: 0-441-01023-7

ACE®
Ace Books are published by The Berkley Publishing Group,
a division of Penguin Putnam Inc.,
375 Hudson Street, New York, New York 10014.
ACE and the "A" design
are trademarks belonging to Penguin Putnam Inc.

PRINTED IN THE UNITED STATES OF AMERICA

10  9  8  7  6  5  4  3  2  1

*For Jack*

# Acknowledgments

SINCERE THANKS TO the many friends and colleagues who advised and encouraged me, including in alpha order: Beth Boord, Patsy Bruce, William and Margaret Buckner, Tim Choate, Mary Helen Clarke, Elizabeth Crook, Deana Deck, Joe DeGross, Dustine Deming, Mary Bess Dunn, Steve Edwards, Laura Fowler, Cindy Kershner, Melany Klinck, Jack Lyle, Bonnie Parker, Nathan Parker, William Parker, Brenna Piper, Brian Relleva, Martha Rider, Nancy Skinner, Allen Steele, Rachel Steele, Robin Warshaw, Ava Weiner, and Tom Wright. And very special gratitude to the editor who believed in me, John Morgan.

The mind commands the body, and the body obeys.
The mind commands itself and finds resistance.

—St. Augustine

WE LOSE OUR lives even as we live them. We forget the moments that formed us, what we were before, and how it was that we changed. So as of today, I have assigned myself this penance—to make a record while I do remember. Because I'm to blame for what happened. Everything was my fault. I knew Merida. I knew how seductive she could be. And still I introduced her to Jin. Maybe I didn't understand Jin as well, not at first, but ignorance is no excuse.

Jin Airlangga Sura was not just a name on my tour group list. Even I, who hardly ever downloaded movies back then, even I had seen his handsome face splashed across the Net. Jin Airlangga Sura, born in wealth, heir to a commercial dynasty. At twenty-five, the same age as me, Jin had already become a preter-famous screen idol with over a dozen movies to his credit. His elegant Indonesian looks and sultry style drove women to acts of mindless worship. When he signed up for my Irian Jaya adventure tour, I barely glanced at the letter he'd attached about what this trip meant to him. I assumed that I knew what Jin Sura would be like.

Jolie's Trips—that was the name of my tour guide service. My extreme adventure tours drew a rich crowd—I set the prices high. Traveling on the Earth's open surface is no stroll in the mall. What with lethal sunlight and toxic atmosphere and the cyclones blowing right out of Hades, your life depends on the right gear. Top-of-the-line airtight surface suits. Custom vehicles. Hardened communications links. Lots can happen on the open surface.

Sometimes people were surprised to find a woman guiding these trips. But once they saw me in action, they stopped doubting. Bien sûr, they may have joked about my scrawny size, or my bristly white hair, or my deviant fashion sense. But they didn't joke about my skill.

I met Jin Sura almost exactly three years ago in Paris, on

the night of November 27, 2125—before the war broke out and changed Paris forever. As usual, Rennie's Airport Bar was sweltering hot and sticky. Can anyone tell me why they kept the humidity turned up so high in Paris back in those days? Anyway, I always met clients at Rennie's before a trip. It was easy to find, directly under the Place Etoile launchpad. The beer was nothing special. The floor was not exactly clean. There was the constant rumble of rockets launching overhead. But the place never got crowded—by northern hemisphere standards.

We had five clients that night, three men and two women. They sat hunched up in their chairs trying not to touch anything and wearing expressions like they expected vermin to crawl up their legs. The gay bodybuilder couple from Nome.Com were holding hands. The slender, thirtyish widow from Greenland.Com was talking to a Net node she kept hidden in her purse. The other woman, an exec from Yev.Com, was closer to fifty but she had a big stout body, fit for action. I wasn't so sure about the bloated bond trader from Canada.Com. He seemed eager, I'll say that. He looked like he'd rather face death than another bond trade.

I drew myself a beer and caught Luc's eye. Cher Luc grinned and mouthed a sentence at me, our private joke. "Vive les Coms!"

The Coms. Without them, we couldn't have stayed in business as long as we did. Before the war, those fourteen commercial dynasties owned all the habitable territories in the northern hemisphere, including surface domes, tunnels and undersea colonies, not to mention the life contracts of all the rank-and-file workers. Only Com executives were rich enough to afford my trips. Born to their positions like royalty, those Commies treated Luc and me like vending machines.

What the hell, they paid in advance. For the next few days, Luc and I would give them their fright show under the open skies. They'd get their money's worth. Yeah, making those soft Commie execs pay me—a tunnel rat—to scare the stew out of them, that made me chuckle.

Dr. Judith Merida was there, too, mooching my beer and glad-handing my clients. The year before, she'd signed on for my three-day/two-night Madagascar excursion. Judith Merida had once been attached to a Com, but somehow she'd fallen out with the top brass and lost her place. Merida couldn't afford my prices after that first time. Still, she kept showing up at Rennie's for the pretrip meetings.

I knew what she was up to. She was trying to snag a rich backer to fund her research. Merida didn't have money, but she had ambitions. She ran a neuroscience clinic in Frisco, California, and she'd earned a reputation for some kind of fad cosmetic nanosurgery. The Commies knew Dr. Judith Merida by name.

In the beginning, I really liked Merida. Short like me, but sensual and curvy, with full round breasts, the way men like. She had thick black hair, pretty Spanic eyes, and a wide mobile mouth outlined in lipstick. She was older than me, maybe a lot older. Ça va, I couldn't guess her age. The whites of her eyes looked like granulated sugar, a sure sign of gene rejuvenation.

Dr. M., I nicknamed her. She always greeted me with a kiss that left a big red smear on my cheek. What a mouth on that woman! "Jolie, you heavenly creature, who cuts your hair? You could frighten the dead!"

She had an earthy laugh and an easy way of getting next to people. Her Spanic accent made her sound way exotic. And when Dr. M. started describing her latest nanosurgery scheme, her mouth would quiver, and she'd fling out her hands. Mes dieux, but she could draw you in. You'd think she had discovered nirvana.

That night, she was shining. "Friends, life is a dream. Sí, everything we're most certain about, what we see, hear, touch and taste—all our perceptions are mere chemical signals manufactured in our brains. They may not refer to anything outside ourselves. Our brains create colors, flavors and sounds that don't exist in abstract reality. Perhaps we're sleeping, dreaming the world."

Merida strutted around like a flirty bar singer, lifting her beer glass. "You've browsed the Science Channel, sí? The physicists know that nothing is solid. This beer, this room, even you, my excellent friends. Just waves of energy. Transient particles. Vibrating loops in vast empty space."

Her eyes smoldered with emotion, and my clients unconsciously leaned toward her. "How do you define the present moment? You can't. It has no dimension. Everything has oc-

curred in the past. We think we remember. But memories—
they're only phantom chains of molecules woven in our brains.
If we can't trust our senses or our memories, how do we know
what's real? What if we're caught in a maze within our own
dreaming brains?"

Merida let the silence lengthen. She pranced among her lis-
teners in the elevated boots that made her seem taller. Slicing
her eyes back and forth, she held them spellbound. "What if
only one of you is real, and all the rest of us are characters in
your dream?" Then she leaned forward and hissed, "You already
know the truth!"

The Commies drew back in surprise. The fat bond trader
spilled his drink on his pant leg. Merida leered at each of them
in turn. "Sí, you know. But the knowledge lurks under the surface of your consciousness. You can feel it like a nagging suspicion, something you've thought about many times, sí? At the
quantum level, your brain registers more input than you realize.
You know the truth! I can show it to you!"

"How?" asked one of the bodybuilders.

"With simple nanosurgery, my friend. I have developed a
nano-sized robot to travel into your perception centers and activate your latent senses. Perfectly safe and painless, I guarantee.
My nanobot will make you smarter than all your friends. You
will gain a new kind of sight!"

The Greenland widow asked for Merida's Net address. The
bodybuilders took it, too, and I saw the bond trader record a
memo in the Net node he wore strapped to his wrist. Those
Com execs were sucking in Merida's scam like a bunch of babies. Dr. M. had them in her palm, all set to put the squeeze
on.

But then everything fell apart. Merida touched the widow's
shoulder. "When will you visit my clinic, señora? Next week?
How about Monday? Let's set the date now, sí?" She was standing too close, breathing in the widow's face. Even I knew the
aristo snobs didn't like that.

"No, that's not convenient for me." The widow backed up
several steps and tripped on the bond trader's foot. When Merida followed, the widow squeaked some excuse and fled to the
ladies' room.

Merida whirled on the others as if they were escaping prey.
Her expression went naked and predatory as she moved closer.

I saw the bond trader's eyes widen. "My friends," Merida raised her voice, "we must set the date. I can make you smarter than God, but nothing begins till we set the date." She pointed her handheld Net node like a gun. "Open your calendar," she said to the bond trader.

He stuffed his hands in his pockets and didn't answer. The bodybuilders became engrossed with Rennie's slot machines. The woman from Yev.Com simply turned her back. Poor Merida, I'd seen it happen before.

Dr. M. just couldn't blend with those Commie snobs. She didn't understand their sense of personal space. Her clothes were a tinge too colorful, and her Spanic accent marred her attempt to sound high-toned. In the end, she scared them.

Anyway, Merida worked hard, and I admired her persistence. I thought, best of luck to you, Dr. M. Fleece your golden geese. Someday, you'll get the funding you need to expand your clinic. So why should I think twice about introducing her to a rich Indonesian movie star with a long, pretentious name? Jin Airlangga Sura.

My assistant, Luc Viollett, was already halfway through the safety talk when Jin made his entrance. Everyone turned to stare. He seemed to expect it. After a weighty pause, the clients starting chattering and pretending to ignore him, but they couldn't stop rubbernecking. Jin Sura had a presence, no denying it. Sir Jin, I dubbed him. In that first glance, I decided he personified the arrogant Commie prick from head to toe.

For one thing, he was wearing the most expensive faux-silk traveling suit money could buy. Second, it fit him like a glove. Third, he stood six feet tall, as stunning as some dark Polynesian god of fire, and I felt sure he knew it.

He graced us with his movie star smile and apologized for being late. While he waited for someone to find him a chair, I signaled Luc to continue. Luc was explaining about the cyclonic winds that constantly blast Earth's surface and the necessity of staying tethered together. All the while Luc talked, I kept eyeing Sir Jin.

By noon the next day, we would be rock climbing in the Sudirman Range of Irian Jaya. It's one of my favorite places. The old volcanic peaks rise above the visible gas layer—that unbroken blanket of greenhouse smog that now engulfs our glorious planet. From Mt. Puncak Jaya, you can actually look down on the yellow muck, and you get a clear view of mountaintops breaking through the smog for kilometers in every direction. There's something euphoric about gazing into the distance, something you never experience living underground or even under domes on the surface. That view gives you scope. Elbow room for the mind. That's worth risking a little gale-force wind and lethal smog, I think.

The whole time Luc was explaining our safety procedures, the guests kept turning to gawk at Jin. He flashed his eyebrows at them. I took note of his manicure, his polished boots, his expensive cinnamon brown tan.

Javanese, his letter had said, though I knew his family managed Pacific.Com, headquartered in Tokyo. Going back to find his roots, he'd written. He seemed troubled. Even a bit melancholy. Something in the line of his mouth. A shadow under his eye. That softened my opinion a little—but not much. I'd met plenty of his ilk—bored, pampered, self-absorbed. The Commie management classes produced little else.

"Who's that dark young lion?" Dr. M. was leaning against me, whispering in my ear. I felt her stiff black curls brush my cheek. She said, "I've seen him before, sí? He's gorgeous. Yum." She made a sucking sound with her tongue against her teeth. "But so dolorous."

"Jin Airlangga Sura," I whispered back. "You know. The actor."

Merida's eyelids drooped halfway, and she moistened her lips with her tongue. "His father is CEO of Pacific.Com. Lord Suradon Sura." Then her pretty eyes sliced toward me. "This Jin is a bad boy. I've seen his face in the scandal ezines."

"D'accord, I'm not surprised," I said. I was liking this dark lion less and less. Jin Sura represented everything I hated about the Commies, wealth, privilege, and self-conceit.

"Well, well. Lord Suradon's wayward son. Introduce us," Merida whispered, squeezing my arm.

"Sure," I said. And with that one thoughtless word, I made the most disastrous decision of my life.

Don't worry, this story isn't about me. You don't want to hear about Jolie Blanche Sauvage, the skinny, bleached white Paris rat, one of the millions of Euro orphans left over after the Great Dislocation. Maybe you've browsed video about the big European die-off in the summer of 2057. That was before they knew how fast the atmosphere was changing, before they'd built enough sealed underground habitats to protect everyone from the toxins. Decades later, even with safe housing, Parisians were still dropping dead.

Anyway, I was one of the leftover kids, one of the deep-Earth tunnel rats. Living in packs, we infested the transit system, begging food and water, stealing municipal air. The only difference about me was, when I was eight, I found an old surface suit.

It was my preter-treasure, my secret. That oversized old suit and helmet allowed me to sneak up through a maintenance well, all by myself, and explore the forbidden open surface. To my astonishment, the open Earth was not a death zone as we'd been warned, but a wide storm-blasted plane full of misty sunlight and strange beauty. After my first visit, the city below seemed blighted and cramped. I took to spending a lot of time up top. Wandering through the smog. Finding things to sell. Learning.

I never planned anything, but gradually I started getting jobs on the open surface. Hardly anyone wanted to go there, ça va? The Com managers hired me for stuff they didn't want to supervise—like foaming communication towers, cleaning out vents, and guiding dome repairmen through the haze. I saved my funds and bought gear on the hot market. Finally, I acquired my first aircar through a freeboot Net site based out of Sydney. The car brought new liberty. I started roaming all over the Euro islands.

Like I said, I never planned any of it, just made things up as I went. Before long, I launched my own Net site and started a tour guide service, Jolie's Trips, extreme surface adventure for individuals of means. For a while, in my own way, I was richer than any of them. And that's all there is to say about me.

This is my account of Jin Airlangga Sura, whose strange pilgrimage I've witnessed in intermittent spurts over the last three years. What happened to Jin was my fault for sure, and I swear by the Laws of Physics, I would change it if I could. But it's done now. Jin's journey began that muggy night at Rennie's. Or maybe his journey began long before. Maybe you could say it began with the Big Bang. Don't worry, I'm not going back that far.

After I introduced them, Dr. M. linked her arm in Jin's and led him off into a corner. They talked for a solid hour. I saw Judith Merida's large, scarlet mouth working nonstop. I saw them laugh and flirt with each other, and when I looked again, they'd grown solemn and strangely intense. This time, Merida hadn't scared off her prey. But I couldn't eavesdrop. I had work to do.

Luc and I were fitting the clients in surfsuits and helmets and boots, showing them how to seal the gaskets, and answering their questions—always the same questions. Luc was good with people. Cher petit Luc. Milk white, dimple-cheeked, he looked like a skinny cherub. Only seventeen, already he knew how to say the right thing.

"Ah oui, it's possible to survive on the surface without a suit, but only for a little while, and you must get the therapy right away. Oui, monsieur, the winds can lift you many kilometers into the sky. That is why we use a safety tether. Ah oui, we've done this before." Luc spoke Net English with a quaint Fragñol accent that everyone adored. Me, I'd worked hard to lose my Euro twang. Ironic, huh.

When everyone else had been dealt with, I called Jin by name. "Mr. Sura. It's time for your fitting."

Jin lifted his shapely dark head and glanced my way with an air of distraction. So patently aristo. Mes dieux, but he set me on fire.

I said, "Luc, you take care of Mr. Sura." And I stalked out to the toilet.

The truth was, Jin Sura embarrassed me. He made me conscious of my broken fingernails. We were the same age, he and I, but in his twenty-five years, he'd lived like a prince, whereas I'd had to claw and fight just to eat. Now here he was, glittering with high Com polish, a movie star no less, whereas I had nothing to show but a pile of used gear and an overabundance of cheekiness. He made me feel raw.

Luc was measuring him for boots when I returned. Watching them, I drew myself a glass of beer and drank most of it—Rennie's Bar was strictly self-serve. Jin shifted in his seat and gave me another view of his perfect profile. Then he glanced at me as if he were seeing my face for the first time. I could tell he was noticing the five-point star tattooed around my left eye like a violet bruise.

He said, "May I ask a question?"

I shrugged and drained my glass.

"Will we see the carvings at Belahan?" He spoke Net English with the soft sibilant accent of the Pacific Rim.

His question caught me off guard, so I didn't answer at once. Hardly anyone knew about those ancient icons carved in the Javanese rocks. That site had been flooded decades ago. I enjoyed browsing the history of surface places, but few people did that anymore.

He went on in what I took to be a patronizing tone. "The Belahan carvings date back to the eleventh century. That's before global warming, before the sea level rose. There was once a coastal kingdom. It could have been paradise—"

"No," I interrupted him. "In the first place, that's in Java. We're going to Irian Jaya, which is a completely different island. In the second place, those carvings are way underwater."

"I thought perhaps a side trip?" He slipped his elegant foot into the boot Luc held. "I'd be willing to pay."

"That's a custom-order tour. You'd need insulated dive gear. That ocean is hot. If you wanted that kind of trip, you should have said so earlier."

Luc grimaced at me and made signs that I should take Jin's offer. But I grimaced back and shook my head. I wasn't in the mood.

"Have you seen the carvings yourself?" Jin asked, in that damned polite tone.

"No." I took another swallow but found my glass empty.

"That's good," he said to Luc, who had just finished tightening his boots.

I said, "Walk around, Mr. Sura. Make sure. We don't want you getting blisters."

Jin got up and gracefully stamped around in the surf boots. He glanced at me with that melancholy smile. "The inscriptions commemorate one of my ancestors. I wanted to see them firsthand. It's a whimsical idea, I know. As if that would change anything."

With a slight shrug, he crossed to the bar where I was standing and lifted the beer nozzle and refilled my glass. "Here's to making the right choices, Mademoiselle Sauvage." He flashed his dazzling white teeth and winked at me. Then he took my glass and put his lips just where mine had been, and he drank till the glass was empty.

THE NEXT DAY, we flew to our drop point in a chartered plasma jump-jet. About midmorning, our pilot—Rebel Jeanne Sabat—touched down on a narrow, irregular rock shelf. It was maybe twenty meters wide, and it stuck out halfway down a palisade on Mt. Puncak Jaya's southern face. The shelf had a high cliff on one side and a sheer drop-off on the other. I'd found that the cliff's angle usually protected this shelf from the vicious Sudirman wind shears, so I called it Tranquility Base. We'd used it before.

Our six guests trooped out of the small fuselage. They were stiff and sullen. Even though we'd outfitted them in the newest lightweight gear, they moved awkwardly. Except for Jin Sura—naturellement, he moved like a dancer. The giddy young widow from Greenland.Com slipped and fell and started singing the most eloquent lullaby of curses. Jin helped her up.

The wind was flinging sheets of grit along our shelf, but far out on the horizon, the sun had turned the smog blanket a lustrous amber. Wisps of smoky dust stirred up in delicate vortexes and cast blue shadows over the denser clouds below. To the south, a herd of rose-colored thunderheads seemed to be galloping toward us in slow motion. I had to stop and stare.

As usual, Luc and I off-loaded the baggage while the clients toddled around aimlessly. We had to hustle because Rebel Jeanne Sabat was antsy to lift off. Rebel Jeanne survived on amphetamines. She never could settle down. We had arranged that Rebel Jeanne would return to this spot in exactly one week to pick us up.

The guests wore helmets equipped with interference-resistant, line-of-sight radios. I ordered everyone to stay close. Wouldn't you know, the bodybuilder couple dug out their little geology hammers and started wandering down the shelf, chipping at rocks. Before I could yell an order, Luc touched my arm. I saw him wink at me through his faceplate.

"Relax, ma chérie. I take care of those two."

Petit Luc. That kid had more savvy about handling people than I ever would. I nodded, and he sauntered off to nursemaid the amateur geologists.

Rebel Jeanne doesn't handle baggage, so I had to finish off-loading the heavy cases by myself. Jin offered to help, but I fussed and said he was getting in my way. He stepped back obediently.

"This is Puncak Jaya, yes? Irian Jaya's tallest mountain?" he asked. "Mademoiselle Sauvage—or may I call you Jolie?"

"Whatever."

"Imagine, Jolie, one short century ago, this mountain rose over five kilometers above sea level. What's the altitude now? It's seventy meters less I think."

He sounded like some balmy narrator on the History Channel. "Puncak Jaya's still plenty high," I grunted, heaving a crate out of the jet's cargo hold.

"Yes, it's lovely," he said. "I can't decide whether to be glad about global warming or disappointed. We've gained and lost, yes? It's hard to know which is better. This island used to be the second largest on the planet, second only to Greenland. Now it's mostly underwater."

"Uh-huh."

"Perhaps you know," he crooned on in that professorial tone, "this island was home to the mythical Bird of Paradise, a creature who spent its entire life flying through the air because it was born without feet."

"That I didn't know." I had to grin despite myself. "You've done your homework, Mr. Sura. A-plus. Now why don't you go gaze at the view for a while. Give my other guests a history lesson. I don't want one of these crates to land on your toe by accident."

Maybe fifteen minutes later, right after Rebel Jeanne blasted off, I realized Luc and the amateur geologists had disappeared around an outcropping at the far end of the shelf. And the winds were picking up. This did not improve my mood.

Whenever I led tour groups back then, I wore a full-function miniature Net node strapped to my left forearm. It was hardened against solar radiation, and its beam could find a Net satellite from anywhere on the planet. On my trips, having a dependable link to the Net was mandatory. So I ripped back the cover flap on my sleeve, activated the cybernails in my right glove, and started tapping the small screen. On Earth's open surface, you can't use voice commands. You have to tap. Anyway, I patched a signal through the Net to Luc's helmet radio to let him know I was trying to reach him. Luc had a Net node on his wrist, too, so he could tap a reply. I signaled for a full minute, but Luc didn't respond. Hell.

"Are they in trouble?" Jin surprised me. He was standing really close. I realized he was touching his helmet to mine so he didn't have to speak through the radio. He'd had the foresight not to disturb the other guests. That should have softened my opinion of him, but I was agitated.

I chinned the radio switch in my helmet. "Get on the tether now! Everyone! Now!"

Then I realized I hadn't unpacked the tether yet, so I did that. Jin helped me shake out the tangles. All the time, I kept checking my Net node screen for Luc's reply. A simple malfunction, it had to be. I unclipped the piton gun from my belt and fired titanium spikes into the rock cliff, then secured the tether in place with carabiners.

"Over here," I motioned impatiently. My Net screen was still not showing Luc's reply, and the winds were getting stiffer, blowing up billows of smog from below. I switched to metavision. That's the adaptive optics that use laser and infrared tomography and magnetic resonance plus a few other tricks to help our feeble human eyes penetrate the smog. Through my metavisor, I saw Jin helping the other guests clip their carabiners to the tether.

"You too!" I yelled.

"What should we do first, secure the gear or break out the safety beacon?" Jin pointed to where the wind was rolling an air cylinder down the rocky shelf.

"I know my job!" I just barely managed not to spit.

I clipped Jin to the tether, then chased the cylinder down. We would need that air. Next, I wrestled the big cargo net out of its bag and flung it over the pile of cases. I'm plenty strong for my size. Gusts were toying with some of the lighter items, so I had to run around kicking them under the net as I fastened the edges down with more pitons. Going by the book for once, I set up a beacon laser. Its bright red beam shot straight up through the whirling smog like a pencil-thin pillar of fire.

A real gale was brewing. My Net screen still showed no response from Luc, and the guests were demanding information. "Stay on the tether," I warned them in my gruffest voice. "If you move from this spot, I will personally beat you to bloody gore."

Luc would have said something nicer. Cher enfant. I'd met him in Paris, when he was twelve and I was twenty. An orphan like me, he'd been following me around ever since. I swallowed my worry and headed toward the outcropping.

The atmosphere was getting murkier by the minute. Suddenly a gust lifted me off my feet and sailed me several meters along the shelf. I landed sliding, grabbing for a hold. My left glove caught in a cranny. I knew I couldn't risk another flight like that. Our climbing gear was still packed in its case under the cargo net, but I carried a spool of emergency monothread for just this sort of occasion. Monothread is tough enough to bear more than twice my weight. The spool at my belt had thumb levers for brake, release, and rewind. I'd used it plenty of times. Lying flat on my face, I shot a piton into the rock, close enough to shower chips against my faceplate. I'm used to working in gloves, even with tiny monothread, so I knotted a couple of quick half hitches around the piton to make a belay.

With this security, I belly-crawled farther along the shelf and eased around the outcropping, reeling out thread and shooting more pitons as I went. The shelf narrowed to a mere ledge beyond the outcropping, maybe a meter wide, and the winds were regularly lifting me off the rock, fluttering me like a kite. Who knows how much time passed before I heard one of the bodybuilders moaning? Metavision is sort of low-resolution, so I didn't see his gloves grasping the ledge till I was right on top of him.

The guy was practically hanging by his thumbs. His bulging muscles had locked up so tight, he couldn't move. The wind had saved him. After flinging him over the edge, it had pressed him into a small declivity in the rock face. He was a big, brawny guy, and it took all my strength to haul him up. He was too numb to speak clearly. I secured him to a piton—

the last one I had with me—and I peered down over the ledge for the others.

Hell and double hell. His significant other was hunkered on another narrow ledge maybe eight meters below, cradling his ankle in both hands and rocking back and forth, oblivious to the fact that the wind could blow him away any second. The background rustle in my radio turned out to be his whimpering. About then, a hard, muddy rain pelted us like a hail of golf balls. The drops carried more grit than moisture, and one of them pitted my faceplate with its force. Thank the Laws, the mud rain stopped as quickly as it had begun.

"Where's Luc?" I yelled into my helmet radio.

"My leg," the guy panted. "It's broken. I fell. It hurts like mad."

Ça va. So much for manly men. Both these guys sported the muscle-bound physiques of hard-core weight lifters. They must have been taking supplements for years.

"Where is Luc?" I articulated each word separately.

The guy with the broken ankle pointed down, indicating Luc was below him, beyond my sight. I think my heart missed a beat.

Funny how fast a situation can get out of hand. There must be another ledge below, and Luc is safe—that's the first thing I told myself because I wanted to believe it. My hands were shaking as I eased over the ledge, and the wind was rushing so hard I could hear it whistling up the face of the palisade, even through my helmet. All sorts of feminine feelings surged through my brain. Motherly love and panic and ferocity. I had to force myself to forget about Luc and to concentrate on making clean, controlled moves down the cliff.

I reached the injured man and clipped him to my belay. Then I couldn't wait any longer. I hung out over the ledge to look for Luc. Oh God O God I can hardly breathe as I record this now. The memory is so strong. A dozen meters below, Luc was clinging to the sheer rock wall with his gloved fingers. The kid was skilled. He'd found tiny handholds where no one else would have found them. I imagined I could see him gazing at me. But his faceplate was cracked, and moisture had condensed inside. Only one thing caused that—hot Earth atmosphere mixing with the breathable refrigerated air inside a surfsuit. Luc was breathing poison.

The cliff dropped sheer as glass into a crevasse maybe a kilometer below. All I could think was, if Luc blacks out, he'll fall. In a heartbeat, I unclipped the injured bodybuilder from my belay. The monothread would support only two. I would have to spool myself down to Luc and haul him up, then come back for this guy later. There were no more pitons to anchor the guy in place, so I told him just to sit tight. The Laws of Physics had protected him so far, and anyway, I didn't worry about that. I leaped over the ledge and rappelled down fast toward Luc.

Monothread slid through my gloves—and then jerked me to a halt. I'd come to the end of the spool! Mes dieux, but I had to stop myself from screaming. About then, a sharp gust swung me out and dashed me back against the cliff. I took the impact with my wrists and dangled for a minute. The bodybuilders were whining complaints in my helmet. I gathered my wits.

Two, maybe three meters below me, Luc lay flat against the cliff. It wasn't that far. I started feeling for handholds and footholds in the rock. If I could just find a position that would support my weight, then unclip from the spool and free-climb down to Luc, and then somehow shove or drag his semiconscious body back up this cliff, three meters, with no belay . . .

The crevasse yawned below. Even with metavision, I couldn't see its bottom. Ideas assaulted me from many directions. Could I reach Luc in time? Could I haul his body up that sheer cliff, fighting the wind, without a belay?

As the muddy rain started pelting us again, a vision of the six trusting clients passed briefly through my mind. If I should die trying to rescue Luc, they would survive for maybe half a day. Six people versus one. Maybe I should have thought through the logic of that, but I'm a doer, not a thinker. What I've learned is, if you want to survive, you have to make up your own logic—sometimes out of thin air. No matter what the chances, I would not give up on Luc.

Gritting my teeth, I rammed fingers into a tiny crevice, pressed my toes against rock and squeezed the carabiner to free myself from the belay. And I started free-climbing down.

"Sauvage! Stay where you are!"

That's when I saw Jin rappelling from above. He was wearing my bright yellow climbing harness. He must have found it

among the gear. I learned later that he'd followed the trail of
my monothread. He descended steadily, like an expert, and as
he dropped past me, I let my body collapse against the cliff. I
saw him clip a safety line to Luc's belt, and I heard him say,
"It's okay. We're coming up."

I cried then. But no one ever knew that.

FOUR HOURS LATER, we were waiting in a Sydney medical clinic, while a cyberdoctor injected Luc with molecule-sized robots to clean the toxins out of his cells. Luc was unconscious. Mucus oozed from his eyes and nose, and his skin had turned an ugly color, but the cyberdoc said his prognosis looked hopeful.

Me, I felt like a piece of garbage. I'd bungled everything. It was Jin who took the time to think things through, to unpack the climbing gear, to call the Australian rescue squad. It was Jin who saved Luc's life. I sat across from him in the clinic cafeteria, resting my elbows on the plastic table, huddling over a cup of horrible cold tea. All around, people were murmuring about the exotic celebrity, but me, I felt ashamed to meet his eyes. Through my negligence, my cher Luc had nearly . . . I had to bite the insides of my cheeks to keep from shaking.

Someone came into the cafeteria, and I turned so fast, I knocked the table and spilled tea. But it wasn't the cyberdoc with news about Luc, just somebody wanting Jin's autograph.

"You love him, don't you?"

"Huh?"

"Luc Viollett. You love him?"

Jin's question caught me off guard. He'd been silent so long. I saw his concerned expression and quickly lowered my eyes. Funny, my other five tour guests couldn't wait to get away from me, but Jin had stayed. I stared at the puddle of pale green tea on the white table. There was no napkin, and in my muddled state, I started pushing the liquid around with my hand. Then I soaked some of it up with my shirtsleeve. I made a big mess.

Jin grabbed my hand and smiled at me in a troubled sort of way, as if he could see right into my heart. His mouth moved, but he stopped short of saying anything. I wondered about that. His uneasiness touched me.

"Mr. Sura," I studied the tabletop and began steeling myself for humiliation. "Thank you for saving Luc's life. I should have said that before."

"People say a lot without words," he replied.

I glanced up again. His black eyes flashed liquid light. Had he sensed my dislike all along? "Sometimes we get things wrong," I said.

He smiled. "You weren't wrong about me. I'm just as rotten as you imagine."

He must have read my embarrassment, because he laughed. He had a pleasant laugh. It lightened my mood.

He asked me questions about Luc, so I told him how we first met. One hot night years ago in Paris, I saw this scrawny little towhead standing on a crate, peddling counterfeit edu-disks. The boy had the slickest line I'd ever heard. He looked like an underfed cherub, but I swear he could have charmed the horns off a devil.

Me, I'm always hoping to learn stuff, so I asked if he had any disks on the Laws of Physics. Luc said I could have three disks free if I would buy two at the regular price. Sounded like a good deal to me. Anyway, while I was bending over his plastic case, pawing through his stock, little did I know he was secretly rifling my backpack.

Then he yelled, "Jesús, Newton and Einstein! You are the Surfer Girl!" That was my Net alias back then. Anyway, I spun around and caught him holding my surface helmet, staring at me in disbelief. He started sputtering in pure gutter-Fragñol, his English all forgotten. "You are my priestess. I know of your exploits in the world above. I worship your feet . . ." and other similar trash. He made me laugh till I hyperventilated. Talk about turning on the charm, he did.

Ça va, I made the mistake of letting him clean my helmet. Next thing, Luc was following me everywhere, polishing my surf-boots, sweeping my cube, sorting my email, managing my schedule. He latched on to me for good.

Jin listened attentively. "Luc is your family, yes? Your little brother?"

"You could say that." The thought made me grin.

Sir Jin liked the story about Luc. I decided he wasn't such a prick after all. Talking about Luc came as a relief, and after that, Jin asked me about me. So I told him some scary trip stories. My "Jolie's Trip" stories were always a hit.

First, the infamous "Jolie's Trip to Mecca." Most of North Africa is just a moving ocean of sand now. On our one and only trip there, we nearly lost three clients in a rogue dune that blew up out of nowhere. That drift stood ten meters high, I swear. Thank the Laws, we'd brought sail-skids to carry the gear, so Luc got the other clients windsurfing the sand waves in those skids, while I hauled the first three out of that monster drift using a souped-up-metal detector. Everybody had a blast. They thought we'd planned the whole thing for their amusement.

I really liked the sound of Jin's laugh. He wanted to hear more, so I narrated "Jolie's Trip to Hawaii," which is a cluster of sunken islands in the bubbly hot latitudes of the Pacific. Usually, my guests on the Hawaii trip are content to hover above the waves in a copter-jet and view the flooded cities with remote-control bathyscaphe cameras. Bathysnorkeling, we call it. But one time, I had this guy—from Nome.Com wouldn't you know—who insisted on SCUBA diving. The Hawaii story has been much embroidered over time, and I can't remember how it really ended, but in the version I narrated to Jin, the guy paid us double the fee because we convinced him the parboiling effect made his skin look younger. Jin laughed so hard, his eyes watered. He said he knew that guy.

I have to admit I started to like Jin. One thing led to another, and I found myself blabbing my plan to settle in the south someday, maybe right here in Sydney. South Australia is part of the Confederacy of Transkei Free States, which also includes South Africa, Zealand, and Antarctica—all the southern landmasses still cool enough to live in. Even before the war, the southern states had never been aligned with the big Coms in the north. Southerners knew how to enjoy themselves. I couldn't imagine anyone starving in the south. But the downside was, no southerners could afford my trips.

"You cater to the rich," Jin said.

That sent me off on a tear. "D'accord, the rich. And what's wrong with that? My expenses are preter-vicious. The gear alone, not to mention transport. And Com execs, they're the only ones who can pay enough. Mes dieux, those scuzzin' Commies have money to spare!"

Jin had touched a sore point. I was always trying to justify my livelihood to myself, and once I got started, I just blundered on, forgetting that Jin was a Commie, too. "Those fat-ass execs hole up in their secure domes calculating their profits, while their so-called 'protected workers' sweat underground. Protected, my eye! Protes are no better than serfs. My parents were protes. The Commies say they take care of their protes. Free air, housing, and meds. But have you ever seen an underground factory?"

"You take the Com money to get even," Jin said.

"Yes! That's it exactly!"

How had he guessed? I'd never explained that rationale to anyone but Luc. Taking money from the scuzzin' Commies was my brand of revenge.

"You're a gall to the system, Jolie. Have you read about trees?"

"Huh?"

"Trees." Jin smiled. I could tell he liked to explain stuff. He should have been a teacher. "Long ago, tall thick plants called trees covered large areas of Earth's surface. Some trees grew over thirty meters high, can you imagine? And very strong. But tiny insects nested inside their huge bodies and sucked life out of them. The homes these insects made in the trees were called galls."

I had to think about that for a while.

Jin's eyes shifted to the ceiling, then to his hands folded on the table. He'd stopped smiling. He went on, in a darker tone. "Yes, Jolie, I have seen underground factories. My father owns quite a number of them. In Deep-Tokyo, I saw a three-year-old girl whose skin had turned gray from lack of light. It's vile, the way we live now. The whole situation is wrong. But what's to be done? If we overthrow this system, the next one may be worse."

He shoved his chair back from the table and stared toward the wall. I knew he wasn't studying the messages posted on the clinic bulletin board. His fists knotted in his lap. "You think I'm rationalizing," he said. "Perhaps you think I should oppose my father and stop what he's doing?"

Actually, the thought hadn't crossed my mind, but I didn't interrupt. Jin didn't seem to expect an answer.

"Perhaps I could stop him somehow. But others would step into his place. Nothing would change. I wish I knew the right course to take. Believe me, I would give anything to know."

When the cyberdoctor finally called, sometime after midnight, to tell us Luc was out of danger, Jin and I were both too keyed up to sleep. So we went for a walk in the Sydney Subterrain. Sydney was brighter and flimsier than Paris in those days. The patchwork market stalls wobbled and swayed as if they wouldn't last out the week. Southern businesses were mostly small-time affairs run by co-ops and health churches. Unlike the Commies, southerners didn't computer-analyze every monetary unit.

The thing about Sydney was, along with the claptrap stalls came plenty of open public spaces with lightwells to the surface. You saw colorful graffiti and laser shows and street performers. Juice bars filled the air with sugary aromas. And people strolled. That's it. They actually strolled. Many of them recognized Jin that night. They pointed and followed us, and some came up to talk. Jin wore a special smart ring on his little finger just for signing autographs. He seemed unfazed by the attention.

Jin wanted to hear music, but he couldn't decide what kind. We peeked into several cabarets, and I think we would have wandered all night discussing pros and cons if I hadn't finally picked one at random and shoved him inside. Bien sûr, he took it with a laugh. And the place was nice. A band of real musicians was playing, and a live human waitress came to take our order. We drank beer, and Jin analyzed the music. He should have been a professor, the way he talked. He told me the longer riffs derived from classic sizz, while the backbeat was pure Transkei rip-rap.

I decided Jin was an interesting guy. That soft Pacific accent was growing on me. In the bar, people were dancing the old-fashioned way, not slinking around in separate colored energy fields, but actually standing together in ordinary space and moving their bodies to the music. When Jin suggested we try it, I agreed. Luc's recovery made me want to celebrate. I would have said yes to anything.

"La Sauvage, you're a fresh breeze." Jin stood smiling at me for a moment when the dance was over. He brushed a strand of stiff white hair off my forehead, and I blushed. Back at our table, we dropped into our chairs and ordered more beer. We were both perspiring a little.

I liked the way Jin pronounced my name, but sometimes I wondered if he was making fun of me. We kept chatting about surface travel and dancing and Sydney, and after the fourth round of beers, things grew a bit unfocused.

"So, your father runs Pacific.Com. Must be plenty wild to have a meta-magnate for a father."

His jaw quivered with sudden tension. I guess I'd put my foot in it. How fast his mood could change. "A father who lets three-year-olds work in factories," he said. "Yes, that's plenty wild."

"At least you have a father. My parents died before I could know them. What about your mom?"

"Mother was fortunate. Like your parents, she died young."

That wasn't kind. Jin swirled his beer, and his expression was so grim, I almost decided to stop right there. But not me, not Jolie Blanche Sauvage. I tried another subject. "Tell me about your work in the movies."

"Work?" His laugh was short and dry. "I'd hardly call it that."

"But acting," I said, "you have to invent a whole world and live in it. That must take a lot of imagination."

He grunted and drained his beer.

"If you don't like it, then why did you choose it?" I asked.

"I'm heir to a Com throne. Who says I get to choose anything?" Jin laughed bitterly. Then he tipped his empty glass on edge and spun it till it wobbled and fell over. I barely managed to catch the thing before it smashed on the floor. I set it carefully on the table between us, and when Jin finally spoke again, his voice was small and hard.

"You might say my father helped me decide on acting. My father is the first head of our family to have a son in 'the entertainment business.' My career embarrasses him. But not much. Not enough."

Jin was glaring at that empty glass like he wanted to crush it with his mind. Right then would have been a very appropriate moment for me to keep my mouth shut, but I didn't. "Judith Merida saw your face in a scandal ezine. So what scandalous thing did you do, Sir Jin? Get high? Break heads and hearts?"

Even though I was inebriated, I noticed the shadow deepen under his eye. He moved the beer glass back and forth, making a pattern of moisture rings on the table. "You guess right, Jolie. Drugs, brawls, sex, the usual crimes of the idle rich. The choices I make require no imagination at all."

Instinct told me that wasn't the truth. Jin was working through some serious trouble, but I couldn't seem to hold my tongue that night. He had just saved my best friend's life, and all I could do was hassle him with stupid questions. Our hands lay near each other on the table. His were dark and elegant, with pale manicured nails. And mine—bony, callused, almost as white as the plastic cloth. I didn't dare touch him.

Without thinking, I blurted, "You're such a smart man. Why aren't you happier?"

Jin uncrossed his legs and sat up straighter in his chair. "Your friend Judith Merida, she says we dream the world. What if the choices we make don't matter? What if we dream a different life with every heartbeat?"

"Don't I wish!" I shoved ragged bangs out of my eyes.

Jin regarded me thoughtfully. "Pretty Jolie." All at once, he gripped my hand. "There's so much to know, Jolie! Twelve billion people on the planet. Are there really twelve billion separate personalities, or is it a trick with mirrors? Are we all the same person? Am I the only one?"

His intensity surprised me. Earlier, he had seemed so—detached. He ran fingers through his hair and continued in a subdued voice. "The way we live is terribly off-balance. And moral sense tells me I have the resources to make things better. If I only knew what to do! But as your friend Judith says, my frail brain constructs layers of distorted perception that lead me in circles. Jolie, I'm tired of dreaming. I need the truth."

What a load of drivel, I thought. But I didn't say so. I didn't want Jin to think I was ignorant. So I said, "You could study science."

His nostrils flared. "Alchemists and quacks. My father hires them by the gross. I've read their reports. The more they discover, the less they know." Jin brushed imaginary dust from his trouser leg with a gesture of disdain. The move was so characteristic of Com arrogance, it had the effect of reminding me who Jin Sura really was. I watched the waitress refill our beer glasses. Jin still held my hand.

"Nobody can know everything," I said. "We're only human."

"I have to know."

Mes dieux, how he lifted that noble chin. Just a Commie prick after all. "What makes you so special?" I snapped.

"That's precisely the question, Jolie. Why am I special? Look at my position, my wealth, my intellect. Even my physical appearance—just look at me. Why have I been singled out for so many gifts?"

Sacred Laws of Physics, what a peacock! I tried to pull my hand away, but he held it.

"I may be the only real person in the universe," he said. "Everything may depend on the decisions I make. But I don't have accurate information. I can't decide what to do!"

Pitiful, I though. "If you're the only person in the universe, what does that make me, a cyberscrawl?"

"You might be a figment of my imagination. Of course you would be convinced of your own reality to keep up the illusion for me."

My jaw dropped. By this point, you can imagine my pique. "So let me guess," I said, spitting saliva, "If everyone is a figment of your imagination, then no rules apply."

Jin swallowed beer and watched me over the rim of his glass.

I sailed on. "The brawls or whatever juvenile behavior landed you in the scandal ezines, so what? It doesn't matter if you hurt people, or shame yourself, or embarrass your father. No one is real but you. Life is a dream."

He said, "I told you before, you were right about me."

"Rotten. That's the word you used."

"To the core," he replied.

"Or maybe you just dreamed that personal history with your latest heartbeat."

I think that caught him off guard. For a long moment, he sat unmoving, searching my face with his liquid glance. Then he burst out laughing. "Jolie, you're a better guide than you know."

He squeezed my hand. Then he kissed my knuckles, and my fingertips, and my rough, callused palm. I'm thin and pale, but people do say I have a sweet face. Anyway, Sir Jin was definitely coming on to me.

I can't deny I wanted him, despite my anger. Jin was a beautiful man, and I hadn't been with a man in quite a while. Female hormones have a mind of their own, n'est-ce pas? His hair felt silky against my cheek, and I could taste the heat coming off his body. My fingers wandered to the back of his neck. I was more than tempted. Then I remembered the way he had flicked that dust off his trousers, and I could picture him flicking me off just like that. So I said something dirty and pushed him away.

"Jolie, have another beer." He spoke through laughter. "Pretty little Jolie. Drink with me."

I had to push him off me again. "D'accord, let's get drunk. That's a real smart way to find the truth."

"Tonight we'll enjoy ourselves. Tomorrow I'll seek the truth."

"Right. Tomorrow. And where will you look? Down in the Java Sea? In those rock carvings at Belahan?"

Jin stopped trying to grab me and fell back laughing. "In California, actually." He tapped his forehead. "Your friend, Judith Merida. She's promised me a little neurosurgery. To enhance my brain. For an appropriate fee of course."

I blinked my eyes in disbelief. "Dr. M.?" Then I whispered, "Don't go."

"Why not? It might be interesting."

For once, I bit my tongue. Who was I to say how a rich actor should spend his time and money? Still, what Jin said spooked me to the core. He started pawing me again. I hadn't noticed before how much beer he'd consumed. He was soused. I grabbed his square shoulders and tried to shake him sober. "Don't go," I whispered over and over. But Jin Airlangga Sura was beyond listening to me.

WE PARTED ON ambiguous terms, and I didn't see him again for a year. In retrospect, I remember that year, 2126, as one perpetual sunset—smoky crimson clouds viewed through my lawyer's skylight in Paris. It was the last year of peace.

Our adventure on Puncak Jaya really shook up the body-builder couple from Nome.Com. They filed a complaint with Uncle Org, the World Trade Organization, and it came to light that I had never formally applied for a commercial tour guide license. That year, I spent more days in court than on the surface. I did take time to download Jin's movies, all sixteen of them. Frankly, I was curious. Jin played romantic leads with a lazy grace, and the cameras loved him. I watched his scenes over and over, memorizing the shape of his lips.

I even searched the archives of scandal ezines. Jin was there all right, but not for the usual celebrity crimes. I'd had a feeling he wasn't the bar-brawl type. It seems Jin liked to produce independent political movies slamming his Commie cousins. He staged them as film noir parables with lots of special effects. Way dismal. But lots of stormy political weather followed each release. One of his movies even got banned from the Net, which I didn't think was possible in this day and age. It must have been a real shocker.

I found out about that movie because Jin got into a public shouting match with his father over it. I watched the archived video of their argument three times—and I observed something really strange. Jin's words had actually been censored! Some of the things he said about the movie didn't come through on the sound track. Preter-weird. This intrigued me, so next I searched every Jin Sura fan site, ezine archive and chat thread I could think of to discover what that banned movie was all about. Rien. Nothing. Not a single reference. I couldn't even find the title. Jin's father must have deployed a mega-slick creepy-crawler program to censor the Net that pervasively. It made me wonder.

Most of Jin's archived interviews were typical ezine trash—dippy hosts asking cliché questions and Jin answering with glib one-liners. But one segment I liked. The dim-witted host asked Jin about the meaning of life, and instead of playing it smug, Jin answered in that precise, animated tone that reminded me of a professor.

"I've been reading about corals," he said. "Centuries ago, small delicate animals lived in colonies under the sea. The young corals budded from the deposits of the old, and though each individual grew only a few millimeters long, the living and dead together built vast, intricate reefs of staggering beauty. Over time, their structures grew so large they created whole islands where many other creatures could live."

"Meta-cool," the host prattled. "Sounds like the mold in my refrigerator."

Jin ignored that remark and continued evenly. "In a way, the corals achieved immortality. Their dead bodies fed their living ones, transforming death into life, and the shapes each individual left behind remained forever a part of the reef's branching pattern. Some of the reefs still exist as fossils even now. The interesting question is whether the corals exercised free choice in the shapes they created. It would be comforting to believe so."

The host bleated some forgettable quip, but I didn't hear it. Jin's answer stayed with me. D'accord, I had to think about those corals.

My browsing turned up reports about Jin's father as well. Lord Suradon Sura, the chief of Pacific.Com. As a young man, Suradon had single-handedly set his Javanese house at the top of the Pacific.Com power structure—and left resentments in his wake. The proud old families of mainland Asia disliked answering to a brown-skinned, round-eyed Islander. In concession, or maybe in snide mockery, Suradon had had his eyelids cosmetically altered to assume the epicanthic fold. I figured a man like that had to be cynical and ruthless, but the archive photos always showed him smiling. He looked positively jolly. Apparently, something about the world really tickled Lord Suradon. I stored these bits of trivia at the back of my mind—who knows why?

Even as I wasted my days in depositions and lawsuits, the Net sang with rumors of insurgency. Rebels in the northern cities. Secret arrests. Hints of barbarism. Just as the year was end-ing, Jin and I met unexpectedly at an airport in Godthaab. Already, Euro had grown restive with checkpoints and curfews, but Greenland.Com's capitol remained pristine, sterile in its opulence, too well policed for any unpleasantness to occur.

Luc and I were herding weary clients through a private gate. We had just returned from a six-day/five-night adventure in the open Arctic Sea. My chalk white hair was matted to my skull. I hadn't showered, and my temper was brittle. This trip had been more than usually fatiguing.

And there stood Jin, holding a jacket in his hand. "La Sauvage. Well, well." His whole bearing radiated glamour. Cinnamon tan. Slim, muscular elegance. Stylish clothes. He crossed his arms and looked me up and down. "The wild one returns from battle, wounded but unyielding."

I was wearing grimy shorts, and my bare knees were scraped raw. A tussle with a submarine tiller in high seas had thrown me against a bulkhead. No big deal. I hadn't bothered with bandages. Suddenly, those scrapes made me feel like a juvenile.

"Your cranium doesn't look any bigger," I challenged, scowling to cover my embarrassment. "No brain enhancement? I expected bulging eyes at least."

"Miracles occur in their own time, pretty Jolie." He smiled with those perfect movie star teeth. He seemed genuinely pleased to see me. "You're just getting in? Let's have dinner. Don't tell me you're tired. I won't believe you."

Considering our previous encounter, you may ask if I thought twice before accepting his invitation. Sure I did. I bought a quick shower and had my eyelashes done and spent way too much on a dress in one of the airport shops. I was ready in half an hour.

At first, Jin couldn't decide what sort of food he wanted. He asked me what I liked, and we surfed the local Net, browsing dozens of menus. Even so, we buzzed past five different restaurants, and he kept discussing cuisine. I began to note a trend. Gorgeous, charming, polished, Jin was certainly all that, but the man had a serious problem making up his mind. Me, I was hungry. My stomach was growling.

We ended up at some posh watering hole in one of those white-terraced buildings overlooking Godthaab's central shopping plaza. Artificial trees swayed in artificial breezes, and lights twinkled in overhead holograms, suggesting a starry sky. The cyberservants were designed to appear human. We drank wine made from real hothouse grapes—the first I'd ever tasted. Is there any wonder it went to my head? Jin asked about my latest trip, and he listened to my answers. He really seemed to be glad of my company. Besides, he was so preter-good-looking. I could not pretend indifference.

That night, he was full of nervous energy. He'd just returned from his latest visit to Merida's clinic, and I could tell he needed to talk about it. He tried to sound glib. Merida, he said, was an aging flirt with dyed-black curls who kept bumping against him and lying through her teeth. Jin mimicked her bawdy come-ons to perfection. Even though I liked Dr. M., I couldn't help but laugh.

He said Merida had located her "neuroscience institute" in an underwater slum. She always was one to pinch a penny. Somehow she'd found dirt-cheap real estate in the ruins of a flooded city offshore from modern Frisco. He explained how, years back, tectonic activity had thrust the whole coastline deep underwater, and the friction of plates rubbing together had given birth to a trio of undersea volcanoes. Her clinic's thick pressurized windows looked out on deep-ocean gloom and intermittent red lightning. Jin said the garish effect suited Merida's place to a T.

He paused while the cyberservants brought our dinners. I'd never seen edibles so daintily arranged on a plate. After they'd gone, Jin told me about Boren, one of the inmates. It turned out all of Merida's patients were brain-damaged California protes whose health care was subsidized by Nome.Com. California was a protectorate of Nome.Com, and the subsidies were Merida's bread and butter. Jin said the protes received basic life support and experimental cures. Sometimes the cures worked.

Merida had implanted a molecule-sized nanomachine in Boren's parietal cortex. On the day Jin met him, Boren declared that he could hear himself think—that the sound was mincing and painful, and that he wanted to make it stop. The two of them shared an enlightening conversation.

Jin had a way of turning the whole episode into a farce, but his stories unsettled me. I'd never imagined Dr. M. in such a sinister light before. Jin's silver knife and fork flashed candlelight as he narrated with urbane wit. But the look in his liquid black eyes told me he wasn't really amused. He didn't tell me everything. I saw his eyelid quiver.

That's when I noticed a pair of tiny brown scars, like a set of parentheses, centered above his eyebrows. Two pale brown incisions no larger than my fingernail. They frightened me. I said, "Surely you're not going back to that place."

He took a bite of his seared plankton steak and didn't answer.

"What are those scars above your eyebrows, Jin?"

His laughter sounded forced. "We've implanted some nano-bots, pretty pet. Don't worry. They're just surveyors. They're designed to measure and map my cerebral energy fields. It's the first step."

"Sacrée Loi! What have you done?"

I think my words came out a shriek. He had let Dr. Merida cut his brain? Dr. M, the con artist? The barroom flirt? I couldn't for the life of me picture little Merida as a real doctor. Certainly not a neurosurgeon. She had never behaved the least bit like a scientist. All I'd ever seen her do was try to run scams on my clients—usually without success. And Jin Sura had actually put himself under her knife?

My kind feelings for the woman evaporated. I'd been naive. I had never imagined Dr. M. capable of real harm. I knew she was after money, but now I saw my charming little friend in a new light. Merida was not just a fraud—she was dangerous. What injury might her quack experiments do to this vibrant young man? Unbelievable, that Jin Sura would risk his very sanity to such doubtful hands. None of his explanations made sense.

When he lifted his crystal wineglass, I saw his hand tremble. "My father has agreed to underwrite a new line of research. Judith and I are partners."

"Your father? I thought you didn't like your father. What new line of research?"

"They're calling it Hyperthought. He thinks he'll make an-other fortune. Father knows an opportunity when he sees one."

"What opportunity?" I leaned closer to examine those inci-sions in his forehead.

We ordered another liter of wine and drank it all, but I could not get Jin to answer plainly. He talked about waking up his brain so he could choose the right course of action. I thought he laughed too much. At times, he seemed manic.

"Which would you rather have, Jolie—peace or freedom? We don't even know if we have a choice! But soon I'll know. Soon

I'll understand what I'm supposed to do with my life. I'm going to know everything!"

Sometimes he spoke so loudly, the other patrons turned to stare. I felt growing alarm for his state of mind. People around us were whispering. Even the cyberservants kept away. When he overturned his wine, I reached across the tablecloth and caught both his hands. His skin felt feverish. By degrees he calmed down, then grew sad. Finally, he spoke in a husky whisper, "Father expects me to fail. But he's wrong, Jolie. He'll see."

"But Jin," I said, "letting Merida dice up your brain is unzipped. How can your father go for this?"

Jin tossed his head arrogantly. A sudden rancor burned in his eyes. "My father approves. That's all." He glanced at our half-eaten dinners and signaled a waiter. "Pet, this place is dreary. Let's find some music."

I awoke the next morning in Jin's arms. We had consumed untold amounts of wine, and in my residual intoxicated haze, everything seemed golden. Jin's hotel room. Dazzling sun through the skylight. Satin pillows on the burnished brass bed. Jin's body. His arms and legs enveloped me in moist, salty warmth. I felt content. Protected. Utterly complete. I didn't want to move from the shelter of his embrace, not ever. Still, some part of me knew this was just female hormones urging me to bond. I knew Jin wouldn't feel the same. He'd slept with me on a whim. Any moment he would wake up and break the spell.

"Mmm," he murmured, moving against me. I stiffened and turned away, preparing for the break. But he moved closer. His tongue touched my ear. His chest slid firm and slick against my back, and his loins pressed my buttocks. We made love again, and slept, and when we woke much later, the sunlight had turned lavender.

"Want to see something extraordinary?" He was munching sporebread and marmalade, dropping crumbs among the satin sheets. We were sitting naked, cross-legged in the unmade bed, facing each other across a breakfast tray. He seemed much calmer.

I said, "Sure."

He leaned back and touched a key in a small hidden console. All at once, the six walls of our hotel room began to flicker with static electricity. I realized they were flat-panel displays. Slowly, the beige panels transformed into scenes viewed through windows. We seemed to be gazing from a lofty tower at the pale white surface of Godthaab—sans the smog. The details were much clearer than in real life.

"What is this, metavision? It's preter-strange." I stood up and twirled around in the bed to see it all.

"It's a live transmission from the surface. Watch, don't overturn the tea!"

He laughed and grabbed the pot when I jumped up and down on the springy mattress. I didn't care about the tea. The view was fantastic. Surface Godthaab was not a wild place—it was an engineer's dream of order. I'd seen it before, though not from this angle, and never this clearly. Paved runways alternated with long straight rows of surface equipment—communication towers, air exchange compressors, photovoltaic arrays. Everything had been spray-coated white—that was Greenland's style. I could see drogue machines and surfsuited workers moving sluggishly among the equipment. Dominating the landscape, three vast domes swelled like glistening jellies.

"Plenty cool!" I spun around, enchanted. But then I noticed the angle of the sunlight. Late afternoon. Much later than I thought. I sat back down and wiped my oily fingers on the hotel napkin and kicked the silver tray aside with my toes. If possible, I wanted to end this little affair on my own terms. "Sir Jin, my next trip starts in two days. I have to find Luc. This has been fun, but us common folk have to work."

Jin caught me in the crook of his elbow and pulled me to his chest. "La Sauvage, the practical lady of business. Break your schedule for once. I'm not finished with you."

The truth is, I adored being with him. I knew this would be our only time. So I fought my battle with dignity for about two seconds, then threw my arms around his neck. Weak behavior, I knew it even then. But my gut still ached with that damned female urge to cling. I hugged him close and felt the sadness welling up. In the hotel's synthetic view, the white domes of surface Godthaab seemed to stretch to infinity.

Jin pointed past my shoulder toward the southwest. "California," he said. "I'm flying out tonight."

The words filled me with dread. How quickly I'd begun to hate Judith Merida. "Jin, you should never go back there."

He laughed at me. "Judith's going to activate my latent senses. Humans have more than five. Oh, believe me, we do.

We receive input at the quantum level. But in our overreliance on consciousness, we deny it or fail to understand it. Egotism, really. The fatal flaw of Homo sapiens. We trust conscious perception far too much."

Scientific mumbo jumbo wasn't what I wanted. I'd taught myself to read by watching Net ads. All the science I knew came from the Nature Channel. But Jin kept talking. He'd switched to professor mode.

"You see, the neurons, the cells in the brain, they generate tiny electrical fields that resonate with each other. And sometimes they oscillate in phase. Think of voices in a crowd all suddenly humming the same chord." I could hear him choosing short easy words to fit my simple mind. Why did he even bother? I said nothing.

"As we receive input, these electrical fields build up and wash around our brains like weather. Imagine cyclones and warm fronts. Invisible rainbows. Silent thunder."

He rocked nervously. His eagerness disturbed me. I stroked his silky eyebrows with my fingers.

"Scientists fixate on consciousness, Jolie. They ignore our unconscious senses. Judith knows all about it. She and I, we're going to play with the quantum states in my brain's electrical weather. She has a way to modulate the quantum charge densities. To tune them, yes? Like a radio. If she's right, I'll be the first human to directly perceive sensations at the quantum level. I'll wake up from the dream. Then I'll understand what to do."

What a lot of rubbish! He should know better than to believe Judith Merida. But his speech had grown rapid and hectic. His enthusiasm reminded me uncomfortably of his manic episode the night before. I had to stay calm.

"That sounds fine," I said, "but why choose Merida for a partner? You told me yourself she lies through her teeth."

Jin lay back in the pillows with a smug expression. I noticed his face and chest were glistening with sweat. "The good doctor suits me. She wants to move fast, and she won't be hampered by ethical prudence."

All at once, I pictured Merida bending over a surgery table, her mouth stretched wide, laughing in that earthy voice. I saw her probing Jin's brain with her red-lacquered fingernails. "Mes dieux, but think what you're risking! Oh Jin."

"Oh Jolie," he mimicked my anxious whine. "Pretty wild one, you worry too much."

I knew he wouldn't be serious now. He wouldn't listen. "What's next?" I asked.

Reclining in the pillows, Jin clasped his hands behind his head and sighed. "Measurements. I fly back to the clinic tonight so we can start recording data. By now, the nanobots will have replicated throughout my cortex."

"Sacred Laws of Heaven!" I threw myself on his chest and squeezed him tight. I pictured swarms of tiny demons chewing through his brain.

"Jolie, don't be afraid for me. Look at the risks you take, yes? I'm not afraid for you."

"You'll be alone with that monster!"

"Judith? I thought you liked the good doctor. You introduced us."

I opened my mouth in astonishment. Odd, I hadn't considered that point before. In my dawning comprehension, I felt muscle-weak.

"Jin, please reconsider. The woman can't be trusted. At least, take someone to watch over you."

"Father will receive updates."

With my face nuzzled against his chest, I couldn't see his expression, but I heard the bitterness. What was going on between Jin and his father? I embraced him tighter and kissed his salty skin. Ignorance made me powerless even to guess at motivations. It was maddening.

"Send me the updates, too," I said on impulse. Why did I stammer on, committing myself without thinking? "If something goes wrong, I'll come get you."

A promise. It was a thing I didn't like, a thing I had vowed never to give to anyone. But already I'd broken that vow for Luc Viollett, and for others. Truth to tell, I wasn't half so aloof from people as I wanted to believe. And there it was, lying between Jin and me like a thrown gauntlet, my promise of help.

"Hmm." He drew back and gazed at me for a moment with an expression I couldn't read. Then he kissed me gently on the forehead. "You're my good angel, Jolie."

"Jin." I didn't mean to whimper. It just came out that way.

He turned toward the southwest, and I looked past him toward the east. In the distance, among the efficient white air compressors, I saw a tiny puff of black smoke, an explosion. A filtration unit flew apart in jagged pieces. That seemed odd.

"Very well." Jin's words broke my reverie. "You'll have the updates, too, pretty pet. You'll be my witness."

LITTLE DID WE realize, as Jin and I made love once more in our artificial tower, that the city below was fragmenting. That puff of smoke I'd seen among the compressors had been the first faint signal. Terrorists had penetrated Greenland.Com. The world had changed.

Toward evening, Jin walked me to the hotel lobby, but a squad of police had blocked the exits. They were scanning everyone. Jin made a scene. "Let her through. She's with me." He flashed his autograph ring and offered bribes, but the police ignored him. I grabbed his fingers as a cop ran a scanner wand over my body. Jin fumed. "Don't worry, pet. This is a farce."

Jin didn't know the universal ID chip in my signet ring was counterfeit. The chip tagged me as a free agent with Transkei credentials. Usually, I could travel through Com protectorates without hassle. I prayed the forgery would pass muster now. But the cop with the scanner barked an order, and they took me into custody.

I lost sight of Jin when two orange-suited guards marched me toward a rail bus with a lot of other terrified foreign tourists. Someone shoved me in and slammed the door. For two days I paced a jail cell, getting out only for toilet breaks. They fed me tube-goo and synthetic coffee, and they wouldn't even talk to me. When they finally said I could leave, it was a lie.

Oh yeah, the guards escorted me out of the security complex, but by the time I made it back to my lodge and found Luc, no sanctioned transport of any description was leaving Godthaab. What's more, they'd locked up my credit account. The smart chip in my signet ring had gone dead. I couldn't pay the lodge bill or access the Net. I couldn't call Jin's hotel. I couldn't even buy a cola from the vending machine. We were stuck.

Thank the Laws, I'm a resourceful girl. I always carry a few extra signet rings with alternative IDs. And I know better than to store the bulk of my money in a public Net account. Maybe

I never attended an edu, but you learn a lot growing up in the Paris tunnels.

Armed with a new ID, I sent an encrypted call to Jin. His hotel took a while to answer, and they couldn't locate him at first. Finally, they patched me through to his wrist Net node.

"La Sauvage, my angel. Isn't the world hilarious?"

I could tell he'd been drinking again, and I heard someone else in the room with him. I didn't want to see who, and yet I strained to hear if the voice was female. He must have recognized my suspicion, because he leaned close to his node's little cam-eye so his face filled my screen.

"You're still my angel?" he asked.

I nodded.

"Sweet Jolie. I don't deserve you. Stay where you are. Godthaab is dangerous now. I'm working on something for you. We'll talk later." And he terminated the link.

He was right about the dangerous part. The city corridors had turned malevolent. All the downtown sections were empty—an unsettling sight. And there was a smell. Godthaab usually cleaned its air with electrostatic microfilters. It never smelled, not like other human places. Paris had its own perfume of yeasty musk. Sydney smelled like fruit. Even on the surface, you could smell a distinctive burnt-sweat aroma in your surfsuit. But Godthaab had always been too sterile for anything as human as smell. Until now.

And the temperature was rising. Somewhere a refrigeration plant must have failed. In the wee hours, Luc and I stole out of our lodge with just what we could carry. I wanted to go find Jin, but Luc cautioned against it. I knew he was right. Jin could take care of himself, and anyway, I didn't want to find him with some other woman. So Luc and I took off through a labyrinth of dark, narrow maintenance corridors, heading toward the seaport.

We couldn't even get close. At least four kilometers out, we ran into a pack of terrified Greenland protes using the same route. They had children and baggage, and the ones we could see were caught up in mob mind, shoving and crushing each other in unleashed panic. We heard wailing ahead. Luc and I backed up fast and got away.

As usual, I didn't have a plan so much as an urge to survive, and I was willing to try anything. So when Luc found a hatch leading into a public corridor, we climbed through. The corridor was deserted. I'd never seen an empty pedestrian belt before. Those wide gray belts had always been packed with commuters. We passed barred shop windows, locked residences. That smell gave me the jitters. We sprinted through the corridor in eerie silence.

"Jolie." Luc pointed up. A surveillance camera pivoted on its mount to watch us, and a red laser beam shot out. It was scanning our signet rings, identifying us. I had one ring on my finger and two more in my boot. The scanner would read them all. Somewhere in the distance, we heard the thud of heavy footsteps coming our way. No wonder the corridors were empty.

"Let's go!" I shouted, racing on, scouting urgently for any kind of opening to duck into.

Luc saw it first, an electrical service shaft with a voice-recognition lock. "Voilà!" he said.

I ripped my handy piton gun from my belt and shot titanium bolts at the hinges. Luc used his fingernails. Alarms went off, but we got the lightweight little hatch open and shimmied inside. A ladder ran straight down, and we let ourselves drop.

For most of the afternoon, we wormed through the tight-fitting electrical service conduits. We went deep—so deep our GPS locators stopped working. With no sense of direction, we kept descending. Finally, when we were too tired to go on, we collapsed against each other and waited. We slept. After a while we woke up, and Luc fished some liquid nutrient tubes out of his backpack.

"Just like Paris, eh, chérie? Shall we dine?" Luc's cheek dimpled. He was enjoying the adventure.

"Yum, my favorite cuisine! Give me the chocolate one," I said.

"Naturellement! I would never stand between you and your chocolate."

When we'd sucked the tubes flat, Luc grinned at me. "Share your secrets, chérie. What's he like, Le Magicien?"

I knew who Luc meant. The Magician was Jin's most popular movie role, a cult favorite. I fluttered my eyelashes. "Aren't you dying to know!"

"Don't play coy, ma soeur. You slept with him. Oui, you're blushing. You can tell your petit frère Luc. Is his cock like a piston?"

I gave him a rough shove that sent him sprawling. "Luc, you're wicked!"

"Mais oui!" He sat up and dusted himself off. "But truly, chérie, why are you mixing with this aristo trash? He is hand-some, but dangerous for you."

"Oh Luc, it was just one night."

Luc gazed at me with his intelligent gray eyes. He had the sweet impish face of a child, but those eyes never missed a thing.

I said, "Luc, he's already found his next lover. He was with someone when I called. Mes dieux, Jin Sura's a world-famous celebrity. I'm nothing to him, I know that."

"Do you, chérie? You're heart is fragile. Sometimes you don't take very good care of it."

"It was just one night, Luc. It's over."

He nodded slowly, studying my face. When he wore that expression, he put me in mind of some wise old monk on the History Channel. I didn't dare tell Luc about the promise I'd made—to come if Jin called. Luc thought I was tough as iron. The idea of disappointing him, of letting him see my weak side, well it made me cringe.

"Let's move," I said, shoving stuff in my pack. So we took another ladder down.

Luc and I spent a month in Godthaab. We tracked the time on our chronometers, and for eighteen days, we scrambled through a dozen levels of automated machinery, playing hide-and-seek with the cops. Robotic equipment pounded above and below us till our very cells vibrated to the rhythm. It reminded me of the Paris tunnels. I felt like a kid again.

In fact, Godthaab's underworks looked almost exactly like Paris. The same brands of automated machinery converted solar and wind energy from the surface into power to clean and re-frigerate the city's air, to distill water from the rain, to illuminate the nutrient vats, and to pump electricity into the citywide grid. And the same brands of robotic repair drogues stalked though like ghosts, fixing what was broken.

Luc and I tapped the nutrient pipes and bled off all the food we could drink. We opened water valves and treated ourselves to marvelous showers. We pulled insulation foam out of the heat sinks and built nests. Ça va, we could have survived down there for years. But then we met the locals.

Four of them. At gunpoint. Two grown men, a woman, and a young boy. Their eyes glinted with suspicion. Luc immediately went into his charm routine and offered chocolate bars. To me, he whispered, "Smile, chérie. You look like the angel of wrath. You're scaring them."

I did my best to warm up my expression, but they were having none of it. The boy slapped the chocolate bars out of Luc's hands and growled. They were small people, with ice white skin and hair the color of dry chalk—like mine. The boy's eyes were pink, and the woman was balding. And all four of them had long thick yellowish fingernails. Way weird. These people obviously lived deep underground in the absence of wide-spectrum light. Runaway protes, criminals, terrorists? We didn't ask, and they didn't say.

So I tried the universal language. I waved a wad of cash.

The woman muttered a patois I didn't understand, and the two men grabbed us. With handheld electric torches, they led us deeper into the underworks, so far down my ears hurt from the pressure. The air tasted like metal. After a long, tense hike, we entered a warren of rusting ducts and air exchange tanks. The seams had been caulked with luminous plastic. It looked as if a child had been scribbling on the walls with lavender glow-foam.

Many people were living there. We passed small domestic scenes, three old men huddled around a stone brazier, a young woman teaching children some game involving stones. Everyone turned to stare at us. Villagers popped up through hatches and slid down chutes to gather around us in a tight, curious circle. They wore a motley mix of prote uniforms and designer fashions stolen from the Godthaab shops. Luc and I nonchalantly fingered our piton guns.

The woman, our hostess, grunted in monosyllables and scrawled numerals on the gritty floor with her finger. The two men stripped us of our piton guns, our cash, our gear belts, our signet rings—including the ones in my boot—and all of Luc's silver jewelry. Cher Luc was a bit vain about his jewelry, and he took that hard.

Afterward, they seemed to expect us to join them. The woman conveyed with gestures and a few words of Net English that our valuables would be added to the common treasury. In other words, these renegades had organized themselves like a Transkei

health church, sans the exercise equipment and nutrition coun-
selors.

After her little speech, they clamped old-fashioned steel
shackles around our ankles—just as a sort of "welcome to the
commune" ritual I guess. About then, I noticed some of the men
ogling Luc and me and licking their lips. I knew what they were
thinking. Scuzz that.

Luc whispered, "Smile, chérie. Stay calm. We still have resources."

When the village people started picking through our gear, an
argument broke out. So much for communal possession. While
they were occupied, Luc nudged me and winked. We quietly
edged into the shadows. Luc still had one tiny silver pin piercing
the only spot on his body the villagers hadn't searched. He used
that to pick the locks of our shackles. The villagers didn't even
notice when we slipped away.

Silent as thieves, we belly-crawled out of the warren, past the
glowing seams of plastic caulk into the safety of darkness. Then
we huddled in a cranny, and I suggested that the best escape
route would be straight up. The villagers wouldn't expect that.
Maybe the Greenland cops had forgotten us by now. Maybe we
could get to the seaport. Maybe should have been my middle
name. See, I'm a girl who always keeps hoping. What I've
learned is, when in doubt, make the boldest leap you can think
of, and you'll usually land safe. Not everyone agrees with that,
I know. It takes resolve.

Luc didn't like it, but he finally agreed with me. He always
does, eventually. The villagers had taken our chronometers, so
I don't know how many hours we spent working our way back
up through the factory levels to where we'd first played merry-
go-round with the cops. When we were maybe four levels below
Godthaab's public corridors, we started searching for recogniz-
able landmarks. We needed to get our bearings and find the
seaport, but everything looked the same. Mazes of oily blue
machinery clanking and whirring, compressing liquids and
gases, throwing off heat.

We'd fled the village people with just the clothes on our
backs, and we didn't have a single tool between us to open the
food or water pipes. So we dined on black mold, and we drank
from oily pools where steam had condensed under the ma-

chines—just like when we were kids. But it wasn't enough. Mes dieux, but I craved a cool drink of water.

In desperation, Luc finally starting yanking at a small plastic water line just where it connected to a pump. When I realized what he was doing, I joined in. We hauled and hauled at it, using our body weight to pull it loose. After several minutes of struggle, the gasket let go, and water blasted out of that little hose like a geyser. I swear by Newton himself, no drink ever tasted better. We were laughing and spraying each other when all of a sudden, we heard a voice. Machine-made. A cyborg.

"Mademoiselle Sauvage?"

Luc and I froze. The plastic water line lashed around on the floor blasting spray, and the machinery kept clanging. "Mademoiselle Sauvage?" the mechanical voice vibrated again.

I looked over my shoulder, and there stood a copper-colored cyborg wearing the uniform of a Greenland cop. Luc bounded to his feet, then slipped in the water and nearly fell. I sprang up and caught his arm.

"Do not fear me," the cyborg said. "I am Ras. I serve Jin Sura."

"You—what?"

"To avoid electrocution, please move one meter left," it said.

Luc and I gawked at the cyborg with open mouths. We were standing in water up to our ankles like a pair of goofy statues. The cyborg pointed, and we looked down to see where the water was just about to spill into an electrical fuse box. As one unit, Luc and I leaped up to a dry platform a meter to the left. A second later, the box scritched and smoked and arced white lightning as water sizzled through its fuses. Close one.

"Jin Sura has sent me to help you," the cyborg said.

If I had to pick the exact moment when I fell in love, that would be it.

The cyborg explained how Jin had deployed him to find us on the very day we disappeared. Ras had been searching ever since, starting at our lodge and doggedly following our trail. He'd tracked us using a DNA scan based on a few hairs I'd left on Jin's pillow.

He—Ras, that is—carried a Net node, cash, two fake signet rings, eight liters of water and a supply of those nutrient caps that taste like melted plasticene. He also carried a message, recorded in Jin's own voice.

"Take care, pretty Jolie. Remember, you're my witness. I'll be in touch."

Ras led us to the seaport through crawl spaces under the factory floors. Four hours of crawling, two hours of sleep, on and off for more cycles than I care to remember. The seaport turned out to be a preter-vicious long way. When we reached the docks, Ras interfaced with a cyborg shipping clerk, who promptly issued us a pair of surfsuits and stowed us away on a hover freighter bound for the south. Five days later, Luc and I were sitting in a public Net stall in Palmertown, Antarctica, breathing the air of freedom.

FEBRUARY IS THE hottest month in the Antarctic summer, and even though the Palmertown city engineers had all their refrigeration units turned full max, the air reeked with salty human sweat. Laws, that place smelled good to me.

About the first thing I did after we arrived was to download some tracer software to locate Jin. While we waited for the results at a public Net stall, Luc and I surfed the news. And stared at each other in disbelief. The unthinkable had come to pass. Full-out civil war.

Throughout the crowded underground cities of the northern hemisphere, protected workers had risen against their masters. Rebel cells long concealed had blossomed overnight. Bombs exploded in Euro, setting off subterranean fires that raged out of control. Greenland.Com had declared martial law. In the Manhattan Protectorates, production lines had been sabotaged. Looters in Asia prowled the corridors, ransacking without restraint. Nome.Com had released nerve gas in the Alaskan worker dorms. Only the Transkei Free States clustering around the southern pole remained stable.

My tracer program found Jin in Frisco, California. Sacrée Loi! He'd flown straight into the war. California was a protectorate of Nome.Com. And Allistaire Wagstaff, Nome's despotic CEO, had the worst human rights record on the planet. I couldn't believe Jin had flown to Dr. Merida's clinic in the teeth of the war. His action smacked of a death wish.

I sent a videomail to his address and waited for a couple of hours at the public Net stall, but there was no reply. So Luc and I checked into the cheapest lodge we could find, and for the next several days, we considered our options.

So much for Jolie's Trips. The outbreak of violence in the northern Coms put an end to my entrepreneurial pursuits. As if I cared about that anymore. Every day brought new horror stories and market gyrations. I kept thinking about my friends in

Paris. I watched the news every second. Caspar Van Hyeck, the CEO of Greenland.Com, made long windy speeches about peace, while Nome.Com's Allistaire Wagstaff erupted with bloodthirsty threats. Pacific.Com's Suradon Sura came on once or twice to denounce the rebels as suicidal fools. Net newscasters raced to air the most graphic violence.

Meanwhile, Uncle Org—the World Trade Organization, our only planetwide governing body—seemed baffled. Uncle Org's thirty-two satellite-based Artificial Intelligence nodes were simply unable to comprehend the situation. The AIs overloaded the Net with their queries into human history. Maybe they were trying to fathom the purpose of war. Since their creation back in the twenty-first century, Uncle Org had managed Earth's commerce with order and reason and stable exchange rates. This situation didn't fit their scenarios.

It was a heady, nervous time in the south. Partisans mounted parades. Speculators ran scams. Southerners discussed the rebellion as if it were a sports contest. And everyone laid bets. A carnival atmosphere prevailed. You could practically taste the adrenaline.

Me, I wandered the bright, cluttered corridors of Palmertown in a daze. My life was in limbo. I didn't know what to do next. These southerners, most of them, had never been to the north. They didn't know the people living in the Paris tunnels. They didn't bite their nails and feel their guts pulled apart every time the Net aired another explosion. Still, how dare they lay bets on this tragedy? I wanted to punch somebody in the face, but I didn't know where to begin. Luc started drinking too much wine, which was way unlike Luc. Me, I stayed up all hours and bumped into walls.

Out of habit, I checked back every day at the public Net bureau for a reply from Jin. And I kept stopping in the open doors of bars, watching the Net news. What was happening to my friends in Euro? And what, by the Laws, could I do about it? I'm not usually one to hang around idle. I guess I was paralyzed.

The tenth morning, the public Net bureau posted a cryptic, text-only message for me, dated February 24, 2127, from the Merida Institute of Neuroscience.

"To La Sauvage. Boren was right. I can hear myself think.

It's a constant warbling bass note. Rapid changes expected. Wish you were here. J.A.S."

The message from Jin came as a real relief, more so than I had expected. He was alive, and that gave me hope. I think the distance and worry intensified my attachment to him. I sent a vidmail back at once, begging him to get out of there. That word from Jin, and the hope it brought, made something click inside me. After I sent the reply, I didn't hang around waiting for an answer. I went to find Luc. I was sick of feeling paralyzed. Luc and I both needed to be doing something. And finally, a notion had popped into my head about what needed doing.

If I'd been born with a little more smarts, I never would have tried this idea. Everything was against it. Ça va, I simply didn't know. My funds were still mostly intact, so first thing, I got Luc sobered up, and we rented a double cube in midtown with room to work. And I painted a sign in glitter-glue on the door: "Euro Rescue Project." Then I started calling friends.

Luc was too young and innocent to know how impractical my idea was. Luc would follow me anywhere. He bought equipment, built our Net site and started sending global vidmail, trying to reach the protes in Paris.

Jonas Tajor, an old acquaintance and totally brilliant geek living in Perth, Australia, helped a lot. Jonas had long curly hair and coffee black skin and a languid way of talking that calmed my nerves.

"Paris? Easy hack, love. We'll bounce a relay through the Aussie Fugue. That's our procession of 720 contrapuntal satellites circling in harmonic low-Earth orbit at 20 degrees to the ecliptic. A true masterwork of southern engineering. Those Norse-arses think they can scramble us out of their hemisphere? Jolie love, we'll go deep. We'll go hard. We'll go wire! We'll interface with the Transatlantic Cable. You didn't know that old relic was still there? Electrons rip!"

Sanguine, that's how Jonas made me feel. He tapped into pirate Net bands and sent queries to the Euro underground. He patched through to wire-based networks I'd never even heard of. He sent pulsed messages through urban power grids. It took time, but eventually we made contact. The Euro protes were living in hell.

Insurgent prote leaders had underestimated the will of the Coms. When work stoppages occurred, the managers simply shut down life support—leaving whole sectors of protes to suffocate in the dark. Food was scarce. Air was undependable. And almost everywhere, the water supply had been compromised. Old, old diseases, with sinister names like cholera and typhoid, were cropping up. Caught in a trap, the protes were beginning to turn against each other. There had been bloody battles.

Our friends Françoise Thou and Victor Bouille were still alive. I spoke to them. But Celeste and Rupert Chalotais, their three little girls, the Herbier brothers, and Uncle Qués, my old mentor in street crime—all dead. So many friends gone, I couldn't even cry. All I knew was that we had to get the living ones out of there. We needed a major airlift. And we needed housing and doctors and food and clothing. I didn't have enough money for all that. Listening to Victor Bouille's thin voice through the static—it made me crazy.

My idea was to run a quick hack on the WorldBank, grab some funds, then buy a cheap car and fly straight into Paris and see what I could do. But another good friend, maybe my best woman friend in the world, talked me out of that. Her name was Adrienne Stroebel.

Adrienne was another Euro tunnel rat like me. Only, instead of Paris, she'd grown up wild as a weed in Nether Berlin. When I first met her, Adrienne had been chopped down and brutalized so many times, you would have expected her to turn ugly and stunted. Not Adrienne. The hard knocks seemed to concentrate her beauty, and when Adrienne's time came to flower, she produced the loveliest, fullest, sweetest-smelling blossom imaginable. At sixteen she escaped to Palmertown and landed a job as a model. You may have seen her in the Transkei fashion ezines. Tall, willowy, with huge azure eyes, lemony skin and a nimbus of frosty hair. She's smart, too, my friend Adrienne, but a little bossy.

"Jollers, we need a financial strategy." It didn't seem to disturb her that I hated that nickname.

"Adrienne, I have a financial strategy. The WorldBank. Half an hour on the Net, and I'm in."

"Wrong, Jollers. Just shut up and let me take care of this. Our cause needs packaging. Poignant visuals. A stirring theme. I'll stage a few small entertainments to seduce the bleeding hearts. I understand how these southerners part with their cash."

She did, too. Adrienne hosted VR séances, hatha yoga chant-ins and other glam charity events. Plenty soon, she raised a pot of money. More Euro expatriates started showing up in our little office in midtown. Hundreds of people wanted to help. Next thing I knew, Luc was organizing committees and banks of Net nodes. Adrienne took care of finances. Jonas handled communications. Rebel Jeanne Sabot—my speed-freak pilot friend—Rebel Jeanne recruited pilots and set up a network of secret rendezvous sites in Euro.

And this local guy Luc met in a bar, Trinni al-Uq, he helped us acquire aircraft. Trinni also got us a bargain on modular jellyfish—you know, those inflatable seafarm units that float on the ocean and harvest oxygen straight out of the briny depths. We anchored three stealth-shielded jellyfish in the Mediterranean to house refugees.

Me, I'm a decent pilot, so I flew the Paris run. I met the protes in an abandoned solar plant built under the Butte de Montmartre. Men, women, children. None of them had seen the surface, and they were nervous, you know. I tried to remember what Luc used to say to calm people down. I made jokes. I helped people put on their surfsuits. The littlest kids we wrapped in cargo bubbles, and I tried to turn that into a game. I led people up top, forty to a load, tethered on a safety line. I remember this one kid, she was so amazed to be walking on the surface, she did a cartwheel, even in her gawky oversized surfsuit. Man, that was bliss to see.

We airlifted almost 30,000 Euro protes that first month. Thank the Laws my friends stepped in. Luc, Adrienne, Jonas and the others, they made it happen. Without them, the rescue project never would have come together. Mes dieux, but they teased me, too. Luc and Jonas called me "Chief." Adrienne called me "the rescuing angel." They asked me about every little thing as if my opinion carried real weight. Plenty soon, all the volunteers in our midtown cube were following their lead, calling me "Chief" and asking me stuff. I made up answers left and right.

Jin sent three more text messages during that time. I saved them, but they didn't make any sense. "Imagine experiencing the world without language," he wrote. "Could we distinguish boundaries if we had no names for foreground and background?" Another time, he wrote, "We label each experience by referencing what we've seen before. A large room, a white person, a sharp stick. Imagine seeing something entirely new. It must be like birth." In his last text message, he wrote, "I will perceive undifferentiated experience, without the intervening metaphor of number. I will see and hear everything at once."

Frankly, that didn't sound like fun to me. I kept sending back vidmail telling him to get the heck out of there. Even as I flew low under the Paris security scans and met those frightened refugees and led them up to the Earth's surface for the first time in their lives, I was thinking about Jin. When I wasn't flying, I was watching his movies. I memorized his every line and gesture. It shames me to admit I even downloaded a sexy photo of Jin from one of those sleazy fan-club sites, and I carried it folded up in my belt. I didn't even tell Adrienne about that.

Have you ever been so obsessed with someone that you feel wired on speed twenty-four hours a day? You're distracted and edgy. It's not exactly a pleasant feeling. All the time I was flying that old Van Gogh copter-jet back and forth to Paris, I imagined Jin was there beside me, watching everything I did. I imagined I was earning his approval.

His first videomail came in April. I was working in the office in Palmertown when the Net node on my arm vibrated. I took the call just like that, thinking it was Luc or Adrienne or Jonas. But it was Jin.

He looked pale, and his eyes were too bright. I bent close to the small screen and adjusted the contrast. His hair seemed wet. He was grinning like a fool. To my surprise, a text box opened onscreen, covering half his face. "Hello, pet." The words appeared letter by letter in the text box, as if he were typing slowly.

"Jin," I whispered, "can you speak?" That text box scared me.

He shook his head, still wearing the inane grin. He really didn't look like himself. Haltingly, he typed, "I have developed an aversion to the sound of my voice."

I braced my arm on the desk to keep my Net node from shaking. Finally, I remembered to activate the holo. Jin's face projected above the screen in a fist-sized, three-dimensional shimmer. I also enlarged the text box and tilted it toward me so it was easier to read. The projection floated like a sheet of white film just above my arm.

"Nonlinear phonemes," he typed with apparent effort. "Nanobots in my astrocytes. Wish you were here."

Just then a shadow fell across his image, and Jin turned his head. A second later, the holograph vanished, and my screen went gray. That last part of Jin's message haunted me. "Wish you were here." He'd said that before. What did he mean by that? Did he want me to come? I tried all day to reestablish the connection.

A month after that, Jonas retrieved a second vidmail from Jin that had hung up in a Net traffic jam and would never have gotten through to me. The date header was gone. Who knows when he sent it. The first part of the message was distorted, and Jonas had to clean it up. What emerged from the shadows was Jin, sitting in half-light, wearing a blindfold.

Again a text box opened. Jonas enlarged it for me, but instead of typed text, what appeared were quivery scrawled letters. Jin was writing by hand, using a slate and stylus. His first word took shape with glacial slowness. It was, "Fear."

Mes dieux, but I clenched my fists till the fingernails cut. Jin in a blindfold sending a message of fear? My imagination ran rampant. Adrienne walked in about then and leaned over the screen to see what we were staring at, but Jonas must have signaled her to be quiet. More words were forming in the text box. I watched the holograph of Jin's emaciated face, shadowed by the black cloth. His hollow cheeks had grown as pale as my own. He pursed his lips in concentration as he wrote. "Fear the light," his sentence read.

"Fear the light? What the hell?" said Adrienne.

Now Jin was scribbling another word. His stylus vacillated, then skipped. "Blind," he wrote. With desperate illogic, I prayed to the Laws of Physics for his safety. Jin's stylus wandered on, skittering like a seismograph. The final sentence was almost illegible. "Blind yourself."

That was the end. "Fear the light. Blind yourself." The message terminated in a rough cut. From the silence that followed, I could tell that even Jonas and Adrienne felt shaken.

Adrienne squeezed my shoulder. "Jollers?"

"It's all right," I answered.

We said little about the message, that day or any other.

Two weeks later, a curtain fell on Euro. Jonas's network started failing. Luc couldn't reach any of his contacts. Adrienne stomped around our midtown cube slapping the Net monitors as if that would make them work better. Apparently, Greenland.Com had detected our covert communications, and they simply shut down the power grids. Only much later did we discover what that meant in terms of prote lives.

From the commercial news channels, we learned that the largest three Coms—Greenland, Nome, and Pacific—had used the rebellion as an excuse to annex and devour their smaller rivals. Now there were no longer fourteen northern Coms, just three. Greenland was claiming all of Euro as its protectorate. Nome had taken over the entire continent of North America. Pacific had annexed the Arctic Sea and a big chunk of mainland Asia.

The "Triad," they styled themselves. When they issued a joint statement, every bar in Palmertown fell silent. We watched Caspar Van Hyeck, Allistaire Wagstaff, and Suradon Sura announce that the conflict was over. Then our links to the north went dead. We heard no more news. Even the commercial channels were stymied. It was as if half our planet had dropped out of existence.

For several weeks afterward, Jonas kept sending messages through the old grids, hoping they'd flicker back to life, but they didn't. The refugees we'd placed in the floating Mediterranean camps were safe enough. Those jellyfish were stealth-clad and self-sustaining. Trinni gave the protes training classes over the Net in how to operate the equipment. At first, we offered to place them in jobs down south, but the protes voted to stay close to home. They elected themselves a central management committee and set up an internal barter system. They could sail their little fleet wherever they wanted, so we decided to let them be.

For a while, we kept flying missions. But no one met us at our rendezvous spots. Then four of our aircraft were shot down in one week, so we called a halt. After that, we just waited. Adrienne's fundraisers started losing money. One by one, our volunteers lost heart and drifted away.

The appalling thing for me was how abruptly everything changed in Palmertown. One day there was a war. The next day, no war. It was over, forgotten, yesterday's news. Even now, I try not to blame the southerners. Those northern cities were no more real to the citizens of Palmertown than some exotic movie. The north existed only on the Net. The people around me had never visited Paris. They didn't grow up in those tunnels. They hadn't lost mothers and brothers. In fact, the war had changed their lives very little. It was easy to forget.

Adrienne was the first to go back to her old job with the fashion ezine. "You did your best, Jollers. It's time to move on." Ever practical, that was my Adrienne. But I knew about the handkerchief she carried hidden in her sleeve because her beautiful azure eyes kept leaking tears.

When my funds ran completely out, Luc found a job in human relations for a big furniture chain, and I signed on with a surface repair crew. We gave up the midtown office, and Luc and I rented a tiny residence cube in the lower city. Typical southern place, it had beige walls, dented drop-down lockers, a coffin-size toilet, and a door with a broken latch. We splatter-painted the walls and floor with fuchsia glow-foam, bought cheap yellow hammocks and fixed the latch. Luc acquired a flat-panel Net node for the wall, and I splurged on an animatronic aquarium. I love those things. But the place never felt like home.

I kept narrowcasting vidmail to Jin. He hadn't left my mind, not for an instant. Long after we'd lost touch with our friends in Euro, I kept badgering Jonas to help me reach Jin. Why, when half the world was disintegrating, did I continue to brood over the fate of one man? Because I'd promised? Because I felt responsible? Because my damned female hormones kept urging me to protect him? As I record this years later, I can tell you the real reason. It's because I have the kind of heart that, once it gets set, it's like concrete. At the time, though, I didn't stop to examine motives.

Jonas said, "You're flaking, love. This obsession is deeply unzipped." But he went to work with a will. Maybe it was the tedium of inaction. We were all feeling it by then. Like a pressure between the ears, and fingers that couldn't stop drumming, and words stuck in our throats that we knew were a waste of breath. Anyway, Jonas did everything he could to find Jin. He hacked Nome.Com's internal datafiles—a stunning feat. Before they shut him out, he downloaded a few terabytes of newsworthy data and earned his five minutes of fame on the Net, but not another word from Jin.

I wasted six weeks on dreary routine, welding surface ducts all day, avoiding the crew boss, checking my Net node every hour. We could only guess the fate of our friends, and no one wanted to talk about it anymore. The carnival was over. We were left with ignorance and dread—and denial. We concentrated on trivial things and pretended that time wasn't passing.

Often I dreamed about Jin. I dreamed Merida had sawed off the top of his skull, and I saw his brain rise up and metamorphose into a furry brown bat. When I woke from those dreams, I prayed that Nome's troopers would march into that scuzzy clinic and spray napalm. My beautiful Jin, he'd be better off dead than transmogrified by that quack Merida. Almost at once, I reversed my prayer and begged for Jin's life.

At night I hung out with Adrienne, watching the Net's inadequate half-news about half a world. What a glum pair we made, drifting through random bars. I guzzled beer while Adrienne sipped some zero-calorie swill and smiled halfheartedly at the men who flocked around her. I put off going home, because I knew Luc would be there, snuggled up with his curly-headed Arab friend, Trinni al-Uq. Seeing them together made my insides hurt. I hadn't snuggled with anyone since Godthaab. Since Jin.

I knew I didn't belong in Antarctica, welding ducts and drinking too much beer, letting my muscles go soft—while half the world might be suffering the fate of the damned. And Jin. What if he were counting on me to come and save him? "Wish you were here," he'd written. Twice. I guess my anguish about prote friends and the captive Com aristocrat got mixed up together. I forgot they were supposed to be on opposite sides. I awoke one morning—July it was, the middle of southern winter—with an idea already fully mature in my head. I couldn't help the people in Euro anymore. That door was closed. But maybe I could still help Jin.

Luc rolled over in his hammock and asked why I was packing.

"Can you believe I've never been to California?" Piling gear in the middle of the floor, I started humming. I felt better than I had in weeks. It was as if my spirit had been wilting, and now it was springing back to life.

Luc rubbed his eyes. "Jolie, please tell me you're not . . ."

I coiled rope around my forearm and grinned at him.

Trinni raised his curly head from Luc's pillow and sighed. "She's going after that Commie." I didn't think Trinni had been listening.

Luc sat up and frowned at me with that wise expression that

always made him seem so much older than his years. "Tell me it isn't so, chérie. Remember the pilots we lost over Paris? California will be the same. You can't get through. They will certainly shoot you down."

"That's why I'm not asking anyone else to go."

"Chérie, your life is worth more than this. What does Adrienne say?"

"I didn't consult Adrienne," I answered, grinning.

That made Luc angry. "You would risk your life for this aristo prince when his people are slaughtering our friends?"

"His people. Not him, Luc. He saved your life, remember?"

"Ma chérie, you know it's impossible."

I just kept grinning. "At least it's something to do."

I LEFT PALMERTOWN on a Monday, early in August, and set course on the shortest arc toward California. I had saved enough of my wages to buy a used aircar—a Durban Bee. Thinking about Luc made me sad. Luc had offered to help me search for Jin, but I couldn't let him. Palmertown had been good to Luc. He was getting a life together, making friends, earning good money. I think he was even recovering from his grief over the war. I didn't want to mess that up. So I asked him to stay put in case I needed backup. He took it in good grace, and we parted with hugs and tears. I even shook hands with Trinni. D'accord, Luc didn't need me hanging around anymore. I experienced a kind of revelation about that. Maudlin stuff.

By design, I didn't tell anyone else goodbye till I was airborne. I knew what certain people would say.

"Jollers, this is not a lucid decision."

"Adrienne—" I tried to answer, but she wouldn't let me.

"Who is this Sura person to you? You hardly know him. Did you forget the war? What about your friends? The project? Jollers, you just spin right around and come home."

"Adrienne, I—"

"You're infatuated with a movie star, Jollers. It's an addiction. That aristo trash won't even remember your name."

"It's not like that. I—"

"You're heading into a war zone, love." That was Jonas.

Adrienne added, "Those Nome troopers will blast you out of the sky. Why do you think we halted the Euro airlift?"

As if I didn't remember. Adrienne was like that, always arguing and giving me advice. I love her dearly, but sometimes you just need someone to agree with you. So I went off-wave for a while and flew in silence through the smog. "Wish you were here," that's what Jin had said. Twice. To keep from thinking about Adrienne's warnings, I fantasized romantic scenes with Jin. Tender words and caresses. I fantasized till my juices flowed. Chalk it up to hormones.

For more than 20,000 kilometers my metavision scanned nothing below but ocean. Near the equator, heat roiled the turbid surface and made the sea look like molten lava. It's hard to believe humans ever lived in that part of the world.

Bien sûr, I couldn't stay off the Net for long, so I linked back up and started moaning my worries. Did Jin really want me to come? Would I be intruding? Adrienne had plenty of answers, none of which were the ones I wanted. Jonas said the rescue project still needed my leadership, but who was he kidding?

After nine long hours, I spotted land. Gigantic rolling waves crashed at the base of a barren mountain range. The Sierra Nevadas, western edge of North America. I followed the coastal mountains north and, in minutes, sighted the dun-colored domes of Frisco, the southernmost habitable region of California. Any closer to the equator, the climate was simply too hot for cost-efficient housing.

Frisco's domes fringed the mountains like leftover sea foam. I circled lower. And then I saw a grisly sight. One side of a big dome had blown out. Debris and bodies littered the plain to the east for half a kilometer. Thousands must have died. I scouted closer and saw human scavengers in surfsuits picking through the wreckage.

All at once, my sensors read surface radar, and a voice rumbled on a public radio frequency. "Durban Bee. You are flying in prohibited airspace. Leave at once, or you will be shot down."

"Jollers, get out of there!" Adrienne shrieked.

Jonas's calm, easy voice said, "Jolie, love, Nome doesn't bluff. Retreat would be wise."

"Move your tail, chérie!" That was Luc. So the petit infant had tuned in! He still cared about me.

I executed a tight turn and fled due east into the desert. When I'd passed safely beyond the horizon of Frisco's perimeter towers, I spotted a caravan of those surface scavengers who'd been picking through the litter from that blown-out dome. I followed their caravan and touched down at their camp. They were living inside a big mound constructed of sun-baked mud lined with the lightweight fabriglass we use for emergency tent shelters. When the surfers saw me waving hot-market cash, they welcomed me in to dinner.

I've met a lot of surface dwellers in my time. They're mostly juvenile gangs. You can't spend your whole life on the surface and expect to live very long. Being young, surfers are often touchy and vain about things you wouldn't expect. You have to approach them with care. But once you're in, it's preter-fun. Surf dwellers know how to party.

Around midnight, they were playing loud sizz music on their homemade instruments, and we were sniffing something they called "mock orange." I guess I was plenty high. There was a small delicate kid with burns all over his face and shoulders, and everybody called him Tan. He kept hovering around me, bragging about a Net link he'd built out of spare parts. He wore a red rodeo helmet, and his breath was ghastly.

"Lady, 'f you need any kinda code, I'm yer man. I've hacked through Nome.Com security hunderds and hunderds of times. I can breach any dern database in the northern hemisphere."

"And I can see through any scam in the solar system," I said. This kid amused me.

"Scam? You think—? No way I'm gonna scam a fine lady surfer like yerself."

I couldn't help but be charmed by the boy. I said, "Bien sûr, and your mother's a priest."

"Yes ma'am. You come look at my gadgets, and you'll see."

I must have been way too full of myself when I agreed to try out his "gadgets." He'd walled off a corner of the mud hut with a torn blanket, and when he ushered me in, a hundred tiny green lights winked at me from a rack-mounted unit that towered over my head.

The boy strutted around tapping at the equipment with his knuckle. "I can do anything on the Net you name. Jus' try me."

On a whim, I said, "Okay, place a video call to Lord Suradon Sura, the Pacific.Com CEO."

"Hell yes ma'am. On time and on the dime."

Tan must have been a genius geek, because the vid call did not hang up in the usual twisted logic of an automated answering system. It pinged right into Suradon's wrist node, and he answered at once. His face loomed massively on the screen. I was stunned. I recognized him from the news. At my side, Tan winked.

"Who is this?" Suradon demanded.

Tan pointed to the tiny video cam-eye which, at that moment, was tight-focused on my face. I must have looked plenty weird to the Pacific.Com CEO. Onscreen, Lord Suradon Sura was every inch the Asian aristo in a buttoned silk suit, whereas me, with my scraggly locks and facial décor—what can I say? Tan was squirming around behind me so full of himself I thought he might pop.

I smoothed my hair with my fingers. "I'm your son's friend. Do you know where he is?"

"Sauvage?" My name sounded brutal the way Suradon pronounced it. To my surprise, he smiled.

The fact that he knew my name should have clued me, but I was feeling way reckless. The mock orange had addled my judgment. "What kind of father are you? You know what's happening to him, and you don't do anything!"

Beside me, the boy Tan bit his finger and shook with soundless laughter. He thought I was playing a prank.

Suradon's good humor died, and the fierce scowl that replaced it cleared my head. He literally thundered at me, "My son makes his own choices, Sauvage. I take it, so do you. Be ready for the consequences." Abruptly the contact terminated, and Tan slammed his fist against his knee, twitching with silent giggles.

"Jollers, are you insane?" Adrienne's voice shrieked from my wrist Net node. "You just gave him your location!"

"That was not smart, love," Jonas said.

"Plenty damn cool, I think." Tan snickered through his nose and crooked his little finger at me—the surfer's gesture of respect.

Luc just sighed. "Ma chérie."

That's when I realized my drug high had vanished. I was trembling.

I spent that night outside in the desert with the surfers. Tan and I lay on our backs, shoulder to shoulder, snugged up in our surfsuits. We were gazing at the heavens, and I let him link into my telescopic metavision. Did he love that! We talked about what the stars must have looked like, once upon a time, back when the atmosphere was clear enough to see through.

Tan, what a chatter-mouth. Plenty bright for a kid. He knew all about galaxy clusters and parallel universes, and he loved showing off his knowledge. Me, I played audience. Tan reminded me of Luc. Anyway, that night I calmed down and got my head straight, and next morning I left behind half my supply of food. The surfers didn't have a lot to eat. They needed it.

You think I was crazy to try breaking into a city at war? Crazy cunning, that's Jolie Blanche Sauvage. Before leaving Palmertown, I'd downloaded a bunch of schematics and cool reference pages about the Frisco area from the Net. At Frisco's western edge, a cliff dropped straight down into the ocean, and under this cliff lay the ruins of another older city, crushed long ago by earthquakes. Jin was right about the clinic's unusual location. Merida's building had been hard-foamed into the cliff face about 100 meters below the ocean surface, right into the rubble of this old city called San Francisco.

The Net node I wore strapped to my left forearm carried a brand-new GPSNS—Global Positioning by Satellite Neutrino Scan. I'd spent a bundle to get this particular model because it would function deep underground. During my long flight, Jonas had programmed it, remotely, to guide me down to the clinic, and already the audio pulse was playing inside my helmet. All I had to do was listen and follow.

Another thing playing in my helmet was the running commentary from my friends on the Net. "This isn't something you can ad-lib, Jollers. What exactly are you planning?" Adrienne could be such a nanny.

I said, "It's very simple. I'll just scramble Frisco security, then hike along the ocean cliff till I'm standing right above the clinic. My maps show a rock wall sloping down for nearly 1,500 meters. I'll dive, find the clinic's fluid intake pipe, and cut my way in."

"What gear are you carrying?" Now Luc was playing nursemaid, too. Sacrée Loi, I'm the one who taught him how to pack! My kit held nutrients, water, hypercompressed air, tools, dive gear, a deepsea inflatable airlock, and a fistful of hot-market cash for good measure. Also one illegal security field scrambler—a going-away gift from Trinni.

"People, this is Jolie Blanche Sauvage you're talking to. D'accord?"

"Spike 'em, Jo." That gruff voice had to be Rebel Jeanne Sabat. At least she was on my side.

I steered the Durban Bee south, skirting just beyond the range of Frisco's scan. I touched down in a saddle among the craggy Sierran peaks and camouflaged the Bee with a holographic field so it looked like a big rock. A few kilometers offshore, my metavisor picked up the telltale gas plumes of active undersea volcanoes. If I could have taken off my helmet, I would have heard the ocean hiss.

My blood was up. I felt tingly. Alone on the surface, with the prospect of a vigorous hike and a swim—and no scuzzing crew boss to order me around! Mes dieux, but it felt right. I hoisted my pack. This should be a no-brainer. I felt certain Frisco security would be preoccupied by their internal troubles. They wouldn't notice one lone surface hiker. Sure enough, my scrambler zapped their security scan, and I waltzed right through their perimeter without a bleep. Standing on the cliff, I gazed down at the choppy ochre sea.

"Are you sure that cliff slopes down evenly?" Adrienne asked. "What about outcroppings? Maybe you should rappel instead of dive."

"I'm monitoring by satellite, and that's not a natural cliff." Luc's voice. "It's a pair of massive upswellings along a fault line. Two grand bulges of sediment almost identical in shape and size. Meta-weird, chérie."

I heard Jonas laughing. "We wouldn't want you to bash your skull, love."

"Double-check your air tank. Do it now." This from Adrienne.

Offshore, I saw gouts of volcanic steam burst from the waves. The ocean fluid looked glutinous and nasty. I swallowed hard and rechecked my GPSNS. The ocean ran preter-deep under this cliff, and I would be going down deeper than the light could reach. Ironic, for a surface-loving girl like me to choose such a direction.

"D'accord." I backed up and got a running start and dove.

The Pacific welcomed me like a hot sulfur bath. Thank the Laws, my suit filtered out the stink. Under the surface, even with a powerful headlamp and metavision, I could see only dim outlines and shadows. Swimming through that murk was like plowing through gelatin. Above me, breakers crashed against the cliff, churning with fleshy clots of refuse. The tide drove me against the cliff face.

Not a single cliff, but as Luc had said, a pair. The underwater forms bulged out from shore like two enormous fists pressed together. My GPSNS signal was pointing me toward the deep canyon that ran between them. Light from the surface shafted through violent eddies boiling in the narrow cleft. I entered cautiously, touching the rock on either side. Powerful currents whacked me against the ridges that gnarled each surface.

"Must be some kind of hardened lava flow," I said.

"Angle downward." Jonas was following my progress with his own GPSNS. "Steeper. You're still too high."

The currents buffeted me as I fought deeper into the narrow cleft. More than once, the ocean hurled me against the cliff on my right, and I had to fend off the craggy rock with my gloves. But my GPSNS signal was getting louder. I broke a sweat, swimming through the turbulence, but at last, my headlamp lit up the clinic's intake pipe, and I grasped the slimy little grille with relief.

"She found it!" I heard someone say, probably Adrienne.

I tried prying the grille off, but that didn't work. Fortunately, I'd brought my trusty seventeen-in-one, multifunction Ojiwa® pneumatic pocket tool. It took me another twenty minutes to wrestle the scuzzin' grille off with the vise-grip accessory. I squeezed into the pipe and followed the schematic that glowed on my wrist screen.

"She's in!" Adrienne narrated.

At the fourth junction in the pipe, Jonas said, "That's the spot, love."

I stopped and tapped. The pipe echoed a comforting hollow sound. "Thanks, Jonas!" The schematics I'd downloaded showed a maintenance shaft just on the other side. Jonas had the same schematics, and he was giving me prompts. Having him there made me feel a lot more confident.

"I've patched into your metavisor signal, love. You don't mind if I upload the visuals to everyone?"

"Sure. I'll give you a guided tour," I chuckled. "Compliments of Jolie's Trips."

It took time to attach the inflatable airlock to the gunky inner lining of the pipe. Uninflated, the airlock looked like a huge condom, and climbing into the filmy thing with my load of gear proved awkward. Adrienne kept giving me useless directions. Finally, I zipped the seal tight and filled the condom with air from my tanks. I made sure to match the internal pressure of the clinic according to specs I'd downloaded. Next I laser-cut a hole through the pipe and into the maintenance shaft. Then I just waited till the glowing metal rim cooled down.

My gloves and boots were caked with ocean slime, and my
hold on the cruddy metal kept slipping. It was dark in there, and
I was trying to sling the muck off my gloves, so I just didn't
notice the stranger waiting inside.

"Jolie!" Luc shouted. "Attendez!"

The stranger introduced himself with a kick-punch to my helmet.

WHEN THE LIGHTS came back on, I lay sprawled and dripping on a grimy floor with this guy standing over me. Massive legs and shoulders. Dirty prote uniform. He held my piton gun, checking it out. I glanced around and saw shelves, boxes, trash. I was lying in a small cube with metal walls and one dim overhead light source. A portable generator growled in the corner. My helmet was gone. When the guy saw me moving, he pointed the gun at my throat, but his finger wasn't on the trigger.

"I am Vincente," he said in thick Spanglish. "Why have you broken into my home?"

"Hey, amigo, sorry. I must be in the wrong place."

Spanglish came easily to me because it had cognates with my native Paris gutter-Fragñol. I sat up fast and skidded backward on my butt till my shoulder pressed against something sharp. I kept my eye on that gun. Pitons in the throat leave nasty scars.

"So, Vincente, this your cube? Nice cube, amigo. Roomy." I was blathering. "Me, I'm looking for a clinic. Merida Institute of Neuroscience. You know about that?"

Vincente tipped his head to one side, and his long heavy hair swung over his shoulder. "Your name?"

He wanted formality. D'accord, I gave him a name. Then I made up some elaborate story about needing to see my cousin in the clinic. I'm no good at lying. Vincente just nodded, giving no indication whether he believed me or not. So I kept talking.

Finally, I calmed down enough to notice the wily humor in his small blue eyes. He was laughing up his sleeve at me. I also noticed that Vincente was old. Tough and brawny and hard-packed, but old. His long mane wasn't the lusterless white so common among deep-Earth protes. No, his iron gray hair had once been black. And his skin was brown and leathery. This man had seen plenty of solar radiation. In fact, he looked like an old surface dweller. Maybe a guide. Maybe someone like me.

"So anyway," I wound up, "Whaddya say, Vincente? Do you know where I can find this clinic I'm talking about? This Merida Institute?"

"You're there." He twirled my piton gun around his middle finger and caught it with the barrel pointed straight at my throat again. He grinned slyly. I watched his finger tease the trigger, then move away.

I exhaled. "Oh."

"Visitors, they use the front door." He hefted the little gun flat in his palm. Then he tossed it onto a counter littered with tools and machine parts, and he lifted a flat blue object. I slapped my forearm. My Net node was missing! Vincente had it. That node contained my quantum computer, my GPSNS, my Net link, my lifeline to the outside world. I sucked air through my teeth.

Vincente had stripped off my boots and gear belt as well. Time to bargain. I unzipped my suit and fumbled in my bra for the wad of hot-market cash. "I've got money."

He watched what I did, then hunkered over the counter to examine my Net node. "What do you want?"

"Like I said, to see my cousin, Jin Sura."

"I will call the doctor," he said.

"NO! That won't be necessary. Please."

But Vincente wasn't making any move to call. He turned his profile to me, and in one quick sweep, he gathered his long hair tight into an elastic band. Then he sat at his work counter, fitted a monocle to his right eye, and began methodically unclipping the cover of my Net node.

"Hey, don't mess with that!" I sprang up, grabbed it away from him, and scurried back to my corner like a rat with cheese.

Vincente heaved a sigh. His broad shoulders rose and fell like mountains. His blue eyes narrowed, and the seams in his face deepened. His squint seemed familiar to me. The mark of a surf-dweller. Someday, I'd probably have a squint like that.

He said, "Give me the box, and I'll show you your cousin."

"Jin is here?" My hope rose. The force of it surprised me. "Where? Take me now."

"Give me the box, or I shoot you."

"Shoot me?" He was making no move for the gun, just staring at me with those crafty blue eyes. All at once, I saw through his act. The man was harmless. "You're not gonna shoot me.

Where are my boots? You give me back my stuff, you old pervert." I found my helmet on the floor. It had a split across the left side where Vincente had kicked me. I scowled and looked around for the rest of my things.

Vincente sat hunched on his stool, shaking his head. "I've never seen a box like that."

I strapped the Net node to my arm, ignoring him.

He said, "Let me look inside. I'll give it back."

I tugged on my boots, sealed the gaskets, and clipped the damaged helmet to my gear belt. Then I brazenly marched over and grabbed my gun.

He said, "Your cousin, I remember him. The prince, we called him. El principe. The brain-dead one."

I froze. What did he say? Creepy old man. I didn't breathe. Very calmly I said, "That's not him. You must mean someone else. My cousin wasn't a prince."

"Fancy young man from Pacific.Com. I remember the name. Sura. Completely comatose. We pumped out his lungs and kidneys every day. I remember El principe."

"That's not him!" I yelled the words in Vincente's face and raised my fist to hit him.

But he didn't react. He watched me with those wily, twinkling old eyes. "Sí, the brain-dead one. He's gone now. The clinic is empty."

"You're lying!"

"Go and look. There is no one."

"You lead the way!" I waved my gun, feeling hope dissolve.

The electricity was out, so most of the clinic lay in pitch darkness. Hot as an oven. The walls sweated putrid oily beads. And there was a stench. Vincente activated a laser torch and started edging down a corridor whose floor rose and fell in uneven ripples. I followed close, pretending to push him along, but really just needing contact. The idea of getting lost in that place made my skin crawl.

What a slum! Merida hadn't invested a cent in fixing this place up. All the floors were buckled and ridged, and the corridors twisted like a maze. We kept going up and down ramps. I wanted to look in every room, but there were so many, squeezed one on top of another in uneven layers. What kind of insane plan was this for a clinic? As we moved farther in, the air grew so stale, it made me cough. All I could see was the blue-white beam of Vincente's torch playing over vacant cots and empty toilet stalls. We found rotting food in the pantry. I almost gagged.

"Let me hold the light," I said, but Vincente stubbornly lifted it beyond my reach. Annoyed, I unclipped a lightcube from my belt and squeezed it. The cube glowed pale green in my palm. I kept stepping on Vincente's heels because I was following too close. Finally, I grabbed his arm and just hung on.

He used a metal key to unlock a door. "The record office," he said. "You'll find information here."

The door opened, and before I knew what was happening, Vincente spun me off balance. I dropped my lightcube and fell through the doorway. He tried to push me inside, but my leg was caught, and he couldn't get the door shut. Pain shot up my side as he slammed the door on my ankle. When I started kicking at him, he took off.

I wedged the door open with a dented aluminum biowaste can, then belly-crawled to my lightcube and grabbed it to my chest as if the little thing would save me. Slowly I sat up and looked around the dim, shadowy room. It was just another clinic ward, not a record office. I moved out into the pitch-black hall and tried to remember the way back—but to where?

My Net node activated at my touch. Its screen glowed like a friendly face.

"Jollers, are you safe?" "What's happening?" "Where are you, love?"

My friends' voices rushed at me like a warm wind. "Relax, I'm blissin'. Thank the Laws of Physics for GPSNS."

"You're lost," Adrienne scolded.

I called up the clinic floorplan, and my location flashed clearly onscreen. "I am not lost, Adrienne. I'm looking for Jin."

A muffled noise sounded in the corridor behind me. A soft drop. Someone was there. I muted the Net node. Now I heard footsteps in front of me, too. And to the right, I saw torch beams dancing against a distant wall. Many footsteps. And voices.

Just then, someone leaped out of a doorway and seized me from behind. My attacker was too strong for me. He covered my mouth, pinned my arms to my sides, and dragged me backward through the doorway. I heard his heavy breathing and recognized Vincente. I struggled and bit his hand, but he wouldn't let go.

"Quiet. You've drawn the troopers, foolish whore. Be quiet or we're dead."

I settled down fast when he said that. Nome.Com troopers. They must have been tracking me all along. So much for my no-brainer. Vincente dragged me awkwardly across the dark room and pressed me against the wall with his body while he used his free hand to open some kind of bin.

"Through here, chica, and be quick!" He stuffed me into the chute, and I crawled forward blindly until he grabbed my ankle and stopped me. "Lie still."

His hand gripped my leg like a vise. I could hear his breathing, and my own. I had clipped my helmet to my belt, and now it wedged uncomfortably under my hip. The steel chute in which we lay felt gritty, and when I shifted to move the helmet, my nostrils filled with an odd-flavored dust. Like charcoal. "Where are we?" I whispered.

"Quiet. Better you don't know."

We lay there for only a few minutes. Then we heard a terrible clatter. Laser blasts. The troopers were shooting their way into our chute. They'd located us, probably by GPSNS.

"Move!" Vincente shoved me forward.

I scrambled ahead in the darkness, kicking my way along the gritty chute. A couple of meters along, I came to the lip of a downshaft and slid my hand downward, trying to gauge its depth. Vincente pushed me from behind, but I resisted.

"Jump!" he said.

"How deep is this thing?" When I heard the first bullet ricochet past my ear, I put doubts aside and tumbled forward into thin air.

I landed in a pool of fine dry powder. It felt almost too soft to bear my weight, and when Vincente landed on top of me, he drove me under the surface. I shut my eyes, held my breath and fought my way up. But it seemed the more I kicked and squirmed, the deeper I sank into the powder. At last I felt Vincente's grip pulling me upward. I couldn't see in the blackness, but I could feel when my face broke the surface. For several minutes, I spit and coughed and sneezed. The powder tasted like ashes.

Vincente must have crawled into some structure suspended above the powder. Even in total darkness, I could sense him hanging above me, holding my wrist, letting me dangle chest deep in the soot.

"Now we bargain, chica. Give me the device you wear, and I save you, sí?"

I lifted my left arm free of the soot, slung open the Net node cover and spoke a command. The screen glowed. "Luc, this is Jolie. You have my coordinates. A man named Vincente is threatening to kill me. Track him down, Luc!"

Vincente laughed. "You're play-acting, chica. No beam can escape this place."

"You've never seen a device like this before," I reminded him.

Suddenly, light flooded the well from above. The troopers had found us. Before I realized what was happening, Vincente hauled me out of the ashes and swung me onto a ledge. Lasers flashed, and bullets rang out. "Quick!" He shoved me toward a narrow slot in the wall. I had to edge sideways to get through, and looking back toward the light, I saw Vincente sucking in his gut to force his large body through after me. Then we dropped about three meters down, in total darkness again. After a few tentative steps, I sensed an uneven stone floor.

"Run!" he said.

"Which way?"

He grabbed my arm, and we ran together blindly, stumbling over broken stones and trash, supporting each other as best we could. Our steps echoed like gunshot. At last, we entered a passage, rounded a bend, and passed through a door. Vincente slammed the door with all his might. Then he switched on a light, and I saw him activate an electronic lock. We were back in his cube again. He sagged against the door panting for breath. Vincente was a strong man, but old.

"How do we get out of here?" I asked desperately. "We can't hide from Nome.Com troopers."

"You led them here." He wiped his sweaty face and scowled at me.

I said, "That's right. It's me they want. Show me the way out, and I'll lead them off."

"Sí," he nodded. "Give me the box."

"The damned box! Is that all you can think of? I need this. I'll send you another one later. It's just a Net node. It's nothing."

"Then give it to me," he said again. Mes dieux, but the man was persistent.

"Look, Vincente, we don't have time for this. I can't survive without my Net node. Show me how to leave, or the troopers will kill us both."

"You cousin, El principe, he is no longer important to you?"

"You said he's not here."

"I know where he lies sleeping. Shall I tell you?"

# The Cliff

LETTING GO OF that Net node may have been the most difficult choice I've ever made. And the dumbest, Adrienne would add. That node was my link to everything I needed to make this venture succeed—my location finder, schematics, reference pages, and, most important, my friends. How on earth did I think I could pull this off alone? Maybe I expected to find another Net node drifting around in the Pacific Ocean.

But if I hadn't traded that node to Vincente, he would never have told me where they'd taken Jin. So I didn't have a choice, did I?

Twenty minutes later, I found myself flushed out to sea in a load of clotted effluent. Vincente had stuffed me inside an old diving sphere and ejected me with the weekly waste. The sphere looked like a hot-air balloon made of glass, about two meters in diameter, with a hatch and a knot of clunky hoses and control devices hanging below. Its segmented walls were made of triple-layer fabriglass interlaminated with ceramic micromesh—hyper-tough, impervious, and supposedly transparent. But time had hazed the walls with fragrant green-gray scum.

As the sphere gyrated down, soggy masses of ocean debris smeared against the exterior like slicks of oil. The sphere's running lights were only marginally helpful in such thick muck. I thought about the crisp clean satellite scans Luc could have transmitted to me, if only I still had that Net node.

Before jettisoning me, Vincente had pumped both the dive sphere and the extra compression tanks full of an exotic oxy mix. My destination, he said, lay at the very bottom of the cliff—1,500 meters below sea level. The war had forced Merida to abandon her clinic. She'd gone deep, into a safe hideaway she'd built years earlier, far down in the old buried city that had once been called San Francisco. "Find the cave at the bottom of the cliff," Vincente told me.

When I made a remark about the rusty pressure regulator

controlling the auxiliary tanks, Vincente acted as if I'd insulted him. "Niña, if the sphere fails, use your surfsuit. Redundancy, sí?" Then he gallantly mended the split in my helmet—where he had kicked me—with a few rounds of duct tape.

Now, rolling through the spume of oily debris, the sphere began to spin in multiple directions, and my body somersaulted inside. I grabbed for the handholds, but they were slick with mold. My helmet slipped out of my hands and orbited like a moon. Vincente had strung ribbons of sinker weights round and round the sphere like yarn around a ball—to make sure I would descend all the way to 1,500 meters. It occurred to me now that this was not the most stable design.

You're going to ask why I would trust such a crafty old liar as Vincente. Bien, you should have seen his eyes shine when he got that Net node in his hands. The truth fairly gushed out of him. That's what my instincts told me anyway. Did I pause to consider his motives? Did I plan ahead in case it might be a trap? No. I am who I am. Adrienne, do you hear this? No point in making excuses after the fact.

On the other hand, I did not believe a word about Jin being brain-dead. The human will to believe is selective. It didn't matter to me that the sea cliff dropped 1,500 meters down, that the sphere was old and brittle, and that if it failed, my surfsuit was clearly not rated for that depth. I had made my choice to do this. My mind was set. And besides, scary trips are my kind of fun.

My first discovery was that the sphere's motor controls were frozen—probably hadn't been serviced in years. By sheer luck, or perhaps the tide, the sphere drifted back to the sea cliff. I couldn't see the cliff well, but as the sphere bumped against it and started moving down, the rock face appeared scabrous with knobs and folds and protrusions. I had more or less stabilized inside the sphere when, all at once, the sea turned blood red. An intense crimson flash from an undersea volcano lit up the cliff. Its size was staggering. It swelled above me, not as one smooth face but as a pair of colossal hemispheres, with that deep turbulent crevice running between. The whole thing was so large, I couldn't see its beginning or end.

I scrubbed scum off the sphere's inner wall to see better. The cliffs were ridged with swollen, twisted folds. Slabs of old highways and broken buildings were crushed in layers of sediment.

It looked as if centuries of civilizations had been compressed and folded together. Abruptly, the red light faded, leaving me in semi-darkness. The volcanic eruption had ended.

That first hour passed slowly as the sphere rolled down the gnarly bulge. The convex walls creaked and hummed with the ocean's mounting pressure, and the deeper I went, the more I thought about my guilt. I'm the one who introduced Jin to Merida. I kept obsessing about that. If only I could take it back. That one wrong choice. If I could just go back in time and change that one little thing.

But what must Merida have promised, to get her hooks into my Jin so deeply? Why had he fallen for her? It made me want to scream. My beautiful Jin, so discriminating, so appreciative of nuances, forever weighing alternatives, perpetually undecided—why had Jin zeroed in so fast on Merida? This ridiculous brain surgery, she promised it would help him find the truth— as if anyone knew what that was. Jin felt some kind of duty, he said, like noblesse oblige. Because he was born way lucky, he felt this mega-urge to help the starving masses. I could admire that. But then this weird conflict with his father got in his way, and he didn't know what to do. Join the human race, Jin Sura. Nobody knows what to do.

"I have to know!" That's what he'd crowed, sticking up his chin, proud as a peacock. As if he really were the only person in the universe. As if the fate of the world rested on his shoulders alone. Mes dieux, what a prick! What an egotistical, infuriating, dear, precious, screwed-up guy! Doubly screwed-up now, because he had only me to come and save him. Poor Jin.

To my horror, I noticed a dimple forming in one section of the fabriglass sphere. Thank the Laws, the sphere's regulator started increasing internal air pressure to help compensate for the extreme forces on the exterior walls. I held my nose and blew hard to clear my ears. But the dimple kept growing. Not good.

For a little extra peace of mind, I tugged on my duct-taped helmet and sealed the gaskets of my surfsuit. My surfsuit was a Cetus XS™, made in South Africa. A meta-primo surfsuit. Like that Net node, it had cost me a bundle. With its internal recycler system and pressure controls, the Cetus was rated for dives down to 900 meters. I was probably approaching that limit, and I still had a preter-long way to go, not to mention a preter-huge cliff to search for one small sea cave. Normally, I would have flipped open my Net node and asked for advice. Mes dieux, but I missed my friends. The full ramifications of losing that node hit me harder than ever. I'd never been cut off from the Net before.

Another hour passed, and the ocean current kept nudging my sphere against the cliff. Then I noticed something truly bizarre. The running lights showed I was now rolling under the cliff, into the shadow of a vast overhang. I checked that dimple again. Ça va, a million tiny white lines now branched out from the flaw. The fabriglass was old and brittle. Would it split? I was trying to recall my reasons for doing this when the sphere caught on something sharp sticking down from the overhanging cliff. Quick as light, I threw my weight to the floor and bounced clear. That was all I needed, a puncture.

Halfway through the third hour, pain stabbed my eardrums. My suit's regulator had maxxed out. It couldn't keep up with the increasing air pressure inside the sphere. I swallowed hard, popped my jaw, held my nose, and tried to blow air into my middle ears to stop the pain. I would have traded my soul for a depth gauge, but maybe it was better not to know.

At that instant, volcanic light flashed again, turning the sea gory red. I looked up through the top of the dive sphere, and the cliff's bulging mass seemed to press down on me like a monstrous growth. Strange objects were embedded in the overhang. Ancient transport vehicles flattened under broken chunks of aggregate. Seams of melted rubber laced with glittering shards of steel. It was a barbarous formation. A layering of cities and mountains folded together in the Earth's moving crust.

I heard a small pop and spun around to check the dimple. Ocean pressure was deepening those tiny white seams into creases. Sacrée Loi, was the sphere about to implode? I could almost taste the sulfuric reek of the sea. Inhaling a careful breath of surfsuit air, I closed my eyes and prayed to the Laws of Physics. The sphere rolled farther under the cliff.

Sometime during the fourth hour, the sphere wedged against something very solid, and the force of the current held it still. My headlamp barely penetrated the gloom. I couldn't see anything. I tried using my body weight to heave the sphere loose, but it wouldn't budge. Every time I tried to move it, the sphere mired deeper.

So I sat down in the slippery bottom of the sphere to wait for another volcanic flash. The recycled air in my suit stank of sweat. I touched that tape on my helmet again, and I thought of Adrienne and Luc and Jonas, who must be a bit worried by now. And I thought about what Vincente had said: "El príncipe. Sí, I remember him. The brain-dead one."

Jin seemed very near. I felt an almost visceral connection with him. We had shared the bond of sex, yes. But since then, I had fantasized so many intimate conversations, told him so much about my dreams and fears, and watched his image so often in the movies, I felt we were mates. I believed we understood one another, and that our destinies lay together. You may think I was an idiot to base so much on so little. Call it an addiction if you like. Adrienne did. But waiting there in the dark to see him, hunkering under the weight of hundreds of meters of ocean, I couldn't imagine being anywhere else. Is it possible a fixation as strong as mine could be all on one side? I didn't believe it. Jin had to be thinking about me, too. If he were still thinking at all.

Bien sûr, no one would mistake Jolie Blanche Sauvage for a genius, I know that. But I do have a retentive mind. I remembered every word Jin had told me about waking up his latent senses. He said we had old, old ways of knowing. Our lizard brains once guided us through the primordial ooze in ways that had nothing to do with sight or sound or smell. He said we still had those old senses, but we no longer recognized our perceptions for what they were. We mislabeled them as instinct or luck. Sometimes, clairvoyance. Sometimes, lunacy. I understood what Jin meant. That's why I knew he would feel me approaching.

Finally, the volcano erupted again. Its brief flash revealed that my sphere had lodged between the huge cliff above and another smaller bulge below. In the bloody light, this lower bulge looked older, more deeply eroded and pitted with age. Fossils stuck out from its crusted face like fragments of memory.

The red light strobed twice more before fading, but among the rough furrows of the lower cliff, I saw the cave. It lay about ten meters south and maybe a dozen meters down. That opening couldn't be natural. Too perfectly round. It had to be a laser bore.

My sphere made another popping noise. I held my breath, listening for the first hint of seepage. I wouldn't last long if the sphere imploded. I had to move into that sea cave fast. Vincente had said I'd find an airlock just inside. That would mean safety. But how could I maneuver the sphere?

I wasted half an hour throwing myself against the walls trying to dislodge the sphere, but when one whole quadrant suddenly puckered inward, I froze. This would never work. I had to leave the sphere. I had to trust myself to the Cetus surfsuit for whatever time it took to get inside that cave. First, I had to find a way to poke a little hole in the sphere and let ocean fluid slowly fill it. Then I could open the hatch and swim out. Sacred Angels of Physics!

No reason to wait here letting my fears build up. I pressed that duct tape firmer to my helmet, sucked a breath of pungent recycled air, and prayed to Newton. Then I used the tip of my diamond-edged field knife to punch a little hole. Right, you know what happened. Pressure split the hull like a soap bubble, and the escaping gas launched me straight up. I bashed against the underside of the cliff so hard, my ears rang, and the gases began dragging me rapidly under the overhang, rushing toward the surface.

If I hadn't whacked into a flange protruding from the cliff, I might have ridden that gas burble all the way to the top—and had the pleasure of feeling my lungs explode. But the flange caught me fast, and I clung to it for dear life. The flange turned out to be a petrified tree stump.

After the initial excitement, I stopped trembling and collected my wits. Pain throbbed in my ears, and my surfsuit was squeezing me like it was six sizes too small. In seconds, the liner began to feel clammy. Was it sweat, or had a seam started to leak? The Cetus XS™ surfsuit was made of Para-Thinsulate® bonded to Kevtex® and reinforced with woven polymer-germanium. Fire-retardant plasticene coating. And silicon seals. Besides, everyone knows those depth ratings always leave a wide safety margin, right? I kept telling myself those things as I dragged my way along the cliff with one gloved hand and pressed the duct tape flat to my helmet with the other.

For five long minutes, I worked toward that cave, plowing through the glutinous pollution that had collected at the bottom of the ocean. Inside my surfsuit, moisture spread down my ribs and legs, and I imagined I could taste sulfur. But it had to be sweat. Sea fluid was so toxic, it would burn my skin like acid, right? Just then a drop ran off the tip of my nose, and the inside of my helmet started fogging. I pressed the duct tape harder. Just sweat. It had to be.

Near the cave, I encountered heat. Even through my surfsuit, I could feel it. For a moment, the ocean cleared, and my headlamp penetrated to reveal a geyser of fizzing gases boiling up from the opening. Almost at once, a red volcanic flash illuminated the cave's laser-cut entrance. When the geyser subsided, I swam in.

Vincente hadn't lied about the airlock. Not far down the passage, I came to a steel wall with a hulking metal door. The odd thing was, as I approached, the door began to slide open. Maybe there was an automatic motion sensor. Bien, I wanted inside, didn't I? So I swam into the lock.

WITH A HEAVY clank, the outer door of the airlock sealed, and air jetted through a nozzle, forcing the ocean fluid out through a floor drain. When the liquid had drained to my chest level, my sensors read breathable air, so I tugged off my helmet and looked at the duct tape. Mes dieux, a corner of that tape had lifted, exposing the gash. The inner lining was saturated with ocean fluid. In another minute, that helmet might have completely failed! I stared at it stupidly. Then I dropped it. The thing was useless, damaged beyond repair. I wiped my damp face with the back of my hand, drew several deep breaths and tried to ease the pounding in my ears.

Slowly, air filled the lock. When the last ocean fluid vortexed through the floor drain, the lock's inner door grated open. Floodlights blinded me. The airlock echoed with dripping.

"Jolie?" I recognized the Spanic drawl.

"Merida." I drew a quick breath. How did she know I was coming? That stupid call I'd made to Jin's father? Or had Vincente betrayed me?

"We've been tracking you by GPSNS," she said.

I felt hyper-lame for not guessing that.

"Where's Jin?" I said.

"You think you've rushed in to rescue him? Jolie, he's achieving everything he hoped for. Come in, pet. You'll soon discover which one of us he prefers."

Her voice vibrated through a cheap amplification system. Oh no, Merida hadn't come to greet me in person. My eyes were adjusting to the floodlights, and when I held up my hand as a shield, I could just make out three tall figures moving toward me. Merida's amplified voice buzzed, "Please allow my staff to escort you, Jolie. We'll meet soon. I promise."

Her "staff" consisted of three featureless cybergoons with gleaming platinum skin and dark gray uniforms void of insignia. They grabbed me, stripped me to my purple paisley bodysuit,

confiscated my gear, and marched me double-time through one
of the strangest corridors I'd ever seen. The first part seemed
new, cheap and plain, but we soon dropped off into an old, dank
cellar, then climbed spiral stairs and passed through a grand hall
with crystal chandeliers and musty carpet. Apparently to save
money, Merida had assimilated random parts of the old city
ruins into her habitat.

The goons prodded me into a small, unpainted cell without
furnishings of any kind. One of them handed me a basket of
moist towels. I put the towels to use. The guards' presence
didn't bother me. I'd learned to forgo the conventions of physical modesty. I dropped my filthy bodysuit on the floor and
scrubbed my skin, scouring away that putrid moisture that might
have been toxic sea fluid or maybe just nervous sweat. When
I'd finished, Merida's towels were stained beyond redemption.

As soon as the three goons left, I checked the place out. Steel
walls as thick as a vault, recessed light-strips in the ceiling,
probably hidden cam-eyes, too. The door was electronically
sealed. No way to escape. All I could do was wait for Merida
to keep her promise. Adrienne, you don't have to say a word. I
know I should have planned, but how's a person supposed to
plan for the unknown?

After a short while, a middle-aged Japanese woman brought
me a tray of food and a thread-bare kimono. She was human,
not cyborg. Fine lines webbed her face, and wiry silver threads
grizzled her raven hair. But she had a sweet, wide, motherly
smile. She placed the tray on the floor and crossed her hands
over her round belly. "The noodles are good. Sorry, no table."

I wrapped myself in the kimono, and the woman helped me
tie the plastic belt in back. The cloth felt stiff and cheap. When
I sat on the floor, she knelt beside me and poured my cup full
of piping hot green tea. Then she smiled and made an eating
motion with her hands and mouth. The noodles smelled savory,
and believe me, I was famished, so I picked up the chopsticks
and dug in.

"Who are you?" the woman asked when I paused to gulp tea.

She had to be a prote, a maid or cook or something. I studied
her as I upended the chipped teacup. She wore a faded kimono
like mine and funny sandals. No makeup or jewelry, no indication of status. She peered at me with kind, blinking eyes. I
decided I liked her.

"I'm Jolie. Jin's friend. Do you know Jin Sura?"

She smiled and shook her head apologetically. "I do not have that honor."

"What about Suradon Sura? Have you heard that name?" I asked.

Her eyes widened, and she spoke solemnly, "He is my lord."

I said, "Huh?"

"I belong to him." She lowered her eyelids. "Lord Suradon sent me here to serve the doctor."

"Suradon and Merida are in league together?" I nearly choked on a mouthful of noodles. Then I remembered. Jin said they'd formed a partnership.

The serving woman was blinking her eyes and biting her lip. My question had upset her. Right. No point quizzing this simple lady. I invited her to sit down beside me, and we began to chat. She said her name was Matji. She told me about her duties in the kitchen and the daughters she'd left back in Japan. I told her about Jin. Of course, she knew of her boss's only son, but she'd never seen him. She never watched movies, she said. That luxury wasn't allowed to kitchen staff.

When I told her how handsome Jin was and how fans idolized him, she fluttered her eyelashes with pleasure. Matji seemed to think Jin's status reflected well on her own, since she belonged to his family. I declare, the woman accepted her slavery without a notion of protest. I didn't want to upset her by arguing.

So I asked her what Suradon Sura was like.

"He is my lord," she repeated, as if that should explain everything. "He guards the people's welfare," she said, and "He loads our table with bounty," along with other trite drivel that sounded like verbatims from a propaganda ROM.

Naturellement, I kept asking for more. Jin's meta-magnate father intrigued me. What was he like close up? How did he treat his servants? Did Matji like him? Finally, she gave me this cryptic reply: "He is a man who seeks to gather the wind in his fist."

When I said, "Huh?" Matji's face crinkled in a merry grin that squeezed her eyes almost shut. She rocked silently on her haunches, obviously enjoying my confusion. I couldn't get her to say anything more about the mighty Lord Suradon.

Pots of tea materialized as if by magic. Matji told me the tea contained a medicine to cleanse my body of any ocean toxins that might have penetrated my surfsuit. That was great news to me, and I thanked her. We talked for a long time. I'm not usually so voluble, but Matji drew me out.

People always loved my scary trip stories, and the more I told them, the more hair they grew. So I told Matji about "Jolie's Trip to Tierra del Fuego." We'd copter-jetted six clients in for an afternoon picnic—only to find a bunch of Cartel pharmacy lords already parked there, negotiating a profit split under a big green flapping tent. Lots of jet-black cyborgs were strolling around with weapons. Wouldn't you know, my numbhead Commie clients starting shooting video. The Cartel took my whole group hostage on the spot, and they sent me back to Greenland to arrange this mega-ransom. They kept my clients locked up for five days, but the loopy execs thought the whole thing was staged for their entertainment. That trip earned me my biggest tip ever.

Matji didn't seem all that interested in Jolie's Trips. She asked about my family. I explained about being a leftover kid, but incredible as it sounds, Matji had never heard of the big toxic die-off that hit Euro when Earth's climate changed. Matji had even less education than me. I told her about growing up in the Paris tunnels with a pack of righteous thieves led by ten-year-old Uncle Qués. Then I described the mystical surfsuit that had changed the course of my life.

Talking about friends in Euro made me sad. That led to the war and the rescue project and my friends in Palmertown. Not surprisingly, Matji hadn't heard anything about the war. Mes dieux, but I babbled. I told her about Adrienne and Jonas, but that just made me miss them more. I grew sentimental about Luc. I told Matji how I'd raised him, and how he'd fallen in love and didn't need me anymore. When I starting getting weepy, Matji patted my shoulder.

At some point, my head began to spin. I lost track of up and down. Then I slumped forward and realized I couldn't see. My eyelids had closed. I must have fallen asleep in mid-sentence. When I jerked awake, Matji smiled. Her face had changed. Her mouth looked wider than before, and her black eyes had grown rounder. She didn't even look Japanese. "Sleep, pet," she crooned in a voice like syrup, as I rolled over and fell into the dark.

After hearing this, you're going to say that I am a deeply

witless and gullible fool. You would be right. I wish it weren't so, but only after I woke up on the bare floor with a pounding hangover did I realize that Matji had been Merida in disguise. She had wheedled out of me every factoid that might possibly be used against me—the names of my friends, my politics, my psychological weak points—she had me cold.

But why, I asked myself. Why did she allow me to enter her secret habitat so easily? What use did she expect to make of me? Clearly, she had something in mind.

I didn't have to wait long for an answer. As soon as I sat up and rubbed my eyes, my cell door opened, and one of the guards appeared with another pot of steaming tea. You can imagine how much I wanted Merida's tea. The guard also gave me a slice of fragrant seedcake, but I threw that on the floor. I wasn't going to ingest anything else in this place if I could help it.

"Jolie, child, you'll be sorry you didn't eat." Merida stood in the door, curling her wide lips at me. My kimono had come undone, and I pulled it together fast over my bare chest.

She said, "Your belt's untied. Let me help you."

I backed off and tied it myself.

"Have your own way." Her cheerful laugh sounded to me like barking.

The three cyberguards had entered behind her. I noticed they were low-budget models, built for strength, not intelligence. One of them flipped open a small folding stool and placed it on the floor of my cell. Then he drew from his chest pocket a flat black case, a Net node. I ogled the thing with a covetous heart as he arranged it on the stool. Merida spoke an activation command, and a holographic projection filled the air above the node. It was Luc.

I held my breath. The image was being recorded by an over-head camera, probably hidden, and I had a wicked feeling it was being transmitted in real time. Luc was sitting in his office at the furniture co-op, searching the Net. I knew he was hunting for me. His favorite silver cybernails gleamed on all ten of his fingertips as he flashed them through a tiny holographic matrix of icons. Luc always preferred the holo-interface. He said it worked faster than voice command. A pretty young boy—not Trinni—was standing behind Luc's chair, massaging Luc's shoulders. Luc grinned at the boy and patted his hand.

When the projection faded, Merida gurgled deep in her throat, an unholy sound. It made the hairs on the back of my neck stand up.

"Your cher infant. So fair and delicate." She spoke with her syrupy Spanic lilt. "You see, Jolie, we know his ways. We watch him every instant. The boy with him, that's Miguel, my agent. Don't make us angry, pet."

"What do you want?" I said. Jin called me "pet." On Merida's tongue, it sounded dirty.

She commanded the Net node to display another scene. I saw my Durban Bee materialize in holographic shimmer. Its camouflage field had been deactivated. It stood naked in full sunlight among the rocks of the Sierra Nevadas, surrounded by Nome.Com troopers. I had counted on the Bee to take me away from this place, once I reached the surface again. I had thought the Bee would be safe.

"Aren't those troopers a nuisance? It seems they've found your ride." Merida's red mouth split in a gloating smile.

Suddenly, my Durban Bee exploded in an orange fireball. "No," I breathed. The troopers were spraying it with napalm. My Bee collapsed in the flames like a wad of blackened tissue. Numbly, I watched it topple over and roll down the mountain. My way home. Gone.

"It appears your stay with us may be longer than you anticipated. Don't worry, pet. Mi casa, su casa."

I snarled.

Merida circled around me, but I wouldn't give her the satisfaction of turning to face her. She spoke another command, and the holographic display changed to show Jin lying motionless in a narrow bed. His face was turned away from the light, and his closed eyes were sunken in shadow. I saw tubes dripping liquid into a port in his neck.

I spoke through clenched teeth. "What have you done to him?"

"He's done this himself," Merida said, circling around in front of me. "There's no medical reason for this coma. He simply won't wake up." She touched Jin's holographic face and sighed. "It's psychological withdrawal."

"Withdrawal from you!" I raised my fist and sprang at her.

She laughed as her guard grabbed me and slung me around in its metallic arms. "Jolie, there's no need for anger. I'm not your enemy."

"I'll kill you, I swear!"

"You a murderess? No, pet. You don't have the strength of character for that."

I wiped the saliva that had sprayed down my chin and glared at her. I knew she was probably right.

"Wouldn't you like to see Jin?" Her Spanic accent thickened. "You can talk to him, sí? He's fond of you. Maybe you can bring him around."

I struggled against the guard's rough embrace. "That's why you let me in? To bring Jin out of the coma?"

She looked me straight in the eye. "Would you rather not?"

"Naturellement I'll help Jin!" I shouted.

Merida smiled, a loose, ugly, quivering smile. She leaned toward me until her stiff black curls brushed my forehead. The guard held me so I couldn't move away. "I knew you would, pet. You have a generous heart."

She turned on her heel, and the guard shoved me after her, out into the corridor. "This way!" she said in crisp Net English.

RIGHT IN THE very next cell to mine, Jin lay unconscious. I couldn't believe I'd slept all night just a wall away from him. Why didn't my lizard brain sing out? Merida didn't stop me when I rushed to his bedside and took his hand. How thin his wrist had grown. No one had cut his hair. His eyelashes were caked with dried tears.

"Jin." I touched his shoulder. There was no response. He lay rigid.

Merida eyed me with an appraising glance and then left. The witch! She hadn't needed threats to force my cooperation—she should have known me better. I took some comfort in that as I pulled a chair up close beside Jin's pillow. The room smelled of chemicals. Blank sourceless light reflected from the steel walls.

"Jin, it's me, Jolie." I squeezed his arm to make sure he was real. I couldn't take my eyes off him. My love, my idol, in living flesh. After everything that had happened, it seemed too much like a dream.

All day I talked to him, sometimes crying, sometimes kissing him, sometimes stroking his wasted body through the paper-thin hospital wrapper he wore. I told him about my funny trip down the double-headed cliff in Vincente's old dive sphere. I explained how Jonas had retrieved that last vidmail and how badly it scared me. "Fear the light. What did you mean by that, Jin? You wanted me to come, right? You said you wished I was here. Bien, I'm here now, Jin. I'm right beside you." He never stirred.

A digital chronometer hung on the wall, the kind medical suppliers give away for free to advertise their products. Every hour, it played a short, brassy jingle. It was driving me nuts. Near evening, a young man came in carrying a tray of sandwiches and a carafe of water. He was small and delicately made, with olive skin and large brown eyes. His long nose hinted at

Semitic roots. He wore a white smock, and though his thick black hair was combed straight back, one springy lock fell over his forehead.

"This is wholesome food," he said when I opened my mouth to protest. "Eat it, please. You must stay strong to help Mr. Sura." He spoke in a soft soothing baritone. I watched him move around the bed and touch Jin's carotid artery with his finger, checking the pulse.

"Can you shut up that clock?" I asked.

He raised his eyebrows and looked at the thing. Then he yanked if off the wall. "I'll take it away if it annoys you. Please call me Hamad. I am Mr. Sura's caregiver."

"Caregiver!" I sneered at him. "What kind of caregiver works in a place like this?"

Hamad lowered his head. His thick lashes fluttered on his cheek. "I am here because I must be. Please don't ask why. It shames me to explain."

What he said puzzled me. I took a seat in the only chair and watched him with a suspicious eye.

"You've had nothing to drink all day, Ms. Sauvage. You must be very thirsty. Please, this water is pure. I promise." He poured from the decanter.

My throat tightened as that clear cool water sloshed into the cup. Mes dieux, but I craved it. When he placed the cup in my hand, I gulped it down and poured myself more.

Hamad nodded, satisfied. Gently, he checked the tubes attached to Jin's body. Then he pulled a slate from his smock and moved from one monitor to the next, comparing readings. I noticed he moved on the balls of his feet like a dancer. He had beautiful hands. When he sat on the corner of Jin's bed and looked at me, I saw green flecks in his irises.

"You're doing fine," he murmured in his deep voice. "This may take time."

"Tell me what Merida did to him." I bit into the sandwich.

Hamad sighed heavily. As he studied Jin's face, his graceful eyebrows knotted. "Mr. Sura is a troubled man. You know this. He's troubled by his limited understanding. He feels a duty calling him, but he cannot see it clearly. Mr. Sura suspects that much of what passes for reality is only a dream inside his brain. He wants what no one else has found—Hyperthought."

"What no one else has found? You mean Merida never tried this before."

Hamad stood up and walked around the bed. His narrow chest rose and fell in another long sigh. "In technical terms, Dr. Merida's procedure should enable Mr. Sura to perceive the quantum-level input to his brain. We all receive—ah—call them 'vibrations.' They come to us through the complex quantum fabric of mass and energy that links the universe."

"Huh? The what?"

"I apologize, Ms. Sauvage. My words are insufficient." Hamad brushed the lock off his forehead, but it fell right back. "The universe consists of quanta—infinitesimal packets of energy. Each of us, each rock and planet and bead of water, every solid object, every aroma and sound and ray of light, we all emerge from this underlying fabric of interchangeable quantum energy."

"Is that where we go when we die?" I whispered, swallowing half-chewed sandwich.

Hamad didn't seem to hear my question. Instead of answering, he took a damp cloth from his pocket and began to wash Jin's face. "These quantum vibrations act on our brains continuously, linking us in a vast trembling web of interaction with every other existence in the universe. Though we're not conscious of this quantum input, it sways our emotions, our judgments, our actions. It binds our world together in complex patterns. This interplay forms the very ground of our being. Poets and philosophers invent metaphors for it. Ah, but Mr. Sura wants to see it face to face."

Hamad paused to refold the damp cloth. Gently, he began to clean the caked tears from Jin's eyelashes. I thought about what Jin had told me earlier.

"He said we might dream a different universe with every heartbeat."

Hamad seemed to consider this. "Who knows? We humans speak so confidently of our facts and figures. Yet our understanding of perception is staggeringly naive. Anything might be possible. I can understand this young man's ardent desire to know. Indeed, who hasn't glimpsed the depths of the night and wondered?"

I pushed the unfinished sandwich aside. "Merida isn't sure about what she's doing, is she? Jin's a guinea pig."

The young man's brows knotted. He stuffed the cloth in his pocket and sat on the bed, facing me. "Dr. Merida devised a new kind of nanobot, a molecule-sized artificial life-form engineered to evolve and learn the quantum language. Over time, the bot was supposed to recognize the nonlinear patterns of quantum energy, then to translate and boost the signals, so to speak, so Mr. Sura could 'hear' them. She—ah—explained the risks."

Hamad's mouth quivered. He seemed so contrite, I felt a pang of sympathy for him. He continued in his soft, sad baritone, "When the doctor injected the nanobots into Jin's frontal lobe, they replicated much faster than expected. They were designed to spread over the surface of his brain as a living neural net, a kind of secondary cerebral cortex, doubling Mr. Sura's powers of cognition. But instead, they penetrated deep into the inner cerebrum and began to populate the astrocyte cells."

"Astrocytes. Jin used that word before. What does that mean?" I gripped the seat of my chair, not totally sure I wanted to know.

"Astrocytes are cells shaped like stars. They're located throughout the brain, and usually, in mature adults, they lie dormant. Asleep, as it were. But with proper stimulus, astrocytes can trigger neurogenesis. That is, they can propagate new brain tissue."

Hamad leaned across the bed and slipped a hand under Jin's cheek. "What Dr. Merida failed to predict was the way her nanobots would awaken Jin's astrocytes. The nanobots entered the sleeping cells and stimulated a rapid cascade of neurogenesis. But the new brain tissue is—not normal. It's—we can't define what it is." Gently Hamad lifted Jin's head off the pillow. "Mr. Sura's brain weighs half a kilo more than it did before the operation."

I must have gasped aloud.

"His brain hasn't swelled," Hamad said quickly. "There's no physical damage, I assure you. The aberrant new tissue has commandeered empty spaces within other cells."

I was too shocked to speak. My eyes wouldn't focus. I couldn't even begin to process the information he'd given me.

Hamad exhaled a ragged sigh. His remorse seemed very genuine. He whispered, "Stay strong, Ms. Sauvage. Talk to him.

You're his best hope now." And with that, Hamad the caregiver left us alone.

Silently, I prayed to the Laws of Physics that, just this once, they might bend in Jin's favor. Mes dieux, but I understood nothing! How I regretted my lack of education. And how I regretted the lost Net node that would have helped me download reference pages. Sleeping star cells. Rapid cascades. What on Earth was this aberrant new tissue in Jin's brain? All I knew was that it must hurt like hell.

I climbed onto the bed and straddled his chest and began to massage his temples. No doubt, Merida was secretly watching, but I ignored that. I just talked to him. Anything that came into my head. The way stars twinkled in telescopic metavision. The clear, clean layer of pure air I'd once found trapped at the bottom of a valley in Argentina. What sunrise looked like from the Karakoram Pass.

I smoothed his long, silky hair that no one had bothered to cut. Working my fingers down the back of his neck and along his shoulder muscles, I critiqued each of his movies, the early thrillers, the one surprising comedy, the dark later pieces that left me baffled. "You're lazy, Jin. You pick good roles, but you coast along on sex appeal. Scuzz that. You could do better."

Then I started interviewing him like some dippy ezine host, and I made up arrogant answers to put in his mouth, mocking his Pacific lisp, hoping to rile him. "Of course, fans worship me. There's a reason they call me a star. My movies pull people out of hell and give them a glimpse of heaven. Ninety minutes at a time."

This and other nonsense rolled off my tongue till my throat felt raw. Every hour, Hamad brought me a fresh carafe of water. I marked time by the regularity of his visits. Hamad's encouragement kept me going, but how long can you talk before you grow stupid? I found myself chattering stray thoughts, dreams. I told Jin my fantasies. I confessed that I loved him. None of it did any good. At one point, I grew so frustrated that I hauled Jin up to a sitting position and began to swing him back and forth, yelling, "Wake up! Wake up!"

Hamad rushed in and made me stop. "Please calm down, Ms. Sauvage! You're overexcited." As he checked Jin's fragile connections to the monitors, he asked me to get off the bed.

"You've been talking more than 20 hours. Time to rest."

I felt a sting on my shoulder and glanced around just in time to see a cybernurse withdrawing a jet spray. "A sedative," Hamad whispered. My vision blurred. Ça va. Lights out.

I woke the next morning, groggy from sedation. Hamad brought me a breakfast of liquid nutrient. Then the three cyberguards—I nicknamed them les trois mousquetaires—the three musketeers—they trundled me down the hall to Jin's bedside, where I began another marathon monologue. We followed this routine for four days. I suppose they were days. Inside that steel room, I couldn't tell for sure. Since Hamad had taken the wall chronometer away, his regular visits were my only gauge of time.

The steel walls reflected fuzzy unresolved images, the white blob of the bed, my vague beige form hovering above. Merida must have scrounged her medical apparatus from some bargain fire sale. It looked like surplus junk from the 20th century. The air smelled faintly of saline and skin salve, and after a while, I couldn't even hear the liquids dripping through the tubes.

On that fourth day, I asked Hamad, "Do you really think Jin's doing this by choice? What could be so horrible to make him deliberately withdraw from consciousness?"

The question upset Hamad. He paced around the room before he finally sat down to face me. "There was pain," he said at last. "Our medications didn't help."

The tremor of Hamad's voice stopped me cold. For several long moments, we sat together in silence. Then Hamad checked the monitors and left.

That day, I tried reminding Jin of his passion to learn the truth. I pandered to his ego. I said he had a special mission, and the whole world was depending on him to choose the right course. I said his brain had sprouted a pair of tentacles with little receiver dishes on the ends, and that he could tune in the music of the universe anytime he wanted. All he had to do was stop dilly-dallying and open his eyes! Bien, his eyelids didn't even flicker.

Then I hit on the idea of his father. I never had understood the relationship between Jin and his father. I just started talking randomly, imagining what such a father must be like. And I got sort of worked up.

"What kind of man makes three-year-olds work in factories? He's a monster. You want to smash his face, right? Knock him down. Stomp him. But he's your father. He gave you life. You feel a bond with him in your gut, and you know he feels it, too. So the two of you can't leave each other alone. You dance around, fencing with each other, giving little nicks and cuts, and Jin, you're always bleeding. Mes dieux, but that's askew."

The door flew open, and a cybernurse rushed in, followed by Hamad. "There's a spike in the alpha waves," he whispered tensely. "Keep going. Mr. Sura is listening."

While the cybernurse injected a stimulant into Jin's bloodstream, I stammered. Knowing so little, what could I say next?

"Speak to him!" Hamad commanded.

"Your father wants you to fail," I began. Who knows where those words came from? "He—he's afraid of you. He pretends to ignore you, but he really watches every move you make—because—because he's afraid you know something he doesn't. If you give up now, your father wins. Don't let him stop you, Jin. Fight him!"

I felt the bed shake. Jin's body started jerking erratically. Whether from the force of the stimulant or from his own effort of will, he'd gone into a seizure. Another cybernurse rolled in, and Hamad pushed me out of the way. I pressed back against the wall as they held Jin down and strapped him to the bed. Hamad adjusted the cocktail of drugs entering his neck port, and the monitors beeped wildly.

"What's happening? What are you doing?" I shouted.

"Get out!" Hamad's rude tone surprised me. I stayed rooted to the spot while he and his cyberteam worked frantically around Jin's bed.

"Father." That was the first faint word Jin moaned. As he said it, his muscles stopped jerking, and he lay in the damp sheets laboring for breath, his chest heaving. His eyes blinked opened, but I don't think he could focus. His thin hospital wrapper was soggy with sweat. He turned his head on the pillow, grimacing in pain. His lips twitched as he tried to speak again. "Father," he croaked.

All at once, the three musketeer cybergoons appeared in the doorway. "Get her out of here," Hamad commanded over his shoulder as he continued to work. One of the guards grabbed me by the nape of my neck and hauled me into the corridor, but not before I saw my friend Hamad transmogrified into the fierce little Dr. Merida, laboring to save Jin's life.

HOW DID SHE do that? How did Merida disguise herself as the gentle Hamad? Did she use holographic projections, hypnotism, hallucinogenic drugs? Or plain old-fashioned stage make-up? I don't know. Once burned, twice burned, how many times would it take me to wise up? Still, Hamad had helped me coax Jin back to consciousness. I'm not sure I could have done it without him—her. Hamad had seemed so caring and sincere—was that a lie, or did Merida really have a gentler side? Mes dieux, but she kept me off-balance.

Two days passed, and I heard no news. The light-strips in my cell glowed constantly, so I had to use my own circadian body rhythms to track time. Uncle Qués had taught me that trick, back when we were kids together in the Paris tunnels. It required an eye-popping ton of concentration, but what else did I have to do?

The three musketeers brought food and bathing towels. They carried my chamber pot in and out. But cybergoons don't say much, have you noticed? With no one to talk to, I fell into a funk.

Merida had used me. I'd done what she wanted, brought Jin out of the coma. I didn't regret that. But now what? I'd served my purpose. Maybe she would wait to see if Jin had really recovered. She might need me again if he relapsed. Otherwise, what would she want with a cheeky, out-of-work tour guide? She said I lacked the strength of character to commit murder. On the other hand, her character seemed plenty freakin' strong. Gloomy thoughts.

Motivating thoughts. I'm not a girl who wants to die young. That second night during dinner, I used my best sleight of hand to evade the surveillance cameras and hide a plastic chopstick up my kimono sleeve. Time was definitely not on my side, so I took up my position at once, nonchalantly crouching against the wall. When the cybernurse opened my cell door to retrieve the dinner tray, I sprang.

One well-aimed jab of my chopstick into its infrared transceiver port, and the little machine succumbed. I dashed into the corridor. Thank the Laws, Jin's door was not locked. He lay in a doze on the bed, restrained by the leather straps and guarded only by another little cybernurse. Alarm bells rang.

I took out the second nurse with a quick chopstick jab and began clawing at Jin's straps. Releasing the buckles seemed to take long agonizing minutes, but when I starting yanking at the wires connected to Jin's body, he woke up and shrieked in pain.

I hesitated. Those alarms were still clanging. The guards would be on top of me in seconds. I had to act. So I grasped the drip tube connected to his neck port and tore it free in one swift pull. Blood spurted from his neck, and I grabbed up a knot of bedsheet to press against the wound. Jin was moaning and weakly pushing my hand away. Crimson blood soaked through the sheet.

"That's arterial bleeding. He'll die in seconds." Merida stood in the doorway. I glanced around and saw all three cyberguards at her back. "You've acted stupidly, pet. Move back and let me save him."

"Move back and let us go," I said.

"He'll die, you idiot. Guards, take her away."

As she stepped aside to let the musketeers enter, I brandished my plastic chopstick, gripped Jin's upper body and aimed the pointed end at his eye. "What happens if I shove this straight up inside his brain?" I said. "Would that mess up your experiment?"

Merida halted the guards with a gesture. For an instant, we hung silent. Bright red blood continued to pulse from Jin's neck, saturating the sheets.

"You won't kill him," Merida said. "Sorry, pet. We've discussed this before. You don't have the courage for murder."

"Maybe I think he's better off dead."

"You're not a good liar, Jolie."

I didn't answer. I just gripped Jin's chest and moved the chopstick nearer to his eye. If my bluff was going to work, I had to show resolve.

"He's bleeding too much." Merida was losing her composure. "Fool! Your stupidity will kill him. Let me close that wound."

I said, "Move into the hall, and you can send a cybernurse to fix him. But don't try anything, or I'll stab his brain and destroy your whole project."

Merida probably figured she could take control at any time, so she humored me and moved out of sight. A cybernurse rolled in and did something very simple that stopped Jin's bleeding. I wish I'd known how to do that.

"He needs a transfusion," the cybernurse reported mechanically.

I quieted the little demon with my chopstick and panted for breath. The guards waited in the corridor. Jin's body had stopped jerking in rhythmic little spasms. He wasn't fighting me anymore. Trying to recall the moment now, I guess my idea was to throw him over my shoulder, run like hell and find some safe hidey-hole in Merida's rambling habitat, to catch my breath and think of a next step. I know. Lame.

But what could I do, leave him there for Merida to play with and wait in my cell till the guards came to kill me? For all I knew, Jin's mind might be locked in an endless nightmare of suffering. This was no time for logic. I felt a ferocious compulsion to get Jin away from Merida at any cost. And I wasn't about to give up.

So I grasped his thin hospital wrapper, heaved him to a sitting position and slipped my arms around his torso, intending to sling him over my shoulder in a fireman's carry. You may ask how someone my size could do that, but I'm tougher than you'd think. I've carried plenty of fat Commies in out of the rain.

However, just as I bent close, Jin's eyes focused on me. "Who are you?" he mumbled.

"I'm Jolie. Your friend. Remember? Jolie Blanche Sauvage. You sent me the messages. I've come for you, Jin."

"I don't know you," he said more clearly.

"Jin, I'm Jolie, the tour guide. You sent for me."

He studied my face carefully. "I've never seen you before in my life," he said.

I opened my mouth in stupefaction. Jin had forgotten me? He hadn't sent for me? He didn't even remember my face? I stood there gawking at him with my mouth hanging open like a fool. An instant later, the guards were on me like viruses. I felt a sting on my neck, caught a quick glimpse of the jet spray, and lights out.

I awoke in another place. My cheek rested on a smooth firm pillow that smelled of citrus. I was lying on my side in a fetal curl, and someone had loosened my belt. I rolled over and opened my eyes on rosy light.

"She's awake."

"The lord must be told."

Voices rustled in the shadows, but I couldn't see anyone. I stretched and kicked at the covers, and that's when I noticed the beautiful sunset-pink kimono that enfolded me. It was embroidered with pale green dragons, and its gauzy chiffon fabric seemed to shimmer. I lay on a thick, cream-colored futon that felt softer than velvet. Above me, yellow and pink drapery billowed from decorative copper fixtures in the ceiling. Tiny russet designs flecked the drapery, like check-marks or flags. I focused my entire attention trying to decipher them.

After a while, I sensed movement beyond the curtains, rustling breeze, a door opening. I sat up and yawned and tried to recall what I was doing here in this beautiful curtained bed. Only then did I remember Jin's bright blood soaking the sheets, and the weapon I'd aimed at his eye. I sat up straight. I might have killed him! That recollection went slicing through my mind just as the bed curtains slid open, and I found myself face-to-face with Lord Suradon Sura.

"Get up, Sauvage. Tempus fugit. You've slept long enough."

As soon as he spoke, I knew he was a holographic projection. His image appeared almost as solid as flesh—except for that slight tell-tale flicker around the edges.

"Where's Jin? Is he all right?" I asked quickly.

"He's recovering from your attack."

"Huh?" I bit my lip. My foolhardy rescue probably did seem like an attack. Or was Suradon being sarcastic? I felt very confused. "Am I still in Merida's place?"

Suradon grinned at me as if he found vast amusement in my questions. His features appeared more Asiatic than his son's. Then I remembered he'd had cosmetic surgery to add that epicanthic fold. He had Jin's liquid black eyes, but they gleamed with a merry light, and jovial wrinkles rayed out across his temples. He obviously smiled a lot. His hair and thick brushy eyebrows glittered silver. Underneath the expensive black suit, he had the same vigorous build his son used to have—before Merida's operation.

"Where's Merida?" I asked.

"Enough questions. My time is short. There's a fuckin' war going on."

From such aristocratic lips, his language shocked me. I fell silent at once. Along with his jovial expression, he carried an aura of command. Literally, an aura. That flicker bleeding out around his hologram was growing brighter by the minute.

He deliberately assumed a stern frown, steepled his fingers together, and looked me up and down until I positively blushed. I pulled the kimono down over my knees and stuffed strands of ragged white hair behind my ears. In the shadows, I noticed cyberservants, standing at attention.

Finally, he shook his head and grunted, "My son chose you?"

Judgmental old bastard. Indignation overcame my nervousness. I jumped off the bed and threatened him with my fists. "D'accord! He chose a no-name tunnel rat to fight for him—because you wouldn't! You said he could make his own choices."

Suradon's lips twitched as if he wanted to smile again, but he held it back. "Jin doesn't even recognize you, Sauvage."

Whoa, that hurt.

He quirked one thick eyebrow. "Can't imagine why not. Who could forget a mug like yours? With that big purple star splattered around your eye? I suppose the boy has so many lovers, he can't keep track."

Wish you were here—Jin had said that twice, I reminded myself. Suradon's sarcasm was throwing me off-balance. I gritted my teeth. "Whether he sent for me or not, he needs help. Any sane person can see that. A father especially ought to see that. Maybe Jin called me unconsciously—with those latent senses or whatever."

"Aw, don't tell me you believe Merida's bullshit." His flickering image enlarged and towered over me, which just made me madder.

"That's right, it's bullshit. And you're letting Merida test it on your own son. Have you seen him lately? Don't you feel any love for him?"

Suradon smirked. "Maybe you wanna attack him with your chopstick again?"

"How dare you," I said. "How dare you make jokes while Merida carves up your son's brain. You must know what she is."

Suradon's eyes narrowed. "She's an investment. Her ideas may be bullshit, but people buy bullshit left and right. If this experiment works, it could mean the salvation of Pacific.Com. Stable life support for millions of families, Sauvage. But you're a free agent. You wouldn't understand what that means."

Suradon glanced at something outside the holo-stage, something I couldn't see. He audibly ground his teeth, and the light bleeding around his holographic image jittered. Then he turned back to me, and the smile he'd been restraining suddenly creased his face. It looked like a bitter smile. "Sauvage, life is hilarious. You think you have troubles. I have troubles you can't imagine."

Life is hilarious. That was Jin's line. I felt my nostrils curl. "Old man, you're worse than Merida. You want to see your son humiliated."

Suradon rocked on his heels. "Fuckin' whelp, a little humility wouldn't hurt him."

"How dare you," I repeated.

"Hey, Jin came to me with this idea. Hyperthought. A profitable new product, he said. Frankly, Pacific.Com needs cash flow. The war is sapping our reserves. We've got enemies worse than your rebels, Sauvage. Greenland wants to tear us apart."

Greenland was his enemy? I thought they were allies. I didn't understand a word he was saying. So I just squinted and tried to look mean.

Suradon rolled his eyes. "Jin promised me this new Hyperthought would save our asses. I'm givin' the kid a chance. You talk about love. How much do you know?"

Suradon stretched out his hand, and a tiny holographic image of Jin appeared in his palm. Jin's pale, thin form twisted restlessly in a tangle of sheets. He seemed in agony. I wanted to look away, but I couldn't.

"Tell me, Sauvage, what you feel for my son, is that love? I call it greed. You want to cling to him and never let go, even if you kill him. And what makes it so damned funny, you don't even know the sonabitch. You're hooked on a character from the Mooovies."

I bit my lip. Suradon's words had the ring of truth. For an instant, I doubted myself. But not for long. "What I feel doesn't matter. Jin is suffering, and you can make it stop!"

"Sauvage, can't you get it through your head? My son is doing this to please me." Suradon tossed the image of Jin in the air like a ball and spun to catch it behind his back.

The old man's complacent grin filled me with rage. I shouted, "Jin thinks you're vile! He told me about a three-year-old girl in one of your factories—"

"Not that damned three-year-old again." Suradon held up the image of Jin and pinched it like a squeeze toy.

"He hates everything you do!" I spluttered, spraying my chin with saliva.

The old man huffed. "He fuckin' dotes on me."

Suradon made me so angry, I started punching his holographic image as if I could rip it up with my bare fists. He sparred with me, dodging my blows in mock fear. "Ha, that was a close one. Come on, girl. Show me your stuff."

"You bastard Commie! Is everything a joke to you?" Despite my best effort, I felt my face pouting up to cry. "Jin is hurting. That's all that matters. Stop letting him suffer."

I swung so hard that I spun off-balance and hit the floor.

"You're his choice, Sauvage. Catch this!" Suradon wound up like a baseball pitcher and hurled the tiny image of Jin right at me. I put up my hand, and an explosion of light filled the room. I felt a wave of heat and saw stars, and when my vision cleared, Suradon's hologram had vanished.

Seconds later, a bevy of cyberservants flocked around me like Japanese butterflies. Their clothing flickered with rainbows, and they wore ornaments in their hair that sparkled with dancing light. Three of them helped me to my feet and led me toward a tall, carved doorway. I kept looking back at the spot where Suradon had been standing. More arguments kept springing to mind, things I wanted to tell him about Jin, but it was too late.

Just as we passed through the ornate doorway, the light turned dingy, and the three geishas morphed into dull, platinum cybergoons. Merida's musketeers. I looked back and saw an empty platform surrounded by blank walls. It dawned on me that the whole beautiful bedroom had been nothing but a holostage. Virtual reality projected from a computer. None of it was real.

IN THE LEADEN light of real space, the three musketeers shoved me down the hallway. Such friendly guys. Their identical platinum faces never betrayed the first hint of expressiveness, and the longest sentence they ever spoke was, "Turn right please." One had a scuff mark on the back of his head, so I called him Scuff, and sometimes I tried to start conversations with him. Not that he noticed.

For the next several minutes, the musketeers escorted me through the preter-spooky maze of Merida's habitat. We caught a ride on a squeaking prehistoric pedestrian beltway that dumped us straight into a dripping natural cave. The cave branched in fifty directions, and I couldn't have guessed which way to go. One of the goons pushed my head down and led me through a low fissure into a rusting steel conduit. We crab-walked through the conduit to an adobe tunnel decorated with finger-daub paintings. Shadows darted up the walls as kerosene torches gave way to clunky sodium lamps strung on cables. This was the most schizoid habitat I'd ever seen. I took note of portals and cross corridors, but it was impossible to memorize such an irrational layout.

It wasn't just the floorplan that made Merida's habitat creepy. There was too much empty space. Before the war, back when my life was sane, I'd spent some private moments up top, savoring the beauty of Earth's surface. But most of the time, I had lived like the rest of the world, cheek by jowl with a few billion other people in some crowded subterrain. As the climate heated up and more people migrated toward the poles, it seemed like our habitats shrank smaller every year. I guess we were used to living on top of each other. That's why Merida's habitat freaked me. Only three live human beings shared this whole rambling structure. Jin, Merida and me. You could hear echoes. The place didn't feel like the Earth I knew at all.

The musketeers led me to the paint-crusted steel door of Jin's cell. I pushed it open, and Jin was sitting up in his cot, wearing the same threadbare hospital wrapper. A nest of monitors and drip tubes surrounded him. The light level was set at low, and Jin stared at me with huge hollow eyes. He wore an old plastic neck brace, I suppose to hold up his cranium, which now weighed half a kilo more than usual. His long black hair lay tangled on his shoulders, and the right side of his face drooped in paralysis. I knew what that meant. A stroke. Mes dieux, had my actions caused that?

Beside him, Merida stood guard. There were stains on her gray unisuit, and a lot of medical apparatus dangled from her belt. She'd lined her pretty black eyes with kohl. Her wide red lips wavered between a smile and a grimace. "We're partners now, Jolie. We may as well be friends."

"When Earth freezes," I said.

She chuckled and plumped the pillows for Jin. I sensed she was hiding irritation. "Relax, pet. Lord Suradon wants you to stay with his son. Much to my dismay, you're to have free run of the place. You made an impression on the old man. That must please you."

I pulled up a chair on the other side of Jin's cot, and he shifted to face me. It was clear he still didn't recognize me. I asked, "So how much is he paying you, Merida?"

She sighed. "Ah, Jolie. Money is just the enabler."

"Yeah right."

"It's true." She smoothed Jin's hair, and he turned toward her as she spoke. "You've always known what I want, Jolie. To build more clinics. To make my procedure available everywhere. People will benefit. They will. You've only seen the side effects. You haven't seen the new capabilities Jin is gaining. Be patient. The gestation is still in progress."

"Liar." I wished she would shut up and leave me alone with Jin.

Slowly, thoughtfully, she smoothed his bedcovers. "You think I'm your adversary, Jolie, but the truth is, you and I are alike. We come from the bottom of the heap, both of us. We know what it's like to go hungry. And we've clawed our way up, despite the odds. We could be sisters."

"Not in this life!" I made a face. Still, her words started me thinking.

"You detest the Com managers," she went on. "They killed

your parents. Now they're killing your friends. I know how you feel." She looked me straight in the eye and spoke in dead earnest. "Jolie, I hate them more."

"You're partners with Suradon," I reminded her.

"I hate him most of all, Jolie. Taking his money is my way of getting even."

She could have stolen the words right out of my mouth. I shoved hair out of my eyes and thought about that.

Merida moved around the bed toward me. Jin followed her with his eyes. She said, "Ask yourself, Jolie, why are you helping this Com lordling when you know his people are murdering your friends?"

Ça va. That hit home. Luc had asked me the same question. Jonas and Adrienne both thought I'd flaked out.

Then she bent over me and breathed in my face. Her lips glistened like a wound. "You think Jin's a good man. On what evidence? His movie roles? You don't know him. You're in love with a fantasy."

I leaned away, but she moved closer. I could feel her breath on my cheek.

"Jin Sura is exactly like his father, pet. They're cut from the same cloth. A pair of vain, selfish egotists, each trying to outdo the other. The old man hates the young one because he's young. And the young one mewls like a pup because Papa never cuddled him."

Merida smoothed my stiff white hair back behind my ears with her fingernails. She smiled at me, knowing I couldn't contradict her. "Suradon and his allies are slaughtering your friends, and yet you risk your life to save his brat of a son. A man you slept with once. A man with whom you have nothing in common. A man who doesn't even recognize your face."

Conflicting urges whirled through my mind. I felt stupid and wrong and confused.

But then Merida grasped my shoulders and shook me. "You and I are on the same side!" she yelled in my face. I felt her nails biting my skin. "Jolie, we can help each other!"

She was hammering the point too hard. She sounded desperate for me to believe her. I am undoubtedly a sap, but by this time, even I had started wising up.

"You're making Jin suffer. And you threatened Luc. No, we are not alike." I glanced at Jin. He right cheek and mouth sagged pitifully. "Don't hurt him any more," I said. Whatever else might be true, I still cared for Jin. That was bedrock.

"Hurt him?" Merida cackled, backing away from me. "You're such a little fool, Jolie. I've made him a god!"

Jin lifted his left hand and drew a circle in the air with his finger.

"I've given him everything he wanted," Merida went on. She was gloating now, strutting around the bed. Pleasure stretched her mouth out of shape and made her ugly. "My nanobot will succeed, you'll see. The whole world will recognize my genius. I'll build a hundred clinics. A thousand! Jin is my supreme creation."

"You didn't create him," I said.

"I made him better!" Merida lifted her chin and glared defiantly.

Jin continued to draw ciphers in the air. I watched for a while, then sadly reached out and caught his hand. "Merida, you've turned him into an imbecile. What will become of him?"

"He'll bring us a revelation!" She laughed in that way that sounded like barking. Then she flounced out of the room, slamming the door.

Jin winced at the noise. Maybe his head was hurting. When I leaned over him and began to massage his temples, he clenched his eyes shut. That's when I noticed a tiny red line circling one of the scars on his forehead. That pair of parenthesis-shaped scars where Merida had first injected her nanobots had nearly faded away. I almost couldn't see them anymore. But now, one of the scars looked inflamed. I spoke a command to brighten the room light, and Jin moaned. Even with his eyes shut, the light hurt him.

"Sorry," I whispered, shielding his closed eyes with my hand. I bent closer and examined the scar. It was outlined in faint crimson. Had it become infected? I touched it, and to my surprise, a bit of make-up came off on my fingertip. Someone had deliberately camouflaged that scar with flesh-colored paint.

By now, tears were streaming from Jin's tight-clenched eyelids, and he was gritting his teeth in pain.

"Dim," I commanded the room lights. "Jin, forgive me."

Then I dabbed at the scar with a sterile wipe. Jin moaned, but I didn't stop till I'd wiped both scars clean. They were both fresh and livid. Someone had very recently reopened those incisions. Merida!

Fury engulfed me. Merida had operated again! She must have injected more demon nanobots—even though she knew she couldn't control them! The first ones must not have wrought enough havoc in Jin's brain to satisfy her. She had to vindicate her research to the mighty Lord Suradon. Apparently the woman would do anything to ensure success. I sprang up and rushed toward the door. All I could think of was getting my hands around her throat.

"S-s-sound," Jin stammered.

His voice stopped me in my tracks. He'd spoken! I hurried back to his side. His face was contorted in agony. "L-l-louder than before."

"Oh my Jin." I bathed his forehead with a damp cloth and rubbed his chest with cooling alcohol. After a while, his suffering seemed to ease.

It was absolutely a miracle that Jin spoke right then and stopped me from leaving the room. If I'd rushed out and confronted Merida, I would have botched everything. I've always been way too impulsive. I needed time to cool down.

As I sat there stroking his forehead, Jin turned his deep, hollow eyes toward me and focused on my face. "The s-surgery worked this time?" he asked.

The question shocked me. He knew what Merida had done to him? He had agreed to this outrage? Sacrée Loi! Merida boasted that Jin had come to her of his own free will, that he wanted what she could do for him. I couldn't deny that. But this wasn't right. Her experiments were killing him. Despite what he wanted, this insanity had to stop.

I wracked my brain for ideas. I would take Jin away from this place before Merida could do any more damage. Someday, maybe he would thank me, or maybe he wouldn't. Anyway, he would live. And he would have his whole life ahead to judge me. If I could just think of a way to get him out of here.

If I'd had my Net node, I could have called Adrienne. She would have known what to do. Jonas would have come up with a million ideas. Cher Luc, he would have put me on the right track. Mes dieux, but I needed my friends! They'd saved me from worse scrapes a dozen times. I couldn't do this without them. I didn't have the intelligence.

Ça va, I moaned for about half an hour and shed a few hot tears on Jin's white hospital wrapper. I hugged him and buried my face against his shoulder, but when I moved to kiss him, I saw he was gazing at me with a totally blank expression. It hit me this was wasting time.

So I sat up and looked around the room. My glance landed on the sterile wipe I'd used to clean Jin's scars. It was still all globby with flesh-toned makeup, and the next thing I knew, I picked up that wipe and dabbed the paint right back on Jin's scars.

See, it came home to me that my preter-vicious Net node was not going to fall down from heaven, and that no one was going to burst through those doors and tell me what to do. I would have to think of something myself. This time, I would have to keep my head and be reasonable and work out the logistics. Laws of Physics preserve me, I would need a giga-brilliant plan. But until I had one, Merida couldn't know I was onto her. I had to keep playing the fool. You're probably saying, for Jolie Blanche Sauvage that should be a breeze.

To this day, I don't know why Suradon ordered Merida to give me free run of the habitat. Maybe it amused him to watch me. Like kids who watch gutter bugs crossing a pedestrian belt. Funny little bugs, they're blind. They can't see all the people stomping around. Sometimes they make it across the belt. Sometimes they get squashed and never know why. I think Suradon was watching me like that. Scuzzy old man.

Anyway, I took full advantage of my new freedom to search every cluttered storeroom and twisted tunnel. Merida surely knew what I was doing. I guess she felt smug about her security. For good reason. It was airtight.

Everything about Merida's place was low-budget, cut-rate and stingy. There were only two laser-blasted exits, the airlock in the sea cave and a pneumatic air chute that ran straight up through centuries of buried debris to the surface. Both exits were securely locked and electronically monitored by her metallic musketeers. I checked out the habitat's waste pipe. It was the size of my arm, no escape route there. Honeycombed plastic filled the air ducts, nothing solid could pass that way. My hope centered on the power plant beneath the kitchen.

I'd discovered an unguarded maintenance hatch in the kitchen floor, marked "Danger: High Voltage." It opened down into an

airlock that exited to the power plant. The airlock meant the
power plant had no breathable air, and that meant it lay outside
the habitat walls, beyond Merida's security. The plant had probably been built in a crawl space beneath the structure. Usually,
when contractors blast rock to build a sealed underground habitat, they leave a rough crawl space around the exterior walls
for safety inspections and repairs. Unless Merida had cut more
corners than usual, her habitat had probably been built that way.

If I could manage to carry Jin down through the power plant,
maybe we could squirm up through the crawl space to the habitat's roof. Maybe I could find the air chute that shot straight up
to the surface. Maybe the borehole around the chute would be
a little larger than the chute structure itself, and maybe there
would be enough free space in the borehole for Jin and me to
scale up to the surface. 1,500 meters. Maybe we could. It would
be the meta-primo scary trip, that's for sure. In any case, I knew
from my deep-Paris childhood that the Earth's crust was riddled
with fissures and caves. One way or another, we'd find a way
up.

The problem was, Merida had taken my surface suit, and I
couldn't find it anywhere. What's more, we would need not one
surfsuit, but two.

Jin's condition was worsening. Though he mumbled words
now and then, he'd grown glassy-eyed and distracted. Often he
seemed to be reliving past events in flashback. He moaned and
tossed on his cot in terrible pain. Sometimes he screamed. Merida seemed honestly concerned, although I had gained a new
perspective on Merida's concerns now. As the days went by, I
watched Jin in helpless worry. I also invented a hundred pre-
posterous and totally unfeasible ways to improvise a surfsuit.

Luck changed when I found my old helmet. One of the musketeers had chucked it into a storage bin. When I found it, the
duct tape had completely peeled away, leaving a gummy residue
around the exposed gash. And the sea liquid in the liner had
dried to a foul-smelling rime.

As quietly as possible, I set about repairing the helmet. First
I soaked it in a tub of bleach in the kitchen for two days to kill
the toxins. I hid the bleach tub under a pile of empty protein
sacks, but that was just pro forma. Merida and Suradon had to
be watching me on surveillance cameras. Next I mended the
gash with surgical glue pilfered from Merida's medical stock.

Would a sealant intended to heal body tissue work on a Kevtex helmet? I didn't know for sure, but it looked all right.

Merida and Suradon probably both had a laugh at the little idiot, Jolie Sauvage, who got so excited about one broken helmet, when she would clearly never find the two full surfsuits she would need to take Jin away. Oh sure, they estimated my intelligence about right. What they underestimated was my resolve.

SEE, I WAS desperate. I thought Jin would die if I didn't get him away from Merida soon. I had to try something. I couldn't just sit on my hands.

Life is a blind run, that's my idea. You can't see where you're going, so every step you take, you have to trust there'll be a place for your foot to land. The minute you start to worry about potholes and pits, that's when you stumble. But as long as you keep sprinting ahead in total blind trust, then you move with grace. Bien, I think that's the meaning of grace.

So I decided to give Jin the helmet and take my chances without one.

What I did was fairly simple. The very night the glue hardened on my helmet, I traded my demure kimono for a more serviceable musketeer uniform—stolen, of course. Then I waited till the wee hours and started a fire in the habitat's main electrical bus. This created a temporary power blackout, which shut down life support. You can imagine how Merida felt about no life support. While she and her cyberstaff were going loco trying to restore power, I slipped through the dark corridors into Jin's room.

"Wh—who?" he stammered, waking at once.

No matter how many times I had come to see him in the last few days, Jin never seemed able to remember my face. Each time I entered his room, he treated me as a stranger. His lack of recognition hurt me, but I'd grown used to it by now. So I said what I always said. "It's me, Jolie. I've come to help you, Jin."

"G-good angel."

I drew a quick breath. "You know me?"

He said, "Know your—voice."

I felt like leaping for joy, but there wasn't time. Grinning like a fool in the dark, I started explaining our situation and feeling for the leads attached to his body. Jin said nothing more. I suppose he was too weak. In the pitch darkness, I disconnected all his monitors and tubes, and sealed the port in his neck to prevent bleeding—a procedure which I had carefully observed and memorized in the past few days. Then I slung him over my shoulder in a fireman's carry.

He only moaned a little. "Where?"

"Away from here" was all I could think to say.

We proceeded down the dark twisting halls to the kitchen. Under the sink I had hidden a pack of purloined odds and ends that might prove useful, an electric torch, air cylinders, nutrient tubes, a knife, rope, some first aid stuff, a mirror for signaling once we reached the surface, plus a roll of fabriglass and my leftover surgical glue. I tied Jin's long hair back with a string and gently fitted the helmet onto his head. Then I sealed the neck gasket to his skin with the surgical glue. That should form an airtight seal. Next I plugged a cylinder of hypercompressed air into the helmet's breathing port and strapped the cylinder to Jin's chest with a strip of cloth.

"Just breathe normally," I whispered. He tried to nod, but his head lolled on his shoulders. I had neglected to bring his neck brace. Quickly I wrapped his limp body in fabriglass and sealed him in with more glue. He looked like a cellophane birthday package, but at least the fabriglass would protect him from toxins. For myself, I'd stolen a second cylinder of hypercompressed air, and I'd jury-rigged a lever to open the valve partway so I could suck at it. The air tended to jet out too fast and sting my lips and tongue, but it was better than nothing. As for exposure to toxins, I'd have to risk it. I couldn't afford to bundle up in fabriglass. That interfered with mobility.

Mes dieux, but I was breaking the cardinal rule of life: Never leave a safe habitat without a surfsuit. Every citizen on the planet had been drilled about the danger of environmental toxins. Yet here I was brazenly exposing myself. Some toxins killed in a matter of hours, but the worst ones, the ones that gave me nightmares, were the slow-acting biochemical molecules that rotted away different parts of your body over many years. If I could just get to the surface in time and find therapy, I'd be okay.

Too late for second thoughts now. I'd made my choice. Whatever was going to happen had already begun. I was sitting on the kitchen floor pondering these things when the lights blinked on. Merida had brought the habitat's power back up. Time to move. Just as well I didn't have longer to think—I might have bailed on the whole plan.

Instead, I hastily cranked open the hatch to the power plant, stuffed Jin down into the airlock, then climbed in beside him. It was a tight fit, and I had to twist around and press against him to lock the hatch. He made a noise, but I couldn't hear him very well through the fabriglass. No time to delay. I pulled the big round ring to start the airlock running through its cycle.

When we tumbled out of the airlock, I felt more naked than ever before in my life. The atmosphere in the power plant was hot, dry and bitingly acrid. It tasted of ozone. I could almost feel my skin crackling, as if invisible poisons were already entering my pores. I had to force myself to concentrate on immediate matters. So I switched on my stolen electric torch and scoped the layout. We'd fallen onto a small steel platform just below the airlock. A deep shaft opened below us, housing two segmented columns of turbines. They were spinning like mad, roaring and throwing off static. An odd ladder of knotted cable hung down between them. I couldn't see how far down it went.

Just then, Jin sagged against me in his fabriglass wrapper, and I had to prop him against the wall. My torchlight seemed dimmer than before, and I noticed black spots in my vision. It could be I wasn't getting enough oxygen. To get Jin away from here, I had to keep up my strength, so I took time to pull the air cylinder from my shoulder pack and put my mouth to the valve. I twisted it open slowly. The air jetted out so fast, it cut my lip.

Merida would know exactly where to look for us, so we had to move fast. I sucked a few gulps of oxygen, then stowed the cylinder and wrestled Jin into position over my shoulder. He'd grown so light, any child might have managed him, and yet I found myself panting. Was it my imagination, or did each breath burn all the way down into my lungs?

Clutching Jin's body, I seized the knotted ladder and clambered down the first few rungs. The ladder swung back and forth under our weight, and my torch kept getting dimmer. Maybe the battery was weak. Plenty soon, it failed entirely, and I could see nothing but the sparks flying from those twin columns of turbines. At least I'd gotten a glimpse of the layout. As we descended farther, hot turbulent breezes told me we were passing close between the spinning turbines.

At that moment, light blazed down the shaft from above. I jerked in surprise, my foot slipped, and I nearly dropped Jin. The airlock was opening. Merida had already found us. She'd activated the overhead lights, and now it became obvious that my sight had narrowed to tunnel vision from lack of oxygen. But the lights revealed something else. In the slick gray wall surrounding the turbines, I glimpsed a small orifice tapering inward. As I watched, it puffed open, then closed up so tight it virtually disappeared. The gray wall looked wet and fibrous. There might be handholds. If I could leap from the ladder between those two turbine columns and find a purchase on that wall, Jin and I might be able to squeeze through that little orifice.

Above me, Merida was shouting orders at the musketeers, and I felt their weight shuddering the ladder. They were coming down after us. "Give me grace," I whispered aloud. Then I cradled Jin's body in my left arm, clung to the ladder with my right, and stretched one leg out between the turbines toward that gray wall. I lost my balance and fell. My shoulder pack slammed against a turbine and burst open, raining out gear. Jin and I pitched forward and bounced into the wall.

Desperately I flung out my free right hand and grabbed for the fibrous surface. Light beams splintered down from above as I clawed for a hold. I heard more shouting. At last, my fingers closed on a rubbery wet tendril, and I gripped with all my might.

We'd fallen a long way. The little orifice I'd seen in the wall was far above us now, but a wet sucking noise drew my attention to another similar one just below us. And there was another off to the side. Two more. Apparently, these pores riddled the wall. I watched this one puff open, then close tight. With agonizing care, I worked down to the little pore and pushed my fist through. It felt moist and fleshy. As if in reflex, the pore yawned away from my fist like a mouth. Before it could close, I jammed my head and shoulder through. Grunting and heaving, I squeezed Jin halfway through the opening with me. All at once, the pore wriggled and writhed and spat us the rest of the way through.

We fell straight down into blank darkness. I locked my arms around Jin's body in what may have been a death grip. How long does a second last? Not many could have passed, and yet it seemed like an eternity before we landed, with a mighty splash, in a body of cold black fluid. The transition took me by such surprise I inhaled and choked.

The air trapped inside Jin's fabriglass wrapper saved us. He bobbed to the surface like a balloon and brought me up with him. For several minutes, I could do nothing but hold on to him and cough and spit and throw up fluid from my lungs.

When I came to my senses, I realized we were caught in a boiling current, and in the inky blackness, perception really played tricks with me. The fluid seemed to be surging up like a fountain, with Jin and me balanced at the very top. Fluid swirled around my body and tugged at my musketeer uniform like a rising tide. We must have fallen into an underground spring or artesian well. Anyway, I wanted off, so I pointed my body at an angle to the boil and started kicking, pushing Jin's buoyant fabriglass bag ahead of me. With much effort, I finally reached a solid wall. Only then did I realize that my lungs no longer burned and that my energy had returned. Whatever else might be in this atmosphere, it seemed to have more oxygen.

In the darkness, my hand located a small flat shelf sticking out from the wall just above the bubbling fluid line. It felt wide enough to hold both of us, so I hoisted Jin up, and pulled myself up dripping wet beside him.

"Jin, ça va?"

He moved, but I couldn't hear if he said anything. At least he was still conscious.

Fluid streamed down my face and neck and got into my eyes. I had swallowed plenty. Some of it still gurgled in my lungs. It had a funny sweet taste, but there was no way to guess what it contained. One thing for sure, it had entered my bloodstream by now.

The spring or river, whatever, it was definitely rising. In just moments, the fluid level had already welled up several centimeters above the shelf where we were crouching. Soon, we'd be up to our chins again. I sat there shivering and thinking. What next, Jolie? The electric torch was lost. Likewise the air cylinders, the food, the climbing rope. I didn't have a single piece of communications gear. I didn't even have a chronometer to tell the time. More than that, I had no clue where we were, except that we were giga-deep in the Earth. Curious place for a sun-loving surfer girl to be.

Wouldn't you know, Jin picked that moment to collapse

against me in a lifeless heap. It was all I could do to keep him from slipping off the shelf. Sacrée Loi, let me speak plainly. I whimpered like a child.

Cowering in the dark, with the fluid rising every moment, I rocked Jin in my arms and begged him to wake up. My first botched rescue had half paralyzed him. What had I done this time? His air cylinder would run empty soon. I had no way to time it. But if I unsealed the fabriglass and removed his helmet, I would condemn him to the same fate I was surely facing— exposure to toxins. Either way, he would die. My doing. My fault. As the fluid level rose to my shoulders, I blubbered away, hopelessly begging him to forgive me. He'd made a bad choice when he picked Jolie Sauvage for his angel.

Every lame move, every preter-inane choice I'd made since leaving Palmertown cycled through my mind like reruns of a bad movie. I used to think of myself as a thrill-charged surfer girl with nerves of iron and the cheek to match. Then I remembered Luc's accident. My fault. Mea culpa. All I ever did was rush into things without a plan, without a notion of the risk. Adrienne had been right, I needed a nursemaid. Mes dieux, but I missed my friends!

It was then I began thinking of delivering Jin back to Merida. The rubbery fibers which formed the walls of this place weren't easy to grip and climb, but I could do it. I could scale back up to that mouth-like opening and find the power plant. Merida and the musketeers would be waiting. So what if they murdered me? Without therapy, my fate had already been ordained by the toxins I'd breathed and swallowed. Better to die quickly. At least, with my last act, I could undo this terrible mistake. Merida might play ungodly games with Jin's brain, but maybe she would keep him alive. Maybe.

Self-doubt is a horrible thing. It saps your energy and keeps you from making the bold leaps necessary for survival. Lucky for me, I'm not a deep thinker. My mind skips along the surface of things, where facts tend to stand out in bright colors. I didn't doubt for long. No, Merida would not keep Jin alive. Call it lizard-brain instinct, I knew that sooner or later, her experiments would kill him. I couldn't give up now. There was no easy way. Somewhere overhead, the open surface waited. I had to get Jin up there and signal for help. Keep focused, Jolie.

With shaking legs, I stood up on the narrow shelf and tried

to hoist Jin's unconscious body over my shoulder. Wouldn't you know, he picked that moment to wake up in a panic. I suppose he was suffocating. Anyway, he began clawing so violently at the inside of the fabriglass bag that he broke out of my grip and fell into the liquid. I couldn't see through the darkness, but I heard splashing, so I dove in and swam for him.

Fabriglass is tough material. You need a diamond blade to cut it—or maybe just a meta-surge of adrenaline. By the time I reached him, Jin had managed to tear a rip in the bag, and it was filling fast with liquid and sinking.

"Jin, relax! Stop kicking!"

He didn't hear me. When he sank below the surface, I dove with him, trying by feel alone to free him from the lethal bag. I felt his hands moving. With unbelievable strength, he tore the rip wider and wider till he'd rent the bag from one end to the other. Then he shed it like an old skin, and we kicked to the surface. He tore the helmet off with so much force, I heard the gasket rip. And I heard him sucking great gulps of air.

"Hil—hil—" he spluttered unintelligibly.

"Jin," I panted, touching him in the darkness to make sure he was there. He shook himself and treaded the fluid with steady, powerful kicks.

"Hilarious!" he yelled at the top of his voice. And then he began to laugh.

THE BLACK TIDE surged around us, lifting us higher, and the walls echoed with Jin's laughter. "This way, pet. We'll cross this river. There's a bridge. And beyond that, a chamber."

"What? You can see in the dark?"

"I hear it," he shouted, still laughing. "Jolie, I hear everything!"

"You can hear a bridge?" I'd browsed video about ancient bats navigating through dark caves. "You mean like sonar?"

Jin laughed even louder. He was swimming away from me. I heard long measured strokes. He seemed to have recovered from his paralysis. Quickly, I followed in his wake.

The surging liquid thrust me bodily against a large outcropping. Its surface was slick and wet and hard to grasp. I felt Jin's hand gripping my upper arm. In one easy motion, he hauled me up out of the fluid and set me on my feet. "The bridge," he said. His strength seemed superhuman, and yet as I bumped against him in the dark, I felt his wasted limbs and skeletal torso. He hadn't miraculously sprouted muscles. What could have produced such a physical change in him?

"Stay close to me, pet. The footing's precarious. This bridge is very old." He snatched the collar of my uniform just as I lost my balance. "Wonderful!" he said. "We must get to the chamber. It's coming clearer by the second."

I clung to him on the greasy, wet structure he called a bridge. The surface felt like gelatin, only it seemed to be creeping around my feet like something alive. I couldn't find traction. How could he see where to stand? I asked, "What's coming clearer, Jin?"

"You worry so much, pet," he answered with wry amusement. His soft Pacific accent touched me to the quick. He sounded like himself again. He said, "Take my arm. I can read your thoughts. I can hear the cells in your body. They make a sort of chittering. The sensations are coming from everywhere. This is amazing!" Then he let out an exuberant whooping laugh. "Hoo-hoo-hoo!"

About then, we both slipped and fell in a sprawling heap together, and my fingers touched down onto the viscous oozy surface. Jin hooted again like a delighted lunatic. "Forgive me, pet. This is hard to get used to. I need time to adjust."

"Jin, stop it." I grabbed his shoulders and shook him. This "bridge," as he called it, terrified me. I couldn't see a thing. The dark was so thick, it seemed as if the very fabric of space were closing in on us. Only the fluid gurgling below gave me a sense of dimension. That and the warmth of Jin's body. His skin felt hot to the touch. I clung to him.

"That base note I was hearing before," he said, "it's fracturing."

"Huh?" I didn't have an inkling what he meant.

"Noise. Feedback. It's like a scream. I have to find the patterns. This is—not what I expected."

A shiver ran up the back of my neck. "Jin, what are you talking about?" I tugged at his arms, trying to get his attention and bring him back to the present.

In response, he sprang to his feet and hauled me up so fast, my breath caught in my throat. "You're right, Jolie. This air is filled with toxins. Come on. Let's cross the bridge. I need to reach that chamber."

He grasped me around my middle and lifted me off my feet like a package. "Chemicals," he said, sauntering through the darkness. "You're wondering where I get my strength. Acetylcholine, adenosine triphosphate, adrenaline, a whole alphabet of brain chemicals. Ha. I can name them all if you like. I just realized I control their manufacture now."

Without warning, he started sprinting along the bridge. I locked my arms around his waist, totally disoriented. He leaped into the air, and it seemed as if we'd never touch down, but he landed perfectly on one foot and kept running. "This is marvelous," he shouted. "Hoo-hoo! I'm in conscious control of my entire brain. I can do anything!"

"Jin, slow down!" I pleaded, bouncing along on his hip.

"You want light, pet? You want to see? Certainly."

I sensed a faint rosy glow. After hours in pitch-darkness, the light came as a shock, and for an instant, my mind reeled trying to comprehend where it came from. Jin still held my waist in the crook of his elbow, so my perspective was way off kilter. I whipped my head around to locate the light source. The glow was radiating from Jin's forehead! Gradually, his whole face grew luminous. Sacred Angels of Physics!

"See what I can do?" He grinned like a goblin. "I can tune my brain's energy to visible wavelengths. This is fun!"

"Stop it! Please!"

"Ah, you're crying. Sweet little savage. Your fear rings in my head. Please don't be upset." The glow radiating from his face subsided, but after that, it never completely disappeared. "We're nearly there, Jolie. Hold on."

"There? Where?"

Jin loped on across the narrow slippery bridge. In the spectral glow, the walls around us sweated and glistened, and when I looked down, I saw the bridge's surface ripple with shades of gray, like colorless rainbows gliding through an oil slick. The river of gurgling fluid lay far, far below. Abruptly, Jin halted and set me on my feet.

His forehead grew more luminous, and I saw him wince and press his temples. "That awful static. It's the Net! The signals are full of cross-talk and echoes. Rumors. Gossip. Cyclones of feedback corrupting the code. No wonder people get confused. I wouldn't have expected Net beams to penetrate this deep in the Earth."

"The Net?" I squatted and clung to the bridge so I wouldn't slip again. "You mean the actual Net? By any chance, can you hear Luc Viollett's voice?"

"Don't worry, pet. We've crossed the bridge. The chamber's not far. I sense its resonance. A focal point of energies. That's where we must go. First, we crawl. Then the chamber. You're still with me, yes?"

"I'm with you, Jin."

The structure he insisted on calling a bridge abutted a rough, furrowed wall. I felt it with my hands in the semidarkness but couldn't find any opening. Jin moved my hands down to the base of the wall, and I felt a whoosh of air rushing from a low horizontal fissure. His face brightened with that eerie flesh-colored light that seemed to issue directly through his skin. He pointed, and I could see the crack running along the base of the wall.

"We'll go together," he said, crouching down.

I dropped to my knees beside him. Then he drew my hand to his lips. "La Sauvage. You trust me."

It was a simple statement, spoken with evident surprise. In answer, I lay down flat on my belly and wriggled into the fissure. The opening was narrow from floor to ceiling, but very very wide in the horizontal plane. Maybe this fissure ran for hundreds of kilometers, an empty gap in the layers of folded Earth. When my eyes adjusted to the thin light radiating from Jin's forehead, I could see hundreds of stalactites dripping, dry as dust, from the low ceiling. Some were tiny nubs, but others had grown long enough to meet their counterpart stalagmites on the floor below. These reminded me of miniature columns in an ancient gothic hall, except they seemed too spindly to support such a vast roof.

Lying on my belly, I had to muscle my way in with elbows and feet. The sharp little stalagmites chewed through my musketeer uniform like teeth. At least the floor was dry. The seepage that had caused these formations must have turned to dust ages ago. Soon, I felt a blast of wind and turned my face to avoid the flying grit. Jin moved in beside me. I could hear the scrabbling noises he made, and that gave me comfort.

Side by side, we pushed through the horizontal fissure for what seemed like hours, wending through the stalactite columns, fighting the stinging headwind that grew stronger as we went. My nose started running, and my eyes streamed tears. I had to use my sleeve as a handkerchief.

The fissure was not table-flat. It rose and fell like the space between two crumpled quilts. Sometimes we climbed almost straight up, and other times we slid headfirst down dusty hillocks. Occasionally the ceiling height increased a little—though never enough to let us crawl on hands and knees. Twice, the ceiling dropped so low, I had to exhale all the breath from my lungs to squeeze through. Jin wouldn't have made it if he hadn't lost so much weight. Ça va, what a place for a surfer girl.

"Can we rest?" I asked, at a point where the ceiling rose a little.

Unaccountably, Jin starting laughing. Soon, his laughter grew hectic, and he spoke through gasps, "Judith's coming. I can hear her heartbeat."

Judith Merida! I sucked a breath and scrambled forward, but

Jin gripped my wrist. "Relax, Jolie. She's a long way off. We can rest a while. Judith's not a threat to us."

"If she catches you—"

"Jolie, your fear stabs my head. Please calm down."

He shifted in the narrow space, then held very still. I knew he was listening to something I couldn't hear. Something real, or just a maniacal song in his brain, how could I know? As quietly as possible, I drew a deep breath and tried to shut down my alarm. Gusts whistled through the fissure, and in the wan light radiating from Jin's forehead, I saw a tiny needle-shaped stalagmite rising from the floor between my outstretched fingers. It looked like a time-frozen rocket launch. For how many centuries had it been forming? Was I the first to see it? I counted my breaths and waited for my heartbeat to slow, but I couldn't keep silent forever. "Jin?"

"Yes?" he said with a distracted air. His face had begun to glow brighter. He must have been concentrating very hard.

"There's something I've always wondered about."

"Yes, angel?" Jin was studying the patterns of nubby stalactites above his head as if he could hear them growing.

I shook his knee to get his attention. "That movie you made that got banned from the Net. What was that about?"

"Movie?" He glanced at me with a puzzled expression. "I'd forgotten it. Why do you care, pet?"

"Curiosity," I said. "Tell me."

"It was a documentary. Based on an eleventh-century Javanese poem called 'Arjunavivaha'." He touched his tongue to one of the little stalactites and made a wry face.

"But why was it banned?" I persisted.

Jin frowned and blinked his eyes, as if the effort to remember troubled him. Then he recited in a singsong chant, "There was once a coastal kingdom, long ago in Java. Green trees waved in gentle breezes. And blue ocean broke on white sand. It could have been paradise."

He paused so long, I had to prompt him. "So then one day . . . ?"

With a brief smile, he continued. "Then one day, Sumatran pirates murdered the Javanese king and enslaved the people. The king's son-in-law escaped into the jungle, where he lived with vagabonds and searched for understanding of Krishna's plan. His name was Prince Airlangga." Jin winked at me when he mentioned that name. Then he broke off a bit of the stalactite and rolled it between his fingers. "Instead of enlightenment though, Airlangga found the jungle was full of hunger and filth and disease. So in frustration, he took up arms to drive the Sumatrans away by force. But on the day Airlangga went to war, he recognized one of the pirates as his own father. And he couldn't fight."

Jin crushed the bit of stone between his fingers. I watched the dust sift to the floor. He seemed lost in thought.

"But that wasn't the end," I said, hopefully.

As if he'd forgotten my presence, Jin glanced at me in surprise. "No, it wasn't. The story goes that the prince prayed for guidance, and the great god Krishna revealed himself in a vision. Krishna said, 'Rise, Airlangga. Take back my kingdom, and make my people safe'."

"So he did," I said. "Airlangga drove the pirates away."

"Yes. And afterward, he ruled Java in peace for 30 years. That part is historically true. When he died, the Javanese people laid him to rest at Belahan, under a carving of Vishnu, the preserver of the universe."

Belahan. I remembered that name. Jin had asked me about the carvings of Belahan on the very first day we met.

"I get it. You're Prince Airlangga, and your father's the Sumatran priate. It's one of those political flicks."

Jin's bitter laughter echoed in the narrow space. "I never had a chance to finish the last scene. But I still have my working tapes. They're stored in a public mailbox at TokyoData. Someday, a hacker will stumble onto them, and then we'll see."

I laid my cheek flat on the stone floor and snuffled dust. Poor Jin.

Abruptly his laughter choked off, and his next words came out more sober. "Jolie, you pity me."

"Uh . . ."

"You think my obsession with my father is pitiable." He remained silent a moment. The light in his face flickered like a candle. Then he drew me into his arms. "Come here, pet. It's interesting, seeing myself through another person's thoughts. Light refracted through a new kind of prism." His fingers moved steadily through my hair, but he was talking to himself. "I know it's a waste of time to care what Father thinks about me. The truth is, he doesn't think about me at all."

"You're wrong," I said, remembering my encounter with Suradon. "He thinks about you a lot. What's between you and him? Why did he underwrite this crazy experiment?"

Jin twirled a strand of my hair round and round his finger. "The second question is easier to answer. Father invested in Hyperthought because he hopes to gain profit for Pacific.Com. That's the reason for everything he does."

"Freaky old pervert," I said.

Jin sighed. "My father treats everything as a joke—everything except Pacific.Com. He's deadly serious about his Com. He needs cash flow, and I knew he would see profit in Judith's Hyperthought."

"And your brain's the prototype? You're the beta version? Oh, that makes sense." My temper was rising. This whole scheme sounded more and more insane.

"He and Judith made a bet," Jin said calmly. "Of course, Father set it up so he can't lose. If Judith's nanobot works, he'll underwrite her global expansion—but Pacific.Com takes the profits. If Judith fails, she's put up her own labor contract as collateral, and she'll have to work off her debt. Can you picture that? Fiery little Judith serving as Father's prote? You see how twisted he is?"

"You must hate him!"

"Relax, Jolie." Jin kissed the top of my head. "I can't decide what I feel. Perhaps they haven't invented the word for what's between Father and me. I only know we're bound together." He ruffled my hair and kissed me again.

I wanted nothing better than to hide in Jin's arms forever. But my mind kept veering back to Merida. She wouldn't be far behind. Now that I knew about her infernal bet with Suradon, I felt even more frightened. Merida would never let herself be anyone's slave. She'd be driven by desperation to win that bet. I could almost taste her fury at me for getting in her way. Sharp and acrid, like the gritty toxic dust that lined my nostrils and burned my eyes. The dust that might already be killing us.

"Jolie, my angel, there's no reason to fear death." Jin combed my hair with his fingers. Then he drew me closer and held my head in his hands and kissed my mouth. He shifted me slowly in his arms and pressed the whole length of his body against mine.

Despite our situation, female urges flared up and down me like bursts of heat. "I know," he murmured, gently ripping open the Velcro plackets of my musketeer uniform. He was wearing only the thin hospital wrapper, and the snaps easily came un-done.

Why, you might ask, did we pick this particular moment to make love? Me, I've always been a spontaneous person, and making love with Jin was exactly what I'd been longing for since I'd left his bed in Godthaab. Jin brought me to life. Nothing mattered to me at that moment but the feel of his skin against mine. The whole planet might have burst inside out like a big kernel of popcorn, and I wouldn't have noticed. Jin thrust into me with a strong, steady rhythm. We grappled together sideways in the narrow space, and he bucked me against the rock till my hip bled, but I barely noticed. Pleasure overwhelmed every other sensation. We cried out in unison. It was as if we shared one mind.

Afterward, as we lay panting in a sweaty tangle, he pressed his forehead to my cheek, and I felt a bright, tingling shock of electricity. Then he pulled away. And it was over.

We didn't speak for a while. I heard him snapping his hospital wrapper, so I wriggled back into my uniform and did up the plackets. I felt full to the brim and totally satiated and— abandoned. How can I explain this? Jin's warm, breathing body still lay within arm's reach. We'd just shared the most magnificent sex of my life. My crotch was still quivering, and the sweat hadn't even dried on my skin. Yet I knew with ab- solute certainty that Jin had gone away from me, and that he might never come back. He had returned to those noises that were haunting him, that singing of the universe or of his own deluded brain.

I couldn't stop the tears that welled in my burning eyes or the sick hurt that settled in my gut. Damned female hormones! The worst was, I couldn't cover my feelings. Jin could read my thoughts if he wanted. But he was lying very rigid, almost hold- ing his breath, and I knew he wasn't listening to my silly woes.

"Is Merida closer?" I asked, because I had to say something— maybe just to remind Jin of my existence.

"Yes," he whispered. "Let's go now. The chamber is just ahead."

WE BELLY-CRAWLED UP another dusty ridge, and just as we heaved over the top, a scent of ozone burned my nostrils, and a pale blue light glimmered ahead. Far in the distance, I could see the end of the fissure, and beyond it—flashes of lightning.

"Don't worry about Judith Merida. She's no threat to us." Jin hauled himself over that last ridge and hurtled down the other side with extraordinary energy. I followed as fast as I could.

"We used each other, Judith and I. Fair bargain. She got what she wanted. Her nanobot performed as promised. Ha-ha, I feel my brain evolving. Soon I'll perceive with crystal clarity. I'll know why I was put here and what action to take."

The closer we got to that lightning, the more unnatural Jin's voice sounded. He slurred sentences together, and his sweet Pacific accent edged to sibilance. "Ha, I hear proteins unfolding. I smell neurotransmitters washing through my cortex. Jolie, I can move calcium ions by conscious command. Ha ha ha!" He clambered down the slope unbelievably fast, throwing up little puffs of dust with his hands and feet.

I crawled after him, panting. "Jin, slow down."

"Oh yes, you're right, pet. I'm a bit manic now. It's a temporary condition. I'm penetrating the atomic level. Soon—ha ha ha—the quanta! Judith's nanobots are working. My father will have to build her clinics around the world!"

When I finally caught up, he was breathing so fast, his nose made little snorting sounds. He started giggling, I mean actually giggling. "Lord Suradon Sura. Oops! You lose! Your son can hear the quanta! He-he-he. Jolie, you'll tell him, yes? You'll keep your promise and tell my father?"

"Jin!" I tried to grab his ankle, but he moved too fast for me. He chortled like a demented stranger.

"Look at this, Jolie. Luminous minerals in the rock. Even you must be able to see this wavelength."

It was true. The fissure widened out into a large, almost spherical chamber with glowing blue walls. I stood up and rubbed my legs to work out the cramps. Cold wind whistled through, wafting a harsh electric smell that made me sneeze half a dozen times in a row. Just as the wind hushed to dead silence, veins of bright electricity crackled through the air. Their brilliant strobes etched afterimages in my retinas. I tried not to rub my stinging eyes because that just made the pain worse.

When the lightning stopped, wind gusted again, whipping my hair and clothing. A low, warbling roar set up and slowly intensified. The cold wind seemed to ricochet around the chamber like a living spirit, echoing with harmonics until the very air resonated with its sound. Abruptly, the wind died and the lightning crackled again. The wind and lightning seemed to alternate in a steady one-two pulse.

"This is the focal point," Jin said, gazing about with open delight. "This chamber, the strange attracter, the exact center of incipience. This is where I must be."

In the blue glow, I saw his emaciated body dart forward with shocking speed and race down the curving floor. His long hair streamed back over his shoulders. Confused, I stumbled after him, but the floor was slick with moisture, and the alternating wind and fireworks disoriented me. I tripped and slid head first down to the lowest point of the chamber, landing in a heap at Jin's feet. He didn't notice. He was gazing at the light show overhead—and listening.

"This place is full of bacteria. Clever creatures. Quite beautiful, really. They've mutated to survive the toxic chemicals leaching through the rock strata."

"Are they dangerous?" I asked.

"To humans? Oh yes. Lethal."

I yelped in alarm. "Where are they?"

"In your lungs, in your eyes, in your vulva. They're everywhere, Jolie. Forty-two distinct tribes of them."

I struggled to my feet and clutched his hand. "Jin, I'm so sorry I've exposed you to this. Forgive me."

He patted my shoulder. "Your fear is misplaced, pet. You haven't endangered me. The instant I recognized the bacteria, my brain manufactured an immune response. A teratrillion new nanobots patrol my system now. The bacteria won't harm me. Jolie, my body can live forever if I choose."

"Can you make an immune response for me, Jin?"

"For you?" His eyebrows knotted. He seemed confused by my question. He swayed and rubbed his forehead. "You're not like me, Jolie. The bacteria have already invaded your organs. A pattern has set up. An exquisite fractal pattern of decay and new birth. Your body is host, and the bacteria are so lively. I wish you could hear them, pet."

He turned away, and I had to scramble around to stand in front of him again. "This immune response, Jin, could I get it from your saliva? Maybe you could kiss me."

He waved his hand. "You, me, the bacteria, even the rocks, we interact in a web of fractal branching. It's beautiful, Jolie."

"Maybe this immune stuff is in your bloodstream," I said. "Could I bite you just a little? The earlobe, say? Just to break the skin. You'd hardly feel it."

Jin tugged absently at his wrapper, and his eyes hazed in thought. He draped his arms around me in an absentminded way. "Jolie, how can I make you understand? Would you kill Luc, even to save your own life? No, you wouldn't. Well, the bacteria are your brothers, too. If I save you, the bacteria inside you will perish. Can that be right?"

I said, "Huh?"

"You're asking me to choose who lives and dies. I can't make that choice," he said.

When he let me go, I reeled unsteadily from the sudden loss of support. My skin felt funny, sort of tingly. I heard Jin mumbling to himself in broken phrases. His words blended with the droning wind until I couldn't tell them apart. All I could do was stand there, weaving in the gusts and wondering: Did he just say what I think he said?

Did he just say he wouldn't share that immune response? He wouldn't save me? He wouldn't choose my life over some scuzzy germs?

Rage and shock and grief got all mixed up, and every square centimeter of my skin prickled with heat. I wanted to shake Jin's broad, scrawny shoulders till his teeth rattled. I wanted to scream at him: Save me, you arrogant prick, because I'm trying to save you!

But I didn't scream. I just stood there choking on mucus and wiping my eyes with my sleeve. That wasn't my Jin, I told myself. It couldn't be. Merida's demon nanobots had possessed his brain. If he were himself, he would do anything for me, just as I would do anything for him. The amount of love I felt couldn't be all on one side. Don't ask me what part of my brain concluded that. I just believed it. I needed to believe. In the squalling wind, I whispered, "It's not your fault."

The next instant, his voice rang inside my head. "Be my witness, Jolie."

The wind had changed. Its roar had begun to rise and fall in an irregular pattern. The lightning as well. The two phenomena pulsed out of sync now, sometimes in opposition, sometimes in unison. Shadows flickered through the chamber, and the blue walls seemed to breathe inward.

Jin drew a pattern in the air, and a million electric bolts shot out from his fingertip. They arced through the chamber like brilliant blue veins and throbbed in a steady cadence. More veins of light radiated from Jin's hand, filling the air with a lacy web. The light strobed so painfully bright, I huddled down on the floor and ground my palms into my swollen eye sockets, but I couldn't block it out.

Then the wind growled, and I looked up. The blue veins shattered into billions of sparkling pixels that danced before my eyes. They saturated the air with witchy little explosions of blue. He lifted his hand, and the pixels gusted away in a wave, like sparks caught in a wind. Jin moved his hand again, and the glowing particles surged farther away. A sphere of empty air widened around him. A third time, his gesture hurled the blue sparkles against the chamber walls, where they splashed like radiant paint.

The walls pulsated with a light so cold and piercing, I could actually hear it screech. I covered my face with my hands, but even so, I sensed the light growing brighter. Then it flared so intensely, I saw the very bones in my fingers. And then darkness. Quiet.

"Interesting," Jin said.

He dropped down beside me on the chamber floor. I was whimpering like an idiot. I felt his knee pressing against me. Slowly, I uncovered my eyes and looked around. Occasional flickers of electricity. Gentle breeze. Jin was sitting cross-legged beside me, staring up at a small hole at the very top of the chamber.

"I h-hear it now. Almost like music. So many strains. Hard to sort out." He rocked back and forth on his haunches. He was speaking much slower than before. "T-t-tons of Earth above us. I hear the pressure. Vectors of f-forces warping the walls." Then he stretched his legs out and lay flat on his back, staring up at the vaulted blue ceiling. "Hold my hand, Jolie. The rocks are singing. You'll tell my father about this, yes? You're my witness."

I took his long bony hand in mine, but he didn't respond to my touch. His gaunt fingers lay dry and lifeless in my grip.

"My f-father," he whispered. "I hear my father, Jolie. He's fighting to save Pacific.Com. The Com's his whole world, and Greenland wants to rip it apart. He's terrified."

Jin sucked a sharp breath and pressed his temple. He was in pain. Whatever anger I might have felt before vanished when I saw him suffering. I felt useless, not knowing how to comfort him. He must have been wrong about living forever.

Jin's words whispered through my mind like thoughts. "My god. I understand now. It's pointless to care if father loves me. What he's doing is depraved. I have to stop him."

Jin opened his eyes wide and looked right at me. "The truth I've been seeking, Jolie, I've known it all along. I have to remove him from power."

Suddenly he laughed. "Father would find this hilarious. Because it doesn't change how I feel. I still want him to love me."

All at once, he groaned and closed his eyes. The pain must have been fierce. His next words came in a rush. "I hear the Earth's core spinning. Loops of molten iron. Whirling. The magnetic fields scream. They scream!" He ripped his hand from mine and covered his ears. "Billions of heartbeats! Cells. Dying. They're all dying! The sound of their fear is horrible!"

With impossible quickness, he sprang to his feet, holding his head in both hands. "The extra dimensions are coming uncurled. I perceive all of them. I see universes swelling like bubbles. Too much input!" He staggered in circles as if he'd gone blind. I followed, but his strength rose from unnatural sources, and I couldn't keep up.

"There is no number!" His shrill cry echoed through the chamber. "It's chaotic. I can't differentiate one sensation from another. I can't find the chord. I thought everything would be clear. I thought—"

He started running straight up the curved wall. When he'd climbed as high as his momentum would carry, he slipped and tumbled down like a broken manikin to the center of the floor again. Then he struggled up to his hands and knees, and swayed as if he might fall over. I ran to catch him.

"The chord," he moaned. "I expected—a single chord. One harmony. But there's only this—screaming. Vortexes forming. Dissolving. Birth. Death. So much willfulness to be. Fear of dying. It's all screaming. Wanting to survive. I can't stand it!"

Without warning, Jin bashed his head against the rock floor. Then he did it again. I climbed on his back and locked my arms and legs around his body, but he'd grown so powerful, I couldn't make him stop. Desperately, I laced my fingers around his forehead, and he smashed my hands into the rock. Mes dieux, but it hurt. When he did it the second time, I heard bones snap, and I let go. Finally, I just lay down on the floor under his head. I don't think he even knew I was there. He pounded his head into my chest, over and over, and I sprawled there, clenching my muscles and taking it—until, thank the Laws, he wore himself out.

He rolled over on his side, and I curled around him. For a long time we lay together, shivering quietly. Then he stretched out on his back again. When I sat up to examine his head wounds, pain stabbed under my ribs and made me cough. It really hurt to move. Both my hands were bleeding. In the dim light, I could see a lot of blood streaming from a gash above Jin's left eye. I coughed again and almost couldn't stop. It felt as if a knife were lodged in my side. I guess maybe Jin cracked one of my ribs.

By the time I got my cough under control, Jin's huge beautiful black eyes were staring straight up at that hole in the ceiling. Who knows what visions loomed there. I pressed his head wound with my filthy, disgusting sleeve to stop the bleeding, and I said stupid things like très bien, you'll be all right, I love you, whatever I could think of. My skin felt hot and itchy, so I stripped off the musketeer uniform. Wearing nothing but my old paisley bodysuit felt better.

"The b-bacteria," he whispered. "They're crying for f-food. They just want to live." A moment later, he looked up at me in surprise. "You sound the same, Jolie. The same as the bacteria. Stubborn." In the dim blue light, I saw his eyes shining. He seemed rapt.

"The quantum fabric wants to take form. And once formed,

it wants to persist. Greed and fear create the pattern."

"And love, Jin?" I tore a sleeve off my uniform to bandage his head. His eyes rolled back and forth as if he were seeing monsters.

"N-not what I expected. No harmony. No single mind. It's gnashing. Turbulence. Ripping. One thing changes into another. Violent."

"Do you hear anything good?" I asked. Dumb question, I know, but still I wanted an answer.

His glance wandered in my direction. "Yes. Yes. It's beautiful."

His skin had gone cold and sweaty. When I kissed the bridge of his nose, his eyes cleared. He spoke with renewed urgency.

"Jolie, you have to remember. There's so much I need to tell you. Understand? You have to memorize all of it."

"D'accord," I whispered, stroking his cheek.

"Help me sit up," he said. So I folded my uniform to make a pillow, and I propped him up in my arms.

He began to talk, stuttering at first, trying to find the right words. Once he got going, the sentences flowed. And even though I understood little of what he said, he seemed lucid. He said there wasn't a word for what he was sensing. It was something like music.

"It's so simple," he kept repeating, although his explanations seemed complex beyond reason. Still I memorized as much as I could. He spoke often of will. "In the beginning is the will to be," he said. "After that, the pattern branches." And again, "One will. Many choices. The quantum fabric builds by branching."

I learned his metaphors by heart without understanding them. He spoke of life as a trail through a bubble chamber and as a mote of quicksilver bursting with starlight. At times he moaned with pleasure as if experiencing violent orgasms. "Greedy life. Everything fights for a place." Then he would cry and claw at his ears. "Milk, blood, shit. I can't endure this rainbow."

Several times, his voice deepened and vibrated in many tones at once. "I have no beginning nor middle nor end," and also, "I am a path." More than once he repeated a kind of chant: "One will. The will to be."

His words terrified me and filled me with hope. My gut knotted up. He painted pictures I could only feel, not see. His descriptions so mesmerized me that I forgot my physical pain.

Delight and sadness flooded through me together, and when he finished, I realized I was weeping.

No, I couldn't understand what Jin said, but I retained his words. It seemed so important to him that I bear witness. Finally, he rested. The tension went out of his muscles, and he closed his eyes. I thought he might be asleep, but I was mistaken. His lashes fluttered open, and he laughed gently. "I hear the solar wind."

And sometime later, he said, "Emotion is a kind of sight, too."

The cut above his eye had stopped bleeding. He lay still and calm, with a faraway look sometimes joyous, sometimes thoughtful, sometimes simply attentive. His skin had grown icy cold. He chuckled softly. "Beautiful stubborn screaming."

In the chamber, the wind and lightning were starting up their alternating routine again, and my own awareness of my physical pain returned in spades. I knew the wind was cold, but every gust seemed to flay my skin like a blasting torch. Jin lay rigid in my arms, and when I tried to move him, he winced.

"Jolie," he said.

"Ssssh."

"Jolie, don't be afraid of death. The quantum fabric is not energy or mass. It's the pattern. One thing changes into another. Only the pattern persists. You are not your body but the path you choose. Your choices affect everything that comes after you, Jolie. You reverberate forever. There is no death. Tell him, pet. Tell my father. He won't care, but he'll know."

"Yes, Jin." I kissed his damp hair.

Much later still, he opened his eyes again. "You're still here, Jolie?"

"D'accord, I'm with you, Jin."

I heard him sigh, ever so gently, and then he did go to sleep.

"CHIII——CAAA!" THE SPANGLISH word filtered down to me through folded layers of sediment. "Chiii——caaa," it echoed, sometimes near, sometimes farther away.

I knew it had to be a figment of my fever. Still I cupped a hand around my mouth and yelled, "Vinn——cente!" Only a wheeze came out.

How many hours ago had I strapped Jin's unconscious body to my back with the torn strips of my stolen musketeer uniform? How long had it taken me to scale the walls of the windy blue chamber and find the opening at the top? In the darkness above, I'd crab-walked through a labyrinth of strange tube formations till my joints ached, and I'd lost track of time.

"Chiii——caaa!" the long syllables reverberated. In my febrile waking dream, I imagined I'd returned to the clinic, where the brawny old caretaker kept stealing my Net node. "Chica!" the imaginary sound wafted through my head as I stumbled into an immense hall of white crystals.

Above me, electricity danced through the sparkling crystal matrix that stretched higher than I could see. The formation seemed to glow from within. Millions of glassy white hexagonal needles spiked out in fans and starbursts and crisscross patterns. In the shifting light, the needles changed from soft opalescence to blazing prismatic rainbows. There was a charge in the atmosphere. My hair stood on end, and my fingers tingled. I leaned so far back trying to see the top of the formation, I nearly fell. Never in my life could I have imagined such a fantastic sight, but I was too tired to appreciate its beauty. Jin's weight dragged at me, and the strips of the cloth harness sliced into my shoulders like bandsaws.

My thoughts stayed basic. The white crystals led up. I wanted to go up. Hence, I had to climb. So I tightened the wrapping around my broken hand and gingerly touched a nearby spike. It felt warm and smooth. I got a good grip and clamped my legs around its hexagonal shaft and started shinning.

Each time I stretched for a higher grip, Jin's body flopped like a corpse in the improvised harness on my back. He hadn't awakened since we left the chamber. At first, I had stopped every few minutes to check his pulse, but now that my own strength was fading, I gave up on that. Every breath sent shooting pains through my chest, and my right eye had swollen nearly shut. But the worst was the rash covering my body. It had started to seep a clear liquid. What could I do anyway, if Jin's pulse stopped?

When I had first torn the musketeer uniform into strips to make Jin's harness, I told myself I would never let Merida catch us. Now I longed for her, for anyone who would save me from my own stupid plan. Could that really be Vincente up there? I yelled his name again, but the sound didn't carry. I couldn't get enough breath in my lungs.

See, besides my fatigue and thirst and broken bones, those bacteria Jin had heard crying for food, they were making a feast of Jolie Blanche Sauvage. Conveniently, the glowing crystals lit up my blistery red arms and legs. In the last couple of hours, my rash had turned rank. But I didn't need to see the lesions to know I was mortally sick.

Truth be told, I'd been hoping all along that I'd get to the surface in time for therapy. I'd pictured myself saving Jin and winning his gratitude and living happily ever after on some movie set. How exactly that was going to happen I had never worked out. Maybe when we got to the surface, the Nome troopers would find us and take pity.

We humans never believe in our own deaths, do we? Not for real, not till the absolute last possible nanosecond. I think, up until that actual last breath, every one of us lives in denial and fights like hell. Me, I do.

At this particular moment, all I wanted was a drink of water. That, and to save Jin. I'd come this far. If I could just survive long enough to get him to the surface and maybe steal or borrow a Net node and call for help, that would make everything right. Then Jolie's Trip with a capital T would be over. I had lived 26 interesting years, known a lot of good people, seen some sights. I had loved and made love to the only man in the world I wanted. How many girls could say that? D'accord, I could let go of life with dignity. It wasn't as if I reasoned this out through some clever philosophy. I just felt it. You know me. Not the brightest light.

But I wasn't dead yet. I could still clasp my knees together and place one bruised hand above the other and shin a few centimeters higher up that preter-vicious white crystal. And that's what I did, over and over like a robot programmed on a repeating loop. My sole focus narrowed down to one clean series of motions.

"Chiii——caaa!" The echo sounded half a heartbeat nearer. "I'm coming for youuu!"

Vincente found me hemmed in under a ledge where the top of my white crystal had branched fractal spikes as thick as a root ball. I was too weak to extricate myself, and both my eyes were so swollen, I could barely see him. He wore a surfsuit and metavisor and I knew he had to be a hallucination. From his gear belt, he unclipped an outlandish implement that looked like a medieval laser blaster. Just before he started cutting me out of my crystal cage, he mumbled something into a flat blue box strapped to his forearm. My freakin' Net node!

"That's mine," I yelled, but no sound came out. Pain doubled me over, and it took all my resolve to twist around and feel Jin's throat for a pulse. There it was, that minute warm throb against my fingertip. Even if this were a dream, I decided to thank the Laws.

Vincente's headlamp blinded me so I couldn't see his features through his helmet faceplate. For an instant, I shrank back. "You're not working for Merida, are you?" I don't know if I said the words aloud.

When his gruff old voice croaked through the helmet speaker, I knew he was real. "Chica, you have less brains than the Pope's own saints. Why you try to kill yourself, eh? Whew, you look odioso. Let go of that bundle now. I will take El principe."

Vincente carried a miraculous amount of climbing gear, but no water except the recycling system inside his suit. "Alto," he said, "we must go up." He rigged a real climbing harness and hoisted Jin's limp body to a higher position. Then he scampered back down and did the same for me. In my hazy vision, the old man seemed to dash up and down the crystals like some tree-dwelling primate.

"We've cut a senda—a path," he said, coaxing me along the

ledge toward Jin's inert body. "Tan is above. He is bringing the water."

Tan? I knew that name. But my mind had gone all muzzy, and I couldn't concentrate. Jin still wore the dirty hospital wrapper, and his thin bare legs were so pale, his skin looked translucent. I wanted to cover his nakedness, but then I remembered that I myself wore nothing but a filthy paisley bodysuit, now ripped in a hundred places.

"Your friend, Tan, he teach me much about the Net. He is the supremo geek. My preceptor. You see him soon, chica." Vincente busied himself making a sort of travois sled out of the improbable gear that kept emerging from his belt. He secured Jin in the sled and attached it to his belt loops so he could drag Jin behind him. Then he slung me over his shoulder like so much deadweight, which in fact I was. Hunkering over, he began slogging up the path he'd blasted with his laser.

Sometime later, cool fresh water dribbled into my mouth. I tasted the plastic tube against my lip and opened my eyes. I saw a bright blue sky with a yellow sun stitched in white thread. It took me a second to realize we were squeezed together inside a fabriglass tent, the sort of airtight emergency shelter we'd often used on Jolie's Trips. Someone had gotten cute with a sun appliqué on the blue ceiling. Now I saw yellow stars and crescent moons sewn on as well.

Vincente removed his helmet and settled Jin onto a folding cot next to mine.

"He's sleepin' sound," said a familiar voice. "You should sleep, too, ma'am." I glanced around, and there was the boy with the burns on his face, the boy called Tan. I remembered him now. Red rodeo helmet. A lifetime ago, we'd counted stars together in the California desert.

Besides our two cots, the tent was just large enough to hold a small collapsible table, a camp stool, and a stack of gear cases. Zipped tight to the door flap was an inflatable airlock, and from the center support pole, an electric lantern dangled. On the floor sat a portable air-recycling unit. I could hear its rhythmic whine.

Green diodes winked from a row of squat black boxes on the table. Tan's computer gadgets. He'd set up a sort of workstation. Vincente leaned against the stack of gear cases and watched while Tan slipped a sharp silver cybernail onto his right index finger and activated a light matrix interface. A cube of holographic icons popped up above one of the boxes. Tan started pointing with his finger, twirling his cybernail through the shimmering dots. Soon I heard Luc's faraway voice. They were exchanging coordinates.

My right eye had swollen completely shut, and the left one ached. I seemed to be gazing through water. Rainbow colors haloed every object, and the electric lantern shot out rays like a star. I coughed, and Vincente hurried over. He gave me the drinking tube, but when I moved to take a sip, I thought my skin would crack open. The whole surface of my body had dried to a hard crust.

Vincente dabbed my lip with the gauze. His hairy form loomed above me like a mountain, blocking out the yellow fabric sun. I heard him whispering in my ear.

"Senorita, we are in a cave, maybe 50 meters below the surface of Frisco. The Doctor Merida, she is close. She come here soon with metal robots and weapons. No, don't move. Lie still and listen, sí? Your friends from the south, they are coming, too. But Merida is closer. This niño and I, we have mined the senda with explosives."

I struggled to loosen my tongue, and I started coughing again.

"Sssh! No, chica. Just listen." Vincente's gentle touch scorched my arm like a firebrand. "The bruja witch, she can't get through. Your friends from the south are coming. Above us, the Nome troopers prowl. They don't know our location, but they search everywhere. We must be very quiet."

I tried to move my lips.

The boy named Tan knelt on the other side of my cot. "Them Nome cops want your hide, ma'am. Yer the Angel of Euro."

Huh? My expression must have shown bewilderment.

Tan grinned. "Lady, you ain't seen the news lately. Them Frenchie protes are taking back their tunnels. They're slammin' the Commies. They got big signs painted with your picture."

Vincente said, "They call you the Angel, chica. Sí, it's true. They even make songs about you."

Tan fretted with the blanket near my feet and then made a quick grab for my fingers. "Ma'am, I just wanna say, it is a real honor to shake yer hand."

I thought this over. My logic had slowed way down, and as you know, it had never been exactly swift. Ça va. The protes in Euro had picked my face for their posters? I bet Adrienne had something to do with that. She was always jabbering about poignant visuals. "Angel of Euro," that sounded like a slogan Adrienne would invent. Funny thing, I'd almost forgotten the war. That rescue project seemed like something I remembered from a movie. Bien, that fight didn't belong to me anymore. Euro would have to take care of itself.

I wheezed out a single word. "Jin?"

"El principe, sí." Vincente frowned. "He is well. The toxins have not affected him." Vincente lifted me slightly so I could see Jin sleeping in the other cot. He lay on his side, and his long hair trailed across his outflung arm.

Vincente settled me down in my own cot again. "Chica, I have given you meds but—"

Tan sighed. "We can't reverse the damage, ma'am. Your skin—it's bad."

Vincente scowled at the boy, and Tan hung his head.

Just then, we heard a deep rumbling growl. The lantern danced overhead, and the whole tent shook. One of the cases tumbled off the stack. Tan and Vincente looked at each other with raised eyebrows, and Tan rushed back to his workstation.

"Ha, we got ourselves a robot!" the boy hooted. "Nothing like good old-fashioned TNT. That'll stop the doc in her tracks." He worked his finger through the glowing light matrix, and I heard him speaking to Luc in a subdued voice.

"All is well, muchacha." Vincente stroked my arm. "You sleep. We must be quiet and wait."

But then Tan came scrambling back toward me. "Ma'am, your friends need to talk to you. It sounds kinda urgent. I think you might oughtta take the call."

I nodded. It was all I could do.

"Sorry, it's audio only. I cain't get the visual." Tan held one of his gadgets near my ear, and a tinny voice piped out.

"Chérie, is it you?"

Luc! Mon petit frère. I tried to speak, but my tongue filled my mouth like a great swollen glob of gum.

"You are well, chérie? We're coming. We will be there soon."

"Jollers? Well, finally." Sweet Adrienne. How I'd missed her gentle presence. "Jollers, you have to speak to Euro. Do it now, Jollers. Our friends think you've betrayed them."

Huh?

"Jolie love, this is Jonas. Adrienne's right, we need you to

say a few words. I'm set to broadcast live. Say something in-
spirational. Tell the Parisians to keep fighting. It's important that
they hear you."

Tan held the gadget to his mouth and asked, "What's up, Mr.
Tajor? The lady's sick. She cain't talk very well."

"Adrienne here, Jollers. Listen carefully to what I say. Those
northern Coms have been counterfeiting your holo-image on the
Net. They've got you telling the Parisians to lay down their
arms. We can't have that."

"You owe 'em, Jo." That was Rebel Jeanne's voice. She
sounded angry. "Your pacifist shit is creeping a mind-blitz on
the comrades. Even if it's not really you."

Huh?

Jonas spoke next, but I could hardly follow his words. "Those
counterfeit holos are wrecking morale. The rebels see you plead-
ing with them to stop the war. They're confused, love. They
don't know what to believe. We only re-established communications this week, and we've tried to tell everyone it's a Commie
trick. We're getting the word out, but the holos look so real."

"Your peacenik speeches've got the comrades de-zoned,"
Rebel Jeanne growled.

Jonas added, "We can broadcast your real voice to Euro now.
I've set up an authentication code to certify your identity. Just
say a few words, that's all we need."

"No silly excuses, Jollers. You have to speak," Adrienne commanded.

The words swirled too fast around my head. I couldn't make
sense of anything. How had I become the center of such a
storm? My friends in Euro thought I'd betrayed them? "I—I—"
Words stuck in my throat.

From the corner of my eye, I saw Tan point to the flat blue
Net node strapped to Vincente's wrist. The old man took it off
and gave it to Tan. The boy crawled under his workstation and
extricated a shiny little tool from the litter on the floor. Sitting
lotus fashion, he flipped open the Net node and started poking
at it. Light from the overhead lantern stabbed my eyes, and I
squeezed them shut. Could I be hallucinating all this?

"Hand her this gadget, Vince." I opened my eyes just in time
to see Tan toss the blue box through the air over my cot. Vincente caught it one-handed and held it open where I could see.
Tan had programmed a small digital slate onscreen, and he'd

improvised a stylus from his shiny worktool. "She can write on it," the boy explained.

Adrienne said, "No, that won't work. We need her voice."

"Maybe," said Jonas. "Let's try it."

"Can you hold this, chica? Write your words, sí?"

I studied the slender tool. About as long as an ink pen, it gleamed like chrome, and one end came to a needle-sharp point. I clenched the stylus in my fist, but Vincente had to clasp his hand around mine to keep the stylus from slipping out of my weak grip. Slowly, laboriously, I scrawled a big question mark. I still didn't have a clue what they wanted.

Luc broke through the chaos of responses. His was the only voice that sounded the least bit kind. "Much has happened, chérie. Till last week, the Parisians were winning the war. C'est vrai! Our friends controlled half of Paris."

Jonas said, "That was your doing, love."

"The tunnel-fighters call you their Angel," Luc continued. "You showed the Parisians how to walk on the surface, remember? The people you saved, they returned to the shores of Euro and attacked from above. Greenland.Com didn't expect that. They weren't prepared. That turned the tide, chérie. The protes started winning."

Huh. I had to think about that. Just then, I went into a coughing jag. Every convulsion felt like razors slicing through my chest. When my breathing finally calmed down, I grasped the stylus again. I intended to write: "I'll talk. Feed me stimulants." But before I'd finished the loop of the I, my Net screen strobed, and a shimmering holo rose into the air just centimeters from my face. Pretty black eyes. Wide red mouth. Merida.

"HAVE YOU ENJOYED your little escapade, Jolie? You know I've tracked your every move, pet. Jin made his breakthrough, didn't he? Tell me what happened."

Merida's hologram drifted above my cot, sparkling with iridescence. All I could see was her mouth. The stylus slipped from my hand.

Merida smiled. "You're full of toxin, pet. I have the meds you need. Save yourself, and speak to the protes in Euro. The Parisians need to hear your true voice. Sí, I've been eavesdropping. The Coms are my enemy, too. I can help you, Jolie. Give Jin back to me."

Tan whispered, "We've lost contact with the others, ma'am."

Merida undulated above me like a wisp of colored smoke. "I'll make you well, so you can lead the protes to victory. We're on the same side, Jolie. Give Jin to me, and I promise to make you well so you can speak."

"Ma'am, them Nome troopers is less than a quarter kilometer away. Luc and Trinni and Miguel, they haven't even landed yet. They ain't gonna get here in time."

Miguel? That name triggered a memory—but I lost it.

"Look at him, pet." Merida drifted toward Jin's sleeping form. "That last episode mangled his limbic function. Unless I treat him, he'll be feeble-minded. I can repair his damaged brain. Can you do that? Admit the truth, pet. He's better off with me."

I tossed my head back and forth on the pillow. Never! I wanted to shout. The pillow's fabric sliced at me like a rasp.

Merida said, "You can't keep him, you little fool. Look at yourself. You're dying. Vincente, give her a mirror."

I felt Vincente's rough hand stroking my cheek. "We're a long way from help, niña. You are very sick. The doctor, she can fix you. Perhaps you consider her offer, si?"

"Who's this Commie actor to you anyway?" Tan asked.

Even if I could have spoken, I'm not sure how I would have

answered the boy's question. If it had been me alone, the choice would have been easy. I would have gladly died rather than let Merida get her hands on Jin. But now Vincente and Tan—and all the people of Paris it seemed—had been added to the equation. Violently, I tossed my head against the thorny pillow, trying to think of another option. Some new place to leap. I just did not want to give up.

"Listen to me, Jolie." Merida's voice sighed in my ear. I could almost feel its whispering heat. "Luc is coming. That's right, your dear little brother. Remember who's with him? Remember?"

A vague fear hovered at the edge of my memory. What did she mean?

"Miguel," she said. "Remember now? My agent Miguel is sitting right beside your cher Luc. Miguel is waiting for my orders. Do what I say, pet."

I recoiled deeper into the cot, away from her smoky hologram. Bien sûr, Miguel. I remembered the name now.

"Uh-oh. We got another call comin' in." Tan cocked his head, listening to a small transceiver plugged in his ear. "It's the dern cops! They found us. Lordy, they got their neutrino cannons trained right on us! Them beams can pass straight through solid rock and give us a instant case of deep-fry. Ma'am, they wanna talk to you pronto. They wanna upload yer signal to their holostage, okay?"

When I nodded, Tan wormed the plug out of his ear and stuck it in mine. Then he pulled something out of a case that looked like a fist-sized wad of orange mesh. I recognized it as a virtual reality sensor net—travel size. He flung it over my head—it wasn't big enough to cover my body. Then he drew it tight around my throat with a drawstring. "This won't hurt," he said as he flipped a little toggle switch. The lights went dim. I saw a swirl of colors, and Nome.Com sucked my digital signal up like cola through a straw.

A man sat in a yellow plastic chair. He held a thick, shabby portfolio of papers on his lap, and he looked inexpressibly bored. Vincente, Tan, and the little blue tent had vanished. Merida's hologram was gone. All I could see were gray shadows in the background and this man in his chair. Me, I was floating. I glanced down at my body, and it wasn't there.

"My name's Richard Sprague. Call me Dick." That was the friendliest he ever got.

The scene was so spooky, I started hyperventilating.

"Relax, it's just VR," the man said.

Bien, virtual space. Transient light waves and vibrating code. The reason I didn't have a body was because Tan's sensor mesh covered only my head. Get a grip, Jolie.

Sprague sneezed. He seemed to be suffering from a head cold. A VR head cold? "Here's the deal," he said. "Nome.Com assigned me to represent you, got it? I.e., I'm your lawyer."

"What do you want?" In VR, I could talk again. That was a plus.

Sprague sighed and scratched his two-day beard. His clothes looked slept-in. "One thing at a time, Ms. Sauvage. First off, our forces have you cornered. You and your friends are illegal trespassers. You might wonder why we haven't executed you."

He'd raised a good point. Why were we meeting like this? Nome had us in their crosshairs. They could annihilate us with a single voice command—and not even leave a mess.

Sprague took his time explaining, but I couldn't really follow his story. He said the big three remaining Coms—Nome, Greenland and Pacific—were "restructuring." Greenland.Com was waging a proxy war against Pacific.Com because Greenland had always been paranoid about Suradon Sura. Bien, that much I could grasp. Greenland had already spun off 19 of Pacific.Com's divisions before Suradon could lift a finger. But back in Euro, Greenland was having way too much trouble with those pesky Parisian rebels. Nome.Com was waiting to see which of its two partners would survive.

So how did paltry little Jolie Blanche Sauvage fit into this world drama? It seems I had Lord Suradon to thank. Suradon had called his old pal, Allistaire Wagstaff, the Nome CEO. In the wee hours of the morning, Suradon had whispered a suggestion. "Rescue the Angel of Euro. Greenland hates her, and the Parisian protes love her. You can use her as leverage."

Funny, huh? I thought Suradon had forgotten me. But on second thought, Suradon probably never let any bit of information stray if it might serve his interests. Ça va. He'd planted his suggestion, Allistaire Wagstaff had listened, and thus far at least, the neutrino cannons hadn't torched us.

Sprague fished a soiled handkerchief from his briefcase and

wiped his nose. "Here's the deal. Nome.Com is making a generous offer. Just record a few holos denouncing violence, got it? I.e., tell the protes to lay down their arms. War is ugly. You'll save lives. And to show our gratitude, we'll give you complete restorative therapy, the best Frisco has to offer."

I glowered at Sprague. "You're already broadcasting those holos. You can counterfeit all you want."

He shook his head. "That's Greenland's gig. It's only a matter of time before the rebels spot the fake. We want the genuine article, got it? The real Angel of Euro. With an ID certificate to prove it's you."

"So you can help Greenland crush my comrades?"

"We want merchandise, Ms. Sauvage. We'll sell to the highest bidder."

"I'll record your holo when Earth freezes," I said. My voice carried way more edgy power than usual. I suppose VR does that.

"Take my advice, unless you get therapy soon—." Sprague pulled a mirror out of his pocket and tried to make me look at my face.

"Scuzz that!" I knocked it away.

He turned his handkerchief over, hunting for a dry spot. "There's more to the deal. I.e., you might want to hear about the other people in that tent with you." He shifted in his seat and squinted at me, expecting a reaction. I didn't move an eyelash. I wouldn't give him the satisfaction.

He opened the thick folder of papers on his lap, then licked his thumb and tabbed through a file. Why didn't the man use a Net node for all that data?

"Let's see. Vincente Ramores and Calvin Hooper. As bona fide protected workers of Nome.Com, these two will be remanded to City General for psychiatric repair."

"Huh? Who's Calvin Hooper?"

"Your associate Hooper is a runaway prote," Sprague said. "Missing since the age of nine. I believe you know him by his Net alias. Tan? Yes. He'll be returned to his factory compound as soon as psychiatric repair's complete."

Psychiatric repair. The Com's euphemism for lobotomy. Their penalty for runaways.

"No!" I yelled, wobbling my disembodied head around. "Tan's not a prote. He's . . ."

Sprague sighed when I couldn't finish the sentence. "About those recordings, Ms. Sauvage. We'll need to do some initial plastic surgery on your face—"

"What about Jin?" I asked. A small pain shot through my invisible rib cage.

Sprague sighed again and paged through the file. "Lord Sura's heir, yes. We have reports on unauthorized brain experiments. Nanotherapy to expand IQ—you know about that? Since the procedure was conducted in our territory, said brain has, ipso facto, become the intellectual property of Nome.Com. I.e., young Sura will be detained pending financial discussions with his father."

"You'll hold Jin for ransom? You gutter mold." The pain in my disembodied rib cage throbbed again. That wasn't right. In VR, I shouldn't feel pain. I said, "Jin comes with me. Tan and Vincente, too. They all come with me, or no deal."

Sprague smiled unctuously. "Then do I understand you to say that if we release your friends, we do have a deal?"

I blinked. That wasn't what I meant. This lawyer was spinning me in circles. Nome wanted to use me against my own sisters and brothers in Paris. No way. This Angel of Euro business—Adrienne's propaganda campaign—I couldn't believe it really meant anything. But Nome must think so. Imagine me telling the Parisians to surrender. The pain cut into my side like a knife.

Sprague was trying to scare me. And he'd succeeded. Tan's brilliance—erased? Vincente—entombed in a factory? And Jin? Suradon might not pay the ransom for his son. He might let Nome keep Jin, and who knows what those sadists would do to learn Jin's secrets. Mes dieux, how did I manage to endanger everyone I cared about?

"Your choice, Ms. Sauvage. In order to obtain a verified identity certificate, you have to record the holos of your own free will."

"You call this free will!"

"Let's not quibble over definitions. Are we in accord? You'll make the holos?"

I gritted my teeth. The pain had spread down my immaterial leg and up through my incorporeal shoulder. My hands and feet felt numb. "Let me think about it, Sprague."

"You're stalling."

Naturellement I was stalling. What preter-bold leap would get me out of this mess?

"Another hour without therapy, and you'll die," he said.

More scare tactics, I told myself. But my head felt thick. Even the simplest train of thought eluded me. Something was happening to my body. Even in VR, those hellish bacteria were eating through my flesh.

The lawyer balled up his snotty handkerchief and smirked at me. "We can make you well again. It's your choice. I'll see you in one hour, Ms. Sauvage. If you survive."

Everybody wanted to make me well. How nice. But there were always conditions. I fell through virtual darkness like a sack of bricks and landed with a thump back in my cot in the little blue tent. A rage of coughing shook me to the spine, and those cracked ribs felt like spears prodding my guts. Vincente held my hand and dabbed gauze at my lips with a look of terrible concern. Tan sat with his back to me, monitoring the screens at his workstation.

Merida? I mouthed the word.

"She waits for your call," Vincente told me. "Chica, I have given you more meds to stop the pain, but I can't stop this sickness in your body. We must bargain with the witch. There is no other choice."

"No!" I managed to wheeze. I would never trade Jin to Merida. Nor would I trade Tan and Vincente to Nome. But I would have to do something. One hour Sprague had given me. And who could guess what Merida might do. They had us caught between the devil and the deep brown sea. By the Laws of Physics, we needed a miracle.

"Luc?" I squeaked.

"We lost contact with the southerners. Tan is scanning for their signal."

Mes dieux, that boy Miguel, he might have his fingers around Luc's throat at this very moment. I tried to mouth a warning. Miguel. You must warn Luc about Miguel. Where was that stylus? I fumbled through the folds of my blanket. Where had I dropped the thing? I needed to write.

"Sí, muchacha, sí," Vincente whispered, "you must rest."

Rest? Was Vincente loco? With gut-wrenching effort, I shifted up on one elbow and gazed at Jin. He still slept peacefully in the cot next to mine. The blanket had fallen away a little, and my glance lingered on the stark, graceful angle of his shoulder blade. How splendid his hair looked, curling in damp strands across his pale skin. I longed to ask him what I should do. But chances were, if I woke him up now, he wouldn't even recognize me. What's this Commie actor to you anyway, Tan had asked.

Why do we make the choices that change our lives? How do we prepare for consequences we can't see coming? It seemed like centuries ago I had flown north in my Durban Bee to find a movie star. That war in Euro didn't belong to me anymore, so I had told myself.

Swifter than thought, I stammered, "Suradon." The swelling in my tongue was going down a little, thanks to Vincente's drugs. "Call Suradon," I sputtered. The Pacific.Com CEO had never been my friend, but he was powerful. And he'd kept Nome from blasting us. Maybe he would surprise me once more and finally help his son. Maybe he would just laugh at me, I didn't know. At least it was something to do.

I AWOKE IN another place. Cool. Numb. Floating. The air smelled of citrus. My skin no longer burned. I opened my eyes on yellow and pink drapery flecked with tiny russet flags.

"She's awake," someone whispered.

"The lord must be told."

I sat up quickly and reached for the curtains—and noticed with astonishment that my forearm had healed. I examined the back of my hand. Smooth white knuckles. I touched my face. Soft as down. I parted the pink chiffon kimono and stared at my naked body. No blisters. No ugly crusted skin. No pain. I felt whole again, new and clean and strong. I drew a deep breath and realized that both my eyes had cleared. I felt light and joyous and full of hope.

Then logic kicked in and reminded me this was a trick—Suradon's holo-stage. Computer-generated illusion—not real at all. Tan had uploaded an old backup file of my holo-image, one I'd stored in my Net node years ago. He'd also unraveled his little orange sensor web and attached the threads to key points on my limbs and torso to give me at least a little motor control on the holo-stage. What's more, he'd improvised an echo loop to disguise our transmission to Pacific.Com, so the Nome troopers couldn't listen in. The kid was a meta-geek.

I drew back the bed curtains. In a shaft of golden light, three figures loomed. Judith Merida, Lord Suradon and Jin.

Jin? How had Jin come to be on the holo-stage? Mes dieux, had Tan uploaded Jin's signal, too? In this preter-vicious VR, Jin had regained the illusion of health. His image must also have been an old backup. Maybe Suradon kept one in archive for just this sort of occasion. Jin's body appeared tall and straight and vigorous, his skin a rich dark cinnamon, his hair thick and wavy and short—just like the first time we'd met in Rennie's Airport Bar. It hurt me to see him this way again.

Suradon and Merida were so intent on their own conversation, they didn't seem to notice when I crept up and sat cross-legged on the floor to watch—even though I moved with about as much grace as a sledgehammer.

"You lying bitch, this is not what we bargained for?" Suradon's face turned crimson. His black Asian eyes glittered with rage, and he tugged at his silk collar so hard, a button flew off. "This is not a saleable product! This is a joke!"

"If you'll only listen—"

"I don't have time for this, Judith. The Triad's in play. Those sharks want to tear my Com to pieces. I should be there, not here."

"But my lord," Merida said. I'd never heard her use that simpering tone before.

"You guaranteed this Hyperthought would sell like candy panties," Suradon thundered. "You said your research would put Pacific.Com back on top. Judith, you know how badly I need cash flow right now—but look at him!"

Both of them turned to watch Jin. He was drawing his ciphers in the air, and a faint smile played at his lips as if he were listening to some sweet private melody no one else could hear.

"Jin, tell your father what you've achieved," said Merida. "Tell him about the quantum vibrations. You heard them, I know you did. Tell him."

"There once was a coastal kingdom, long ago in Java," Jin chanted softly. "It could have been paradise."

"He's reciting a fairy tale." Suradon's sarcastic laughter split the air. "I'm fighting the battle of my life to save Pacific.Com, and my heir recites make-believe! I knew this would come to nothing."

Jin focused his eyes on his father. He tilted his head with infinite melancholy, but he didn't speak.

Suradon hammered his fist into his palm. "To think I had my ass-wipe ad agency work out the marketing plan!" He gestured, and a sheaf of holographic projections spilled through the air like pliant sheets of film. Each one displayed moving graphics. They were Net broadblast ads for Hyperthought. I caught one or two headlines: "Instant Intelligence." "Bulk Up on Brain Power." "Secrets of the Quanta Revealed." When Suradon snapped his fingers, the ads crumpled into little wads and popped out of existence.

"My Lord Suradon, I've been running remote brain scans for the past half hour." Merida lifted her chin, and her own sheaf of projected images fanned neatly through the air in a regular grid. They showed bright blue MRI slices of Jin's brain, with scarlet dots blinking in every section. Merida pointed with her fingernail. "You see the red glyphs? Those are nanobot concentrations. First, the bots propagated an auxiliary neural net throughout Jin's cerebral cortex. Then they wove through the cerebellum and penetrated the limbic system. Approximately 15 hours ago, Jin's brain activity soared to unprecedented levels."

"Green trees waved in gentle breezes," Jin's voice drifted softly, "and the blue ocean broke on the white sand."

I recognized those words. He was quoting that old Javanese poem about Prince Airlangga.

Suradon laughed. "You've made him a clown, Judith. This is not apotheosis. This is Vaudeville. Admit it, darlin', you screwed up."

"Listen to him, Lord Suradon, please!" Merida clutched Jin's arm and drew him farther into the golden light. "He's trying to tell you."

Suradon rolled his eyes and crossed his arms with a great show of impatience. "All right, son. Now's your chance. Tell me what you know about quanta."

Jin shifted vaguely in my direction, and I saw a melancholy shadow deepen under his eye. Hesitantly he stuttered, "The p-prince couldn't fight."

"Bullshit," Suradon huffed. "Brain enhancement, my ass. Judith, I can't present this. The Triad would eat me alive."

"But our agreement—" Merida whined.

"The boy can't even speak properly. Your experiment is fucked, Judith. You lose the bet."

"Bet! Is that all he is to you, old man?" I couldn't hold back my anger any longer. I jumped up and marched into the light— listing a bit to the left like a top-heavy manikin. "Jin is your son!"

Suradon turned a scowl on me like a gathering of storm clouds. "He's no worse than before. Too damned cocky for his own good."

"La Sauvage," Jin whispered, pointing in my direction. "Witness."

"Yes, that's right." Merida's scarlet mouth stretched into a smile. Her pretty black eyes flashed at me. "You were there when Jin's brain activity peaked. You saw it all. Tell Lord Suradon what happened, Jolie."

Suradon steepled his fingers and looked down his nose at me. "Jolie Blanche Sauvage, Angel of Euro. My son does make interesting choices. Greenland posted a reward for your death. You're plenty gutsy to call me."

Between Merida's smile and Suradon's ominous smirk, I was getting way more attention than I wanted. Plus, with Tan's improvised motor controls, I was having a lot of trouble standing without falling over. Malgré tout, I had to speak. "Will you help your son or not?"

"Help him? I'm the one with the problems." The old man lifted his hands theatrically. "The Triad wants to bust up my Com. That's millions of people and half a continent of infrastructure, not to mention the retained capital. Generations of my family spent their lives building Pacific.Com. You're asking me to play favorites, to put my son ahead of everyone else."

Merida purred. "You're in a pretty fix, pet. Tell Lord Suradon what happened to Jin, and we'll save you as well as your friends. You'll be well again. Nome won't bother you anymore. And you can make that speech we were talking about earlier, to you know who." She pretended to be talking behind her hand so Suradon wouldn't hear. "Oh, and your little brother Luc will be fine. No more worries, pet."

Mes dieux, but I hated Merida at that moment. She knew all my buttons, and she pushed hard. Although Jin had asked me to tell his father, I hesitated. Anything Merida wanted I automatically opposed.

"Speak, girl!" She grabbed my hair and jerked me off my feet. Even in the holograph, I felt her nails dig in. "Your comrades think you betrayed them. And they're right, aren't they? You ran off to pleasure yourself with an aristocrat. All those children suffocating in the tunnels. Did you forget them, pet?"

I tried to fight her, but I think Tan had cross-wired the sensors. My arms swung around loose, as if a marionette were pulling my strings. I yelled, "Let me go, you witch."

"Running after a rich prince when your friends are dying in

the war. That doesn't look good, pet. People know you by the choices you make." Merida released her grip on my hair, and I stumbled. The floor came up hard and hit me in the chest. I wasn't getting any better at this motor control.

Merida said, "Make the right choice now, pet. Tell us, and save your friends."

"Tempus fuckin' fugit." Suradon's words exploded above me. "I have a meeting, ladies. Can you hold the catfights? Sauvage, do you have something to say?"

I lay sprawled on the virtual floor. When I looked up, Suradon and Merida glared down at me with shining, ravenous eyes. Their eagerness frightened me. I realized that for different reasons, they were both equally anxious to hear whether Jin had made a breakthrough. For a moment, I bit my lip and said nothing. Then I heard Jin speaking inside my head. A memory? Imagination? He said, "Jolie, keep your promise. Be my witness."

"D'accord," I said aloud. As calmly as possible, I sat up and crossed my legs, pretending a confidence I didn't feel. I squinted up at the pair of them. They were hunching over me with their heads nearly touching, two black vultures silhouetted in the golden light. I spoke to Suradon. "Jin wants me to tell you, so I will. But I'm asking for your promise. Will you protect my friends?"

"Sí, pet, and we will make you well again." Merida's Spanic accent got thicker when she poured on the charm. "You can go back and do your duty in Euro."

I ignored Merida and spoke only to Suradon. "There's one other promise I want."

Suradon's eyes narrowed fiercely. "Do you think you can negotiate with ME?"

Excellent question. Who was I to make terms with the head of Pacific.Com? I wasn't exactly bargaining from a position of power. Still, I carried on as usual, ignoring the obvious. "After I tell you what happened, you'll let Jin leave with me. That's what I want you to promise."

Suradon hooted and clapped his hands.

Merida sneered. "We don't need to make bargains with you."

"Hmm, I don't know, Judith." Suradon grinned. "Perhaps my son would be better off with this girl. She claims to love him." He ducked when Merida whirled to glare at him.

"That's ridiculous. She'll be dead in minutes." Merida wiped her palms on the cloth of her suit and made a visible effort to regain control. Contorting her lips into a smile, she linked her elbow through Jin's and continued more smoothly, "My Lord, I'll redesign the nanobot. I already know what direction to take. Jin will be magnificent, and Pacific.Com will be rich. You'll see. We don't need this girl."

Suradon was still wiping laugh tears from his eyes. "I wanna hear Sauvage's story."

"Jin asked me to tell you." I pushed myself up from the floor and stood with my legs planted wide to keep from staggering. "He wants you to know, Suradon. Just promise to let me take Jin away from her."

Merida marched toward me and bumped her chest against mine. She kept walking into me, forcing me to step backward. It was all I could do to stay on my feet.

"Stupid slut. I can take Jin to higher planes of consciousness. Can you? That's what he wants. To learn more and more about the nature of the universe. Can you show him that? This last episode injured his thalamus. I can heal him. Can you make him well? No. If he stays with you, he'll be a doddering imbecile for the rest of his life."

I shoved Merida back. "Jin stays with me."

Suradon chuckled. "Greedy, Sauvage. You wanna keep my son an invalid so he can't leave you. And you call that love. That's rich."

Suradon's words shot through me like a bolt. His mocking laughter drummed in my ears. Is that what I wanted? To keep Jin dependent on me? No, I wanted to keep Merida's fingernails out of his brain. She had no intention of healing him. But . . . but . . . The old bastard's accusation confused me.

"What do you call love?" I shouted back defensively.

Suradon's laughter died as quickly as it had begun. "I don't use the word."

His hulking image towered over me, but I forced myself to face him. I was not going to let the old bugger stare me down. As we locked glances, his accusation reverberated through my mind. Greedy, Sauvage?

Had I been wrong to drag Jin away from Merida? He wanted that nanosurgery. I knew how burdened he felt by all his wealth and talents. His compulsion to do the right thing hounded him, and he honestly believed Merida's nanobot would help him make up his mind. Maybe the nanobot worked. Maybe Jin really had heard the universe singing in that blue chamber. Who was I to say? Jin had never once asked me to take him away from Merida. "Wish you were here," those were his words. Maybe just an idle greeting from a movie star to a fan. Was I simply addicted to a screen idol? I started second-guessing.

Suradon's stare burned into me like a searchlight, and I sensed that I should say something. He was wavering. He might actually give in and let Jin leave with me. A few well chosen words might tip the balance in my favor. But was I asking for the right thing? Scenes from the blue chamber reeled through my mind. My beautiful Jin. At the height of his vision, he'd seemed euphoric and all-seeing. If I took him away now, would he live out his life as a muddle-headed freak? Who was I to make that choice for him?

Faster even than the answer formed in my mind, I said, "Jin stays with me."

D'accord, someone had to choose. And I'm not the girl to drag things out forever. It came down to this. Merida didn't care if she killed him, whereas I would do everything to keep him alive. Call me greedy, arrogant, stupid. You would be right about all of that. Still, if Jin stayed alive, maybe someday another doctor could cure his brain damage. Maybe he wouldn't be as muddle-headed as Merida claimed. Maybe someday he'd be well enough to make his own choices. For now, at this moment, I chose for him.

"I want him to live," I said.

Gradually, Suradon's burning stare dissolved into a tired, wrinkled smile. He remained silent only for a moment. Then he snapped his fingers like a magician. "Agreed, Sauvage. You may keep my son. Now tell us what happened."

"Lord Suradon, you're making a mistake." Merida rose on the balls of her feet as if to attack.

"Quiet, Judith. Let the girl talk."

Merida gnawed her red lips and glowered at me. Her eyes glittered with anger, but she settled back and said nothing more. Suradon crossed his arms and tapped a finger impatiently. Jin waited with lowered head. So I told them everything. I repeated what Jin had said in the chamber, quoting him word for word as nearly as I could recall, even what he'd said about his father. It took some time, and when the telling was done, I felt drained.

"My nanobot worked! I win! You owe me, old man!" Merida danced around like a fire-flame, gloating with delight. "You owe me! Upload those Net ads. We'll air them tonight. I'll set up a chain of clinic franchises around the globe. Everyone will want my Hyperthought!"

"Mystical crap," Suradon said, working his fists. "This is not a scientific breakthrough. It's a psychotic hallucination. I can't take this to the Triad."

"You know the truth when you hear it. My nanobot worked!"

"It's bullshit. The boy was raving."

"Jin goes with me now," I reminded them. Jin had stepped backward out of the golden light. I saw him only in shadow.

"Suradon, she can't have him!" Merida rose on tiptoes again and balled her fists. "I won our wager, and I demand justice. He's mine!"

"Go now, Sauvage," Suradon thundered at me.

"To hell with you!" Merida's holographic image ballooned out larger than Suradon's, and the whole holo-stage went topsy-turvy. "You think you can change the terms of our bargain, old man? We had a deal. I get Jin."

"You get what I say," Suradon boomed. Their projected images overlapped in a weird interference ripple. I struggled to keep my balance.

"And what'll you do to stop me?" Merida's image started strobing. "You'll do nothing. Impotent old fraud. Jolie Sauvage called you for help. The poor child thinks you have power over me. That's the real joke."

The colors on the holo-stage marbled together like liquid paint. I lost all sense of balance. My pink chiffon kimono streamed into the golden light, and my body started melting into the floor. Out of nowhere, Merida filled my vision. She was breathing in my face.

"Sorry, pet. Lord Suradon has his own battles. He'll forget you the minute you're out of his sight."

Far away, I saw Suradon arching one bushy eyebrow. "Judith, I've got a meeting. Are we done here?"

A rainbow rippled and exploded, and I barely caught Merida's last words. "This isn't over, pet." Then solid white light expanded around me, and everything vanished. I fell into a velvet black whirlpool. Another holo-stage exit. I should be getting used to it.

"JOLIE." SOMEONE SHOOK my shoulder. I knew that voice. Merida! Mes dieux, but she had caught us after all! I wanted to scream and grab Jin and run, but I couldn't get my eyes open. They were glued shut. I tried clawing at them, but I couldn't find my hands.

"Jolie," the voice came again, and this time it wasn't Merida but Luc. "What gear did you pack, chérie? Did you forget the waterproof matches?"

"Luc?" I whispered. But someone kept jogging my shoulder, and the whole world quaked up and down. Go away. Leave me alone. I couldn't get enough breath in my lungs to speak.

I woke up coughing. Tan was leaning over me, holding a gauze bandage to my lips and looking concerned. "Lady? Can you see me?"

Yes, I could see a little better than before. Vincente's meds must have reduced the swelling around my eyes. The electric lantern dangling from the tent pole no longer bristled with long sharp rays. My friends had wrapped me up in sheets like a mummy. I felt hot and constricted. I tried to loosen the winding sheets, but I didn't have the strength.

"Aw, ma'am, now don't mess with them sheets, okay? What happened with that Commie lord? You were gone a long time. He made us upload Jin's signal, too. I rigged another holo-interface outta spare parts. I hope that was okay."

I felt dizzy. The sheets were wrapped too tight around me.

Vincente smoothed my hair. "Chica, the bruja witch, she's coming. She figured out how to disarm our explosives. Your amigo, the Asian lord, will he help us?"

Merida was still coming? She'd disarmed the mines? But Suradon had promised to let everyone go free. Surely he would do something to stop her. This cot felt so lumpy, and the sheets were making me hot. How clearly I remembered the feeling of being whole and healthy on that holo-stage. But that was a dream. This nightmare was real. I couldn't wake up from this.

"We're onwave with Luc Viollett," Tan was saying. "The whole dern world knows where we are now. No point keepin' silent."

"Luc?" I managed to wheeze.

"Yes, ma'am, Luc and Trinni and Miguel. They're comin' as fast as they can. Got some kinda stolen military stealth jet. Plenty cool."

Luc and Trinni and—Miguel. My heart sank.

"Chica, will the Com lord help us? Your friends will land soon, but they have many meters to descend before they reach us. The witch, she is very near."

I swung my head back and forth. Instinct told me Merida had been right, that Suradon had already forgotten me. He was all bluff. About now, he'd be walking into that Triad meeting, grinning and spouting his bullshit. Oh yes, the mighty Lord Suradon would think of some way to save his precious Com. That was mega more important than one trifling son. Suradon be damned.

"She's here!" Tan yelled. In that same moment, the tent's inflatable airlock zipped open, and Merida stepped through—in the flesh.

"What an amusing party!" She removed her helmet and unzipped the collar of her glossy black surfsuit. "Vincente, you gutter cur. You teach me the value of trusting human servants. And who's this? What an ugly face you have, boy. You look like a maggot."

"Senorita Judith—" Vincente began.

"None of your fawning, dog! I see you've salvaged this tedious bag of bones. Jolie Blanche Sauvage, ha! Better toss her in the recycling bin. She's putrid. Where is Jin?"

My ears pricked up. Jin was no longer on the other cot? I swung around to look, and the cot wasn't even there.

"What about them meds for Ms. Sauvage?" Tan asked. "You said you'd bring 'em to trade."

"The meds are just outside. Where is Jin? My instruments no longer pick up his signature." Merida tromped around the tent, knocking things over. Then she grabbed Vincente's throat. "How have you hidden him from me, you old mongrel?"

"El principe is dead," Vincente replied, choking. He tried to pull her hand away from his windpipe.

"Dead!"

"As a dern doornail," Tan seconded.

"Quiet, maggot! Vincente, explain this to me. Where is his body?"

I couldn't find my breath. Had Jin died while I'd been capering around on that hold-stage? My chest heaved so violently, I sat straight up. Suddenly there was motion, and terrible pain. I guess I must have tumbled out of the cot. Tan knelt beside me on the floor and fumbled with the sheets that trapped me like a mummy. "Lady, you okay?"

"Forget that plague of a girl. Where is Jin!"

"Señorita—"

"Don't señorita me!"

Sprawled on my side, I felt strangely heavy and awkward. Tan seemed to be nudging me under the cot, maybe to protect me. All I could see was his thigh. He was wearing bluejeans. Above me, Vincente kept talking.

"A very strange thing, Señorita Judith. When El Principe die, his body it turn to dust, and the wind carry it away."

I heard a slap. Merida's elegant black boots danced around Vincente's scuffed workshoes. The old man was backing away from her. More slapping sounds and choking. Tan nudged me farther under the cot.

"Lie to me, you vulgar beast! Where is he? Tell me or I call my guards. Vincente, you know what they can do."

Tan stood up slowly.

"Sí, sí," Vincente was saying. Merida had him backed into a corner. "I tell you the truth. El principe, he—"

Tan sprang forward. I heard Merida gasp, and then she started barking her ugly laughter. "A jet-spray? Stupid boy, you can't poison me. My blood is full of antidotes. I've made myself immune to . . ."

Then a thump. Merida fell flat on the floor not ten centimeters away from me. Maybe you think it was rude, but I don't care—I spat in her face. My mouth worked well enough for that.

"Be quick, niño. Tie her. I go outside and look for the meds she brought."

"Don't you worry, Vince. I'll truss 'er up like a dern bale of kelp."

Tan grabbed fistfuls of my winding sheet and tugged me out from under the cot, but when I gasped in pain, he stopped and let me lie still. "Sorry, ma'am. You can just rest on the floor for a while."

"Where's Jin?" I wheezed, but my voice came out a garbled cough.

"It's a botanical sleep aid," Tan said, as he wrapped duct tape around Merida's arms and legs. "I synthesized the herbs myself. Archaic biochemistry I found on the Net. Kinda neat." He wagged his head with unabashed pride. "Thing is, it'll wear off soon."

I barely focused on what Tan was saying. Infuriating boy! Why wouldn't he speak about Jin? What had become of Jin?

Tan bent over and whispered in my ear, "That Commie actor guy, he was a spy for the rebels, wasn't he? That's why you was helpin' him."

When I tried to speak again, it turned to hectic coughing.

"That's all right, ma'am. You just rest. Vince and me, we got the situation handled." He grinned and whispered in my ear again. "What we did, we recorded Merida's voice so we could fake an audio command. Heh-heh, we sicced her robots onto them Nome.Com troopers. That'll teach 'em where to aim their neutrino beams."

Finally, Vincente returned. He must have gone outside on reconnaissance because he was holding his helmet in one hand. "I'm sorry, chica. The bruja she brought no medicines for you. She always lies." Gently, he lifted me in his arms and laid me down on my cot again. The pain was all gone now. I felt cold. I worked my mouth and felt froth drooling from my lips. Surely Vincente understood what I wanted to ask.

He put his lips to my ear. "Be still, chica. The prince lives. He's in that sheet with you."

Huh? Those lumps in the cot. At last I understood. Jin's body was wrapped tightly against mine. That's how they'd hidden his biological signature from Merida's scan. They'd camouflaged it with my own. Oh mes dieux. I bet Tan thought of that.

"We leave him there a bit longer, sí? To fool the Nome.Com troopers? They are scanning us. We make them wonder, sí?" Vincente's blue eyes shone with moisture. He looked disconsolate as he studied my ravaged face. "I'm sorry, niña. I'm so sorry." He cradled me in his arms and rocked me. "Your friends come soon. I have prayed to Saint Einstein."

"Thank you," I rumbled, though the sounds I made weren't words.

When Vincente released me, I snuggled deeper into the sheet, imagining Jin was caressing me from behind. Merida said I had only a few minutes to live. An icy chill was spreading through my body, but I couldn't die yet. I still had things to do. My mind felt like mush. Who would take care of Jin now? I was lying on top of him. My weight might be crushing him. Vincente and Tan were busy searching Merida's pockets, so they didn't notice what I was doing. Looking back, I think that rolling over in that narrow cot to get my weight off Jin was the most excruciating thing I ever did. But I felt a tremendous lightness afterward. Vincente's words sounded in my ear like a blessing. The prince lives.

"Yaaaah!" Merida's arm ripped free of the duct tape and struck Tan a savage blow. I heard a fleshy thud as the boy fell back against the gear cases. Before Vincente could react, Merida tore her other limbs free. For such a small woman, she showed astonishing strength. She must have been hopped up on adrenaline. In one quick move, she sprang to her feet and barked her ghastly laugh.

"The prince lives, does he? In the sheet?"

Duct tape trailed in shreds from her surfsuit as she flew at Vincente. He leaped aside, but not quick enough. Merida landed a staggering kick-punch in his belly, and he sank to his knees. Tan rolled over and moaned. Merida turned when she heard him, and her glossy black curls shook as she started kicking him in the ribs and gut and head. He shook like a rag doll, and I knew he'd lost consciousness long before she stopped kicking.

Then she came at me. She raised her hand, and time seemed to stop when I saw the razor-sharp surgeon's scalpel clutched in her fist. Then her blow fell, slicing through my sheet and grazing my crusted skin. In three strokes, she cut the sheet away and threw me aside like garbage.

"Jin, my beautiful Jin. Are you all right?" She held his head in both her hands and kissed his eyelids.

I tumbled to the floor next to Tan. The poor boy had been horribly battered. Blood oozed from cuts all over his body.

"Ah, what have they done to you?" Merida was checking Jin's pulse, speaking in a voice as soft and soothing as Hamad's.

She opened one of his eyelids. "The fools. I'll save you, Jin. Relax now. It's me. Judith."

The tent floor was gritty with sand and rock chips. I pushed myself up with my elbows and struggled into a position where I could see Vincente. He sagged motionless against the airlock. Merida's blow had knocked him unconscious. Then I saw Merida flip open the cover of a sleek black Net node on the belt at her waist.

"Miguel. Go ahead as planned," she said. "And don't leave any evidence."

Miguel. Merida's agent. I imagined his fingers circling Luc's throat. Maternal fury surged through me. I had to stop her! Her helmet had rolled into a corner near me, so I slithered over and grabbed it. Merida couldn't leave the tent without her helmet. I would hide it somewhere. Maybe I could lie on top of it.

"You're pathetic, Jolie." I turned and saw her glaring at me with that wide ugly smile.

She stepped across Tan's body, yanked the helmet from my hands, and dropped it over her head. The neck gasket sealed with a soft click. Then I heard her laughing inside the helmet. She must have activated her speaker. She raised the scalpel and punched a hole in the tent wall. Then another and another.

Sour atmosphere jetted through from outside, foul and toxic. As the gases seeped into the tent, it hit me that neither Vincente nor Tan was wearing a protective helmet. Merida had just exposed them to the same toxins that were liquefying my skin. Sacrée Loi! I grabbed the tent pole and pulled myself up.

Merida snorted. "You want to fight me, pet?" She casually put her scalpel away in her belt pouch, then thumped my chest with the back of her hand. I toppled backward. But I didn't fall. I clung to a tent pole and coughed. Just then I happened to notice I was naked, but that was a truly trivial point.

Merida snorted again and turned her back to me. As she gathered Jin in her arms, my glance fell on a shiny little worktool lying on the floor under my cot. My stylus. Its sharp point gleamed in the lantern light. When I hobbled over to get it, Merida laughed.

"Give it up. You're a rotting corpse."

She shoved me with one hand, and I fell in a heap, but not before I'd swept up the little stylus. Now I gripped it in my fist and tried to push myself back up, but my hands and knees kept slipping out from under me on the gritty tent floor.

"You're dead, Jolie."

Merida lifted Jin like a child. She stepped over me and carried Jin to the airlock. She had to kick Vincente's heavy body out of the way.

"And by the by, your friends above are dead, too. Nasty accident. Too bad about cher Luc." Then the airlock zipper stuck, and she bent down to work it free.

Impotent fury overwhelmed me. I had no strength left. I kept pushing at the floor, but I couldn't get traction. I was beyond caring about the pain.

Merida took her scalpel out and slashed the zipper open, snickering under her breath. "Jin chose me, not you. He came to me of his own free will. Others will come, too. You'll see. People will want what I can give them. You could have been part of it, but you were too foolish to understand."

Merida carried Jin into the airlock and started unzipping the outer door flap. "No," I wheezed.

She turned to smile at me, that pretty Spanic smile I used to think so charming. "He's mine now."

All at once, female hormones raged through my veins. Primordial instinct galvanized my muscles and filled my heart with savagery. I pushed myself up and lunged. I knew I'd have only one chance. Merida was caught in the small airlock with Jin in her arms. She couldn't dodge me, but she raised her hand to fend me off, and I saw the flash of her scalpel. Still, I dove face-first against her, driving the little stylus home as hard as I could, praying my aim was true. When I collapsed at her feet, I saw its gleaming tip wedged behind her left eye. I'd buried it deep.

For a long time, I couldn't take my eyes off the sight of Merida's dead body. She had slumped to a sitting position, her hands spread open, the pale palms facing up. No scalpel. She must have dropped it. One bright thread of blood trickled down her soft cheek. Jin lay sprawled in her arms. Together, they reminded me of some ancient marble statue of a mother and son.

A moment ago, she'd been a living soul, and now she lay dead. By my hand. Without a thought, without hesitation, I had taken away her life. Once, she gloated that I lacked the will to commit murder. And there she lay. I crammed knuckles into my mouth and bit down hard. There was a sound of guttural moaning. I realized it was me.

Did the fever of sickness stir me to take that next step? On impulse, I reached out and grasped the end of the stylus. Merida's face wasn't all that far away. I barely had to shift forward to touch her. With an involuntary cry, I tugged, and the shiny little tool came loose in my hand. Why did I wipe it on the cloth of Jin's filthy wrapper? As if that could clean it.

With leaden movements, I grasped Jin's arm and laid his wrist bare. The needle-sharp stylus scratched his skin, severing one of the small veins just under the surface. Blood beaded up immediately from the scratch. Did those crimson drops carry the immune response that would save my life? Some primordial sense deep in my brain urged me to try it. I touched a drop with my finger and smeared red blood across my lips. Warm sweet saltiness. Yes, it had to be true. I knew in my heart that Jin's blood would cure me. So I fell forward and sucked. Someone had to choose who would live and who would die. Me, I chose.

THE NEXT INSTANT, Jin pushed himself up to a sitting position and rubbed his head. He didn't seem to notice Merida's lifeless body. He just smiled and started humming. I was too stunned to react. The tune he hummed seemed strange and familiar at once, and somehow it soothed me.

Jin scooped me up in his arms. Mes dieux, but he'd grown strong. "Rise, Airlangga," he murmured with a smile. Was he making a little joke?

He carried me to the cot and wrapped me in a blanket. Then he sat on the floor beside me with his back against the gear cases. He seemed oblivious of Tan's unconscious body curled on the floor. I tried to speak, but my tongue still lay huge and flaccid against my teeth. So I gave up and relaxed against the pillow and stared at the yellow fabric sun stitched to the blue sky. Jin's soft humming blended with the whine of the air recycler. For the first time in a while, I felt peaceful.

I closed my eyes—for only a moment it seemed—but when I opened them, jagged rocks were rushing past my face. Someone was dragging me along the floor of a dark tunnel. I cried aloud.

"Lady, I'm sorry." A hand closed over my mouth. "You gotta be quiet, okay?"

Tan. I recognized his breathless whisper even though his helmet lamp blinded me. The last time I'd seen Tan, he'd been lying unconscious in the tent.

"Tan?" I choked out the words. "Are you hurt?"

"Don't worry about me, ma'am. A few bruises ain't gonna kill yours truly." He was wearing a full surfsuit, and his voice emanated from his helmet speaker. Now he started moving again, dragging me along in the travois sled Vincente had made for Jin. Where was Jin?

I tried to ask questions. My throat was clearing. My tongue didn't feel so swollen.

"Please, ma'am, you gotta keep it down. Them dern Nome troopers has got us surrounded. I'm projectin' mirage signals all through these rocks, so they can't tell exactly where we are. But we gotta stay quiet. And we gotta get up top fast and find a clinic. We all been exposed to toxins."

"The immune response," I said, but he didn't hear me.

Ahead, Vincente whispered, "Niño. Through here. The senda."

My travois swung up on its end. As I tumbled out, someone caught me around the middle and shoved me upward through a rough laser-blasted tunnel. I bit my lip till it bled, trying not to cry out.

Vincente pulled my arms, and Tan pushed from below. We struggled up through Vincente's laser-blasted "senda" for what seemed like years, but I don't remember how we came to the room. Maybe I dozed again. When I regained my senses, I was staring at the ceiling of Vincente's metal cube. We were back in his room in the neuroscience clinic! I felt warm. I flexed my fingers. My muscles were working again, and I could see fairly well. Yes, I knew it was true! Jin's blood did carry the immune response!

Tan and Vincente were still wearing surfsuits, but they'd removed their helmets. They huddled over the worktable in the corner, doing something to a black box. I whispered to get their attention.

Vincente raised his shaggy head. "Chica, you feel better?"

I sat up and pulled the blanket snug around my shoulders. "Where's Jin?" I whispered weakly. And then I saw him. Jin was standing in the shadows near the worktable, thin and pale, wearing nothing but that dingy hospital wrapper. Yet his face glowed with absolute joy.

"Jin," I breathed. He didn't look my way. Instead, Vincente lumbered over and knelt beside me. They had spread a pallet for me on the floor.

"So, so," the old man whispered, stroking my forehead and grinning. "You are better. Saint Einstein and the Laws of Physics have granted our prayers. The bruja, the witch, you stabbed her a good stroke, niña. Sí, you saved us. We left the witch to rot." Vincente spat on the floor.

"The doc surprised us." Tan spoke without looking up from his worktable. He seemed to be ripping the guts out of his black box. "Guess that botanical sleep aid wasn't so brilliant after all. But we located your friends again. They've landed."

Luc. A memory flashed—Miguel. I remembered the words Merida had whispered into her wrist node: "Go ahead as planned. Don't leave any evidence." She'd ordered Luc's execution!

I clutched at Vincente's collar. "Luc! She's going to murder him!"

Vincente looked at me as if I were raving.

A scritch of arcing electricity blotted out my next words. Tan whooped. "Dern Nome troopers think they can track my signal. Just watch this!" A holographic light matrix shimmered in the air above the box he'd been eviscerating. Deftly, he slipped a single cybernail onto his right index finger and twirled its point through the luminous icons. "Take that, boys! I'll fry your skinny metal butts."

Tan stopped short and cocked his head, listening. He said, "Un-huh. Yes sir, Mr. Viollett." Then he swung around to me. "Ma'am, can you talk to Luc?"

Luc was still alive? I grabbed the Net node from the boy's outstretched fingers. "Luc, mon cher, are you all right? Is Miguel with you? You have to stop him, Luc. Listen to me, he's an agent—" My words tumbled out rapid-fire, but Luc was speaking at the same time.

"Chérie, calm down. Miguel is gone. How did you know about Miguel?"

"Huh? What happened?" I stammered.

Luc chuckled. "Miguel was a customs agent, investigating Trinni's import trade. C'est vrai, we saw through his secret. We played him like the cat and mouse."

"Half hour ago, Miguel takes a call on his node." That was Trinni speaking. "Next thing, cool as you please, he climbs through the airlock and ejects."

"We saw his parachute open," Luc said.

"Sleazy jade. I don't care if he spied on my business, but he tried to seduce Luc." Trinni sounded peeved.

"Chérie, you are better? You sound good," Luc said.

"Yes, yes, yes," I repeated dopily. Relief warmed my soul. Luc was safe!

The line chattered with several other voices. Adrienne's was loudest. "Where have you been, Jollers? Do you think we're

playing mumblety-peg out here? This is serious. Now stop goof-
ing around, and speak to our friends in Euro. Jonas, are you
onwave?"

"Here, love. Ready to broadcast. Tan, can you cloak the signal
from your end?"

Tan leaned over and spoke into the Net node I was holding.
"Well, Mr. Tajor, I cain't actually cloak it. I can bounce it
around a dern echo loop though. Works good enough."

"No choice. We can't lose any more time," Adrienne said.

Vincente pulled the node from my hand and spoke. "Amigos,
can you not wait until the Angel is safe? The Nome troopers
are very close, and they are not known for their kindness."

"Jollers, you know the situation. You decide. Every minute
we wait, the Parisians lose more ground. And lives."

"Never you worry," Tan said. "Miss Sauvage is a dern iron
lady. She'll stand up to them Commies, whatever it takes."

Whatever it takes. Tan spoke with so much youthful confidence, it made my heart ache. Did he realize what Nome would
do if they captured him? Vincente's expression told me he had
a plenty clear idea.

"Just a few words," Jonas said. "We'll make it quick."

Aside to me, Tan whispered, "Don't worry about Vince and
me. We'll take care of ourselves. You just talk." He put the Net
node in my hand and nodded. He expected so much.

I glanced at Jin. He leaned against a metal cabinet, gazing
into space, lost in his glorious quantum song. I believe his face
had started emitting light again. He looked radiant. I loved him
so much in that moment. All I'd ever wanted was to save Jin,
and yet, one more time I was about to make a choice that might
kill us all. Protect a few dear friends close at hand, or help
millions on the other side of the globe? There had never been
any way to avoid such choices. I saw that now. D'accord, suck
it up, Sauvage. You can't play favorites, even for love.

I said, "Are you ready, Jonas?"

"Go, Angel. You're onwave."

I squeezed the node tight in my fist and enunciated as clearly
as possible. "Hello, Paris." Then it occurred to me that I hadn't
planned anything to say. "Um, this is Jolie Blanche Sauvage.
I'm a tunnel rat. I guess you've heard of me. Bien, the thing is,
the Commies are preter-lame. They're fighting each other like
a bunch of babies. You're going to win. Just don't give up. No

matter what happens, keep fighting. And um, this is really me. Those holos were a trick. So, that's all."

"Perfect!" Jonas said. At least I thought it was Jonas.

But Tan raised his eyebrows and shook his head. "It's a dern intruder. Someone's hacked our signal."

Had Nome triangulated our location already? They would be aiming their cannons in seconds. They wouldn't hesitate to torch us now. Any moment, we'd feel the neutrino blast.

"Good job, Sauvage. I couldn't have scripted a better speech myself."

Mes dieux, but I recognized that blustering voice. That was Suradon Sura! I almost dropped the Net node. "You wanted me to say that?"

Tan was flipping icons all through his light matrix. "Who's talkin', ma'am? I cain't get a ID."

"Who is that, love?" Jonas asked.

"My compliments to your geek friends," Suradon boomed. "The Euro protes are picking up your broadcast now. Hot damn, it's stirring them up. They'll oust those Greenland dickheads in a week."

"You planned this?" I couldn't believe it. Then the truth dawned. "You used me to get at Greenland. This is nothing but Triad politics."

Suradon's laughter ricocheted around Vincente's metal cube. "What are you complaining about? Your Euro pals get their islands back. We'll see if they can run things better than Greenland. It should be entertaining."

"Evil man, you got what you wanted," I said. "Now, keep your promise."

"Whoever called you an angel? You're a greedy little savage."

I gripped the Net node so hard, its plastic case cracked. "Your promise, Suradon."

"Yeah, okay," he said. "You might thank me for sending that fake message that got Miguel out of the picture. But never mind. I don't expect gratitude."

"You did that?" I sat up a little straighter.

"That and more. My people fragged Nome's security system. A giga-feat of geek, I might add. You and Jin can walk outta that sewer anytime you please. Nome thinks they can hold my son for ransom? Screw the cocksuckers."

Just then, a pinpoint of light flared on one of Tan's screens. It began to spread and brighten. Then it jetted out from the screen and swelled into a luminous holographic projection of Suradon. His Asiatic features expanded to gigantic proportion. Tan and Vincente sidled toward the far walls. Tan's eyes were so big, the whites showed all around his irises, and Vincente fidgeted as if he needed to take a piss. I knew Suradon was trying to intimidate us. I'd seen that trick before.

"Give me a break, old man. I've been sick."

Suradon's eyebrows twitched. I could tell he wanted to grin. "You're right about that, Sauvage. You look like crap."

"You have to protect Tan and Vincente, too," I said.

"Sauvage, it's never enough with you. I give you my only son, and you still want more." With effort, he smothered his amusement and assumed a stern scowl, steepling his fingers and arching his eyebrows. For a long time, he studied me. He was making me really tense.

"Hell, take the prote dogs. So what if they're Nome property. And do something about your complexion, Sauvage. You're falling apart."

"Yes," I beamed.

"Just remember I'll be watching. If you think I don't care about my son, you're mistaken. Guard him. You hear what I say? Guard him from Merida. I expect regular updates."

"Merida's dead. I killed her." I lowered my eyes.

Suradon broke out in a hoot. "You think Merida's dead? That's rich."

He didn't believe me? I opened my mouth to protest. I'd seen her dead body. But before I could speak, Suradon's image vanished.

He kept his promise though. Maybe he'd been keeping it all along. I'll never fathom that man. After Tan and Jonas ran independent scans to make sure the way was safe, we walked out together, the four of us, straight through the front door of Merida's clinic, up the service elevator, and into the heart of downtown Frisco. As we searched for the nearest exit, we passed cyberguards frozen in mid-action and humans slumped unconscious on the floor. Surveillance cameras failed to swivel on their mounts. If Suradon had done this, he'd pulled off the hack of the decade.

When we entered an air chute, I felt the buoyant cushion of

air lifting us upward. At the top level, we cycled through an airlock. Tan and Vincente wore their surfsuits, and they worried because they didn't have extras for Jin and me. When I told them about the immune response, they thought I was delirious.

Then we were outside on the surface. A moist gust of atmosphere touched my bare skin. It whipped my hair and filled my nostrils with pungence. A lavender glow suffused the eastern sky. For the first time in my life, I saw the dawn with unshielded eyes. To be on the open surface without a surfsuit! I felt unfettered. Joyous. Even brazen. All at once, I wanted to rip my blanket off and race across the plane. I managed to stifle the impulse.

As we walked across the windy launchpad, Jin's dark hair streamed straight back over his shoulders. He was singing now, in a language I didn't recognize. We advanced through ranks of police cars and rail buses tied down with steel guy wires. No one stopped us. We didn't see a single guard. In the distance, a weird brown jet with flat, stealth-clad wings crouched at the end of a runway. Its hatch lifted at our approach, and a ladder descended to the ground. Tan insisted on letting me go first.

"Chérie!"

"Luc!"

There he sat in the cockpit, mon cher petit, wearing that old surfsuit with the Jolie's Trips logo silk-screened across the chest. And Trinni al-Uq was sitting beside him. Scarcely believing my senses, I reached out to take Luc's gloved hand, thanking the spirits of Newton and Ptolemy and Niels Bohr that the Laws had combined to produce this miracle. But Luc was staring at my face. This was the first time he'd seen me since the bacteria attacked. His expression spoke volumes.

I wanted to ask so many questions, but even though I could talk now, my tongue floundered. I moaned and squeaked, and I might have fainted from sheer joy if Jin hadn't piped up. "Rise, Airlangga," he said with a whimsical sigh. For some reason, that made everybody laugh.

While Vincente buckled me into a seat, Luc snapped open his med kit. I explained that I didn't need any meds, but no one believed me. Trinni closed the hatch and readied the jet for takeoff. Soon, real sunlight warmed my face. Its smoggy rays streamed through the jet window. Luc fed me fruit juice and intravenous drips of painkillers, so I got a real buzzy high. Jin held my hand, and I grinned at the irony of our reversed roles. Now and then, Trinni slipped worried looks in my direction. Luc seemed plain horrified. Didn't they realize how happy they'd made me? I tried to tell them, but those painkillers made me giggle too much.

Only Jin seemed content, humming his little tune and smiling down at me, now and then whispering, "Rise, Airlangga," then laughing softly as if it were our own private joke.

All the way back to Palmertown, I pressed my cheek to the glass and let that yellow sunlight explode against me. It burned through my closed eyelids and glowed bright orange on my retinas, flooding me with hope.

WE FLEW DUE south in Trinni's stolen jet. We got away clean.
That was one year ago. Maybe you think this is the end of the
story. I thought so, too.

But nothing ever ends. As soon as we landed in Palmertown,
my friends grabbed a rental van and rushed me to a clinic. They
were so worried, they ran red lights. Luc even yelled rude words
at a pedestrian who stepped in front of our van. That was a first.
Despite my protests, I spent two months in cell hygiene therapy.
The docs wanted to write a paper about me. They couldn't believe I survived the toxins. They said the only thing that kept
me alive was sheer brute faith and stubbornness. But I knew
better. I knew the immune response in Jin's blood saved me.
Saved my life, at least. Though it didn't my skin.

Now I'm wrapped up in these funny synthetic epidermal
graphs. When I catch myself in the mirror, I have to giggle. A
meat sausage in a wig, that's me. But I can move around fine,
and Jin doesn't care what I look like.

You may be asking, why didn't Jin share his immunity with
me earlier? Don't hold it against him. I don't. See, Jin's perspective is way broader than most of us can comprehend.
He's moved beyond our selfish, human-centered worldview.
To him, those bacteria and his friend Jolie were exactly the
same—beautiful organisms trying to hang on to life as long as
possible. He felt it wasn't his place to alter the natural course.
And also, let's be frank, Jin has a slight decision-making dis-
order. Ça va.

Jin and I live in Sydney now. I have a job working for Syd-
ney.Edu. I guide field trips and teach surface survival skills to
freshmen and sophomores. We don't travel all over the world,
we just camp out on Sydney Topside, but the kids love it.

Vincente has a cube one level down. He helps me with stuff
like shopping, fixing the sink, getting Jin bathed. Tan attends

Sydney.Edu. He's studying communication theory. I predict that boy will go far.

Luc stayed in Palmertown. He and Trinni and Adrienne launched their own fashion ezine, and they're grabbing raves on the Net. Their styles mesh, you know? By the way, Luc eventually told me more about Miguel. Remember, Merida's assassin?

Turns out the boy made an entrance at some post-edge gallery opening and started flirting with Luc. Trinni nearly came to blows with him, right there in the hot buffet line. But mon cher Luc, he could see inside people. He knew Miguel was faking the scene. He figured the boy was a customs agent spying on Trinni's hot-market import business. Trinni was furious, but Luc convinced him it would be fun to play cloak and dagger. I think Luc could charm a cyclone if he tried. Anyway, Trinni got paranoid and made Luc wear concealed body armor night and day. When I heard that part, I had to stop and give Trinni a big slobbery kiss. Trinni and I, we get along better these days. I told them it was Lord Suradon Sura who called and got Miguel to parachute out of their jet.

So much for my friends and me. Up north, the rebels liberated Paris. You can imagine how we celebrated. But since then, the workers haven't taken any more ground. Bien, the big three Coms are still sending out ludicrous statements about peace and productivity, and it makes you wonder what numb-nut is running the show up there. Jonas and Rebel Jeanne moved to Paris about six months back. They send me the real news.

They say Greenland's dominance over Euro is broken for good, but Nome still holds North America, and Pacific.Com dominates the Arctic Sea and parts of East Asia. Yes, Suradon's still hanging on. He and his cronies still toss their protes around like poker chips in their endless games to steal control from each other. I picture those kids in the California desert, scrounging for crumbs and frying in the sun, while their relatives fade away like ghosts in Nome's underground factories. It's pretersick.

At least Paris is free. From what Jonas says, things are plenty wild back in my old hometown. The Parisians have set up all sorts of trade guilds and health churches and food co-ops. Their teleconferences last for hours. Parisians always did like to argue.

They're having trouble with supply distributions, and they squabble over the tax question. One thing they agreed on right away, though. They executed every Commie manager they could find.

Just outside the Place Etoile launchpad, the Parisians erected a monument. I've browsed photos, and the thing looks heinous. It's got two upright posts, grooved on the inside and connected by a crossbeam at the top, with a sharp, angled blade that slides down mega-fast if you let go of the rope. It's an antique decapitation device. Jonas says it's a reminder to the Commies not to come back.

Sometimes Jonas sends me music vids he records in the Paris cafés. Seems a lot of musicians are sampling my Angel of Euro speech. It's comic how they've spliced and dubbed and recycled that old thing in a hundred different rip-rap versions. No one would mistake me for the Angel of Euro now. I look different.

Jin's fine. He's happy. He likes orange juice and sizz music and soft wooly scarves draped over his head. He can stare at the fountain in Sydney's Domain Dome for hours. And he likes to go for walks up top. Jin has regained his health. He's beautiful and strong, you wouldn't believe it. He looks like a movie star again, and lots of people recognize him. Thank the Laws, he didn't lose that smart ring for signing autographs. He still seems unfazed by the attention. Jin doesn't talk much, but he can say a few words when he wants to.

Like last Sunday afternoon. We'd put on our surfsuits for a hike up top. Yes, we wear surfsuits. The docs can't find a trace of that immune response in either of us. They say I dreamed the whole thing. Personally, I don't think they know what to look for, but to play it safe, Jin and I both wear suits when we go up top. Anyway, last Sunday the atmosphere was glowing bright amber. As we strolled through a field of windmills, we watched patterns the smog made vortexing through the blades.

I said, as I always say, "Do you recognize my face today, Jin? It's me. Your old pal Jolie."

As usual, Jin was humming and gazing into the distance. His mind seemed a million kilometers away. Out of nowhere he murmured, "People say a lot without words."

I laughed aloud. I love it when Jin talks. "You're right, Jin, but use words today. Your voice makes me happy."

As if he were moving a giant weight the size of a planet, Jin shifted his attention toward me. He probably couldn't see me very well through my helmet faceplate, but I squeezed his gloved hand. When I felt him return the pressure, my mind rocked. He hadn't done that in months.

"Jolie."

He spoke my name. He recognized me. Two hot tears spilled down my cheeks. This was a good day.

"Shall I tell you a story?" he whispered.

"Oh yes, Jin. Please tell me a story."

His glance wandered away, and he cocked his ear as he often did, listening to sounds and voices I would never hear. He paused so long, I thought he'd forgotten me, but that didn't matter. I didn't really expect him to tell me a story. I took his arm and guided him a little farther along the path. To my surprise he spoke again, in his soft Pacific accent, with that singsong rhythm that reminded me so much of a professor.

"There was once a coastal kingdom. Long ago in Java. Green trees waved in gentle breezes. It could have been paradise. Then came the pirates."

So many words at once! I was blissed to the marrow. This would keep me smiling for weeks. I linked my arm through Jin's and squeezed his shoulder, hoping he would go on. But he had finished. Other sensations distracted him. We reached the edge of the windmill field, and he stared out toward the northern sky. In the west, a rusty haze marked the sunset. Quietly, we stood together gazing through the electrified fence. Wisps of smog swirled around us.

"That's a beautiful story, Jin. That's your Javanese poem, isn't it?"

He answered readily, "Arjunavivaha." Then he started humming his melancholy tune.

What a wonderful day. I didn't want it to end, but the light was already leaving the sky. I touched Jin's shoulder to steer him around for our return walk to the airlock. But he stood firm, staring at the northern sky.

"Home," he said.

"D'accord. Let's go home."

When I touched his shoulder again, he raised his arm and pointed north. "Home."

I sucked a quick breath. This was coming out of nowhere. Could Jin want to return to Pacific.Com? What a crazy idea. It was just a coincidence that he pointed north. I gripped his shoulder and pivoted him around to face me. "We live in Sydney now. Remember?"

Something had changed in him. His eyes were focusing. He looked at me with recognition, and his brows knotted. For the first time, he seemed to notice the changes in my face. Abruptly, he clasped me in his arms. He moved so suddenly, our helmets bumped, and I stumbled against him. Jin was very strong. He held me tight, and I almost couldn't breathe. But he hadn't embraced me like that in a long time, and I didn't want him to let go. I was already sobbing with joy when his voice rang inside my head.

"Jolie, it's time. I need you now."

"I'm right here, Jin. What do you need?"

His voice whispered through my mind like a thought. He was singing, in a language I didn't recognize. Yet the meaning went straight to my brain without the clumsy metaphor of words. He was singing that poem.

"When Krishna revealed himself in a mighty vision, Airlangga saw the universe as one radiant fabric of light. There was no beginning, nor middle, nor end. And the great god Krishna spoke in chords of bright music. 'Rise, Airlangga. Take back my kingdom. I am you and your father and all creatures together. We must divide and do battle before we arrive at peace'."

Jin's song flowed through me like physical heat. I must have swayed because his arms tightened around me. Amazing. Had he spoken, or had I only imagined that ancient song? Gently, he touched his helmet faceplate to mine. "It's time," he said. Then he turned to face the north.

I blinked at the radiant smog and tried to make sense of what had just happened. What did he mean, time to rise against his father? I tugged at his arm. "That's just a goofy old story. So what if you have the same name as that prince? We live in Sydney now. We're happy. Jin, I want it to last."

He pointed at the northern horizon, and his eyes misted. "Rise, Airlangga," he whispered under his breath.

"Oh my sweet Jin, you couldn't rise up to find the toilet without me. What are you thinking?"

"It's time," he whispered again. "This is my choice."

Holy Gods of Physics, why couldn't the universe just stand still and let me be happy? Hadn't we earned a little peace? I grabbed Jin's shoulders and tried to make him look at me. "You want to fight your father? But you don't have an army. What about weapons and transport? I know those protes are suffering in the north. Mes dieux, I want to free them as much as anyone. But Jin, the Coms are so powerful—"

"It's time to make a movie."

"Huh?"

"I need you to produce."

For a minute, all I could do was gawk at him. Produce a movie? Bien, it wasn't the craziest thing I'd heard him say, but it was preter-loco. I figured he was flashing back to his old life. So I shook my head and tried to think of a gentle way to tell him he wasn't rich anymore, but right then, he did something deeply and truly astonishing. He winked at me.

Bien, that was last Sunday. Since then, life has been a little crazy. Jin is changing.

He talks in complete sentences almost every day, and he surfs the Net. He's been ordering all kinds of stuff on my credit card. A voice pad, virtual library subscriptions, an ergonomic chair— it scares me to think about the next monthly invoice. Scares me and thrills me, too. Jin has started smiling again. He never forgets my name anymore. When he holds my hand and browses the documentation on his new chair, I feel myself singing from the inside out. Jin is waking up! The trouble is, he's serious about this movie.

I called my friends for advice, but they're impossible. They're actually encouraging Jin about this movie nonsense. Adrienne loves the "Arjunavivaha" poem. She looked it up on the Net and got a full English translation. Now she quotes passages at me. She calls it the quintessential manifesto for worker revolution.

Jonas surprised me the most. He said, "Your friend's right about the timing, love. The northern protes are fed up to their eyelashes. All they need is one spark. A movie like this, starring the son of a Com CEO, I think it may ignite the flames. Love, we should do this."

Tan has already posted news about the upcoming movie on all the Jin Sura fan sites. The working title is—you guessed it—*Rise, Airlangga.* (I voted for *Prince Airy and the Evil Pirates* myself.) Anyway, it's a period piece. Tan is pumped. He and Jonas are negotiating the underground distribution rights as we speak.

Can it be I'm the only reasonable mind left in this crowd? "Think of the consequences," I keep saying. "Set aside the fact that we don't even know how to point a camera. What if we make the movie anyway, and it works, and the protes start fighting again? Those Coms are brutal. Think what they'll do!"

"But we have a new assault model, Jo. The Angel Maneuver. While the workers fight in the tunnels, we attack from up top." Rebel Jeanne Sabat said that. Even Rebel Jeanne has turned against me.

Luc hacked the mailbox at TokyoData and retrieved Jin's working tapes, and everybody met at our place four nights ago to watch them. We all thought they were preter-cool, but Jin is picky. He's completely rewriting the script. Since that night, he's taken over our living cube, and he won't let anyone but me come near. He spends half his waking hours talking to his voice pad, and the other half staring at the animatronic fish in our aquarium.

Luc and Trinni, they've got their ezine staff handling the auditions. They're hiring grips, gaffers, re-mixers, post-producers, caterers. Adrienne's finding the money. They've leased some raw studio space in Palmertown and registered a new domain name, Angel Flicks. They really believe this movie will make a difference. "Media is mightier than the sword," Adrienne keeps saying, although no one can figure out what she means.

Me, I'm leading an expedition to Java to find those old Belahan carvings. What else could I do? Jin asked me personally. He said we need original footage. He said computer generation won't do. He said, "I need you, pet," and he looked me right in the eye. Am I the girl who could say no to that?

So I'm pulling together a recording crew and wrestling with the problem of operating holo-cams 100 meters deep in the broiling hot ocean. Mes dieux, but it's Jolie's Trips all over again. You can't see the floor of my sleep cube. It's stacked half a meter deep in gear, and I find myself singing all the time. The universe can't stand still? D'accord.